CW01465504

EAST END LOTTERY

By Kim Hunter

Kim Hunter

Copyright © 2014 By Kim Hunter

The right of Kim Hunter to be identified as author
of this work has been asserted in accordance with
sections 77 and 78 of the Copyright, Designs and
Patents Act 1988.

All rights Reserved

This is a work of fiction.
Names, places, characters and incidents originate
from the writers imagination.
Any resemblance to actual persons, living or dead is
purely coincidental.

Table of contents

FOREWORD

"Unseen in the background, Fate was quietly
slipping lead into the boxing-glove."

P.G.Wodehouse

PROLOGUE

Thomas Reginald Mortimer was born on Hillside Drive Edgware in the summer of nineteen fifty seven. His mother Martha, a slightly backward girl as it was termed in those days, worked as an assistant to the housekeeper and was seduced late one night when her employer had returned home drunk. Henry Granger was well known in the city and had made a fortune trading in stocks and shares. A real ladies man he had never married and used women as objects to satisfy his sexual desires. Martha had gained her employment on the recommendation of her aunt who was also a housekeeper at another large house in the area. In all honesty her mother had been glad to see the back of her daughter as she wasn't 'quite the ticket upstairs' or that was the saying she was fond of using. When Henry Granger had forced himself upon her, Martha had struggled at first but allowed him to continue when she was told she would lose her job if she didn't comply. The housekeeper, a Ms Mumbycroft who originated from Hull, was a fair but hard taskmistress and she'd heard the commotion but didn't dare intervene. Waiting until Henry had finished having his way; she had crept into the room and placed her arms around the girl. Martha was inconsolable and after Ms Mumbycroft had cleaned her up and made her a cup of hot sweet tea, she was instructed never to go upstairs after dark again and from now on the two women would share the same bedroom. It turned out to be a case of closing the stable door after the horse had bolted, as within three months it was clear to anyone that Martha Mortimer was well and truly in the family way. A meeting was arranged between Mr Granger, Ms Mumbycroft and Martha's mother and aunt. When a large amount of money was passed into Ruby Mortimer's hand it was agreed that after the baby was born it would be placed in the orphanage on Sefton Avenue and offered up for adoption. Martha wasn't consulted and on the night she went into labour Ms Mumbycroft placed a gag in her mouth to stifle the screams. It took twenty two hours of intense pain before Thomas came into the world and for a lot of that time Martha was left to cope alone. Henry Granger still expected Ms Mumbycroft to take care of his daily needs whether r a baby was being born downstairs or not. Returning to the bedroom and seeing that Martha had delivered the baby herself, Kathy Mumbycroft cut the cord and then whisked the child away. Martha never got to hold her boy or say goodbye but in all honesty she didn't really understand what had happened and had gone into shock. It was agreed that if the family kept their mouths shut and the baby was never mentioned again, then Martha would be allowed to stay in the employment of the Granger household.

Over the years Thomas came to hate being in the children's home and his report contained the words 'a strange child who has difficulty associating with the other boys' and girls'. It had been noted many times that he had a spiteful streak especially with the younger children and it was probably the reason that out of all the visitors to the orphanage, not one had chosen to adopt him. There were only a couple of occasions when he had bonded with other children but when they went it just made young Tommy Mortimer more aloof, especially when he saw how happy each one was as they were being driven away by their new family. He would often disappear after school hours and his favourite haunt to spend time at was over at the allotments that were situated just off Deans Lane. He would steal as much fruit as he could get his hands on and sell it back at the orphanage for a half penny a time if he was lucky enough to find any buyers. If none of the children had any cash then he would just let it rot rather than give it away. From an early age Tommy had decided that when he grew up he would make as much money as he could, rich people seemed to rule the world or at least that's how it appeared through the eyes of a young boy. At the age of fifteen he was placed on an apprenticeship at Keller's wood yard over on Hazel Gardens. Tommy hated every second of it and the only light relief came in the form of days out working at the convent on Priory field. George Brown was Tommy's foreman and noticed straight away that the boy had an eye for the opposite sex. Sitting Tommy down, George told him in no uncertain terms that he was welcome to look but he must never touch. Seeing all the pretty young girls arrive each day for school was torture and there was no way Tommy would ever be able to obey the orders he had been given. June Turner was a cheeky young girl with flaming red hair, who was roughly the same age as Tommy and what prank he didn't think of she sure did. They were a mischievous pair and June could only be described as a thorough tease. Deliberately touching him, she would then rebuff Tommy when he made any advances. June's smile was seductive and her big hazel eyes would cause stirrings in Tommy's loins that he found hard to control. Just lately the only thing he could think about was sex and it was driving him crazy. Finally after a couple of weeks of messing about and when June had led him along once too often, he took matters into his own hands. The door to the old coal shed was open and pushing June inside he roughly forced her up against the wall.

"Tommy you'll make my dress all dirty, get off!" It was as if her words went unheard, Tommy was aroused and placing his hands on her bottom he lifted her flimsy cotton dress and roughly pulled down her panties. Unbuttoning his trousers, Tommy let them fall to his ankles as he nudged his way inside her. The feeling was fantastic and for a few seconds he thought he had died and gone to heaven.

"No Tommy, no I don't want to!" It was all over after a few jerky moments and Tommy then pulled out. He had never felt anything like it and the fact that he had forced himself into her made it all the more exciting. It had been rough and short but none the less June Turner's virginity had definitely been taken. This was the first time Tommy had raped a girl but it certainly wouldn't be the last and from that day on he was hooked and couldn't wait for his next experience. Luckily for him it was payday and after collecting his meagre wages he didn't even bother returning to the orphanage. Unbeknown to him June Turner had been too scared to report the assault to anyone and had just prayed that it wouldn't result in a child. Thankfully for them both and unbeknown to Tommy, her prayers were answered. Tommy boarded the first train to London and made his way to Bethnal Green where he laid low for a few days in Weavers Fields. Sleeping in the bushes wasn't ideal but he had to make what money he had stretch as far as possible.

Acer Goldstein ran a flower stall Monday to Fridays on Wentworth Street market and then on Sundays he would move his whole setup around the corner to Middlesex Street or Petticoat Lane as it is better known. Acer had spotted Tommy several times on his way home from work and it was obvious that the boy was hiding from something or someone. After striking up a conversation he gave the boy his leftover sandwiches which Tommy greedily devoured. The man's act of kindness was thankfully received and when Acer offered Tommy a job on his stall, the young boy was elated.

Tommy Mortimer always referred to this meeting as the best day in his life and was always indebted to the old Jewish man who had asked no questions and had given him a chance. Days were spent running errands for Acer and the other stall holders, who would always tip him generously. Before he knew it Tommy had reached his twenty ninth birthday and as Acer Goldstein had retired two years earlier, Tommy was now running the stall alone. It didn't pay a king's ransom but it was enough to get by on and he loved the atmosphere and banter. In all honesty, every time he thought of moving on something stopped him as he couldn't imagine doing anything else. All of the other stallholders loved him but they always made sure that their wives and daughters were kept at arm's length. Arriving for work one cold December morning, Tommy had just finished erecting the stall when he was approached by a tall smartly dressed man who was making inquiries regarding the whereabouts of a certain Thomas Reginald Mortimer. Even after all these years Tommy was still on his guard and wanted to know who the man was and what he wanted with Thomas. Geoffrey Harper had worked for Latimer & Fulcher for years as an investigator and had come across this scenario many times before.

"I can assure you Sir that Mr Mortimer is not in any kind of trouble."

Geoffrey handed over his business card and as he tipped his trilby hat, informed Tommy that if Mr

Mortimer would like to call in at his office he may find there was some beneficial news to hear. Tommy didn't reply but when the man was out of sight he studied the card. Latimer & Fulcher were a firm of solicitors working in officers on Gresham Street right in the heart of the city. When a customer enquired about a bunch of roses Tommy went into sales mode and pushed the card into his pocket. It wasn't until later that day when he had almost finished packing up that he thought about his early morning visitor again. It was just after three, so quickly finishing the job in hand he caught the tube from Liverpool Street to St Pauls. Luckily it was only three stops and after leaving the tube he had less than a five minute walk to reach his destination. Latimer & Fulcher worked out of a very small but smart office that consisted of a reception area with two private rooms leading off. Tommy introduced himself and instantly the young girl who manned the desk disappeared into one of the side rooms. Within seconds a small grey haired man appeared and held out his hand.

"Good afternoon Mr Mortimer I'm David Fulcher." Ushering Tommy through the door he offered him a seat in one of the small side rooms.

"I must say Mr Mortimer you're a hard man to locate; we've been trying to find you for over six months now."

Suddenly Tommy had visions of June Turner trying to find him to extract some kind of maintenance payment but then that was years ago and surely she would have tried long before now, or it could be his long lost kid trying to find him, that's if there was a kid.

"Maybe I am but I'm also a busy man, now can you cut to the chase and tell me exactly why you wanted to see me?"

"Please forgive me I must apologise and yes of course. Now for many years this firm has represented a Mr Henry Granger."

Tommy shrugged his shoulders as if to say 'the name doesn't ring a bell'.

"I can see I'm not making a lot of sense Mr Mortimer. We represented Mr Granger on legal matters regarding his business dealings but we didn't participate in the drawing up of his will. Unfortunately Mr Granger passed away last year and we were instructed by the probate solicitors' to locate you and pass over your inheritance."

Tommy sat bolt upright, was he hearing right, had someone left him some cash.

"It seems Mr Granger wanted you to have this." David Fulcher handed Tommy a manila envelope and then stood up ready to see Tommy out. This was all happening so fast and there were still questions he wanted answering.

"I don't know what's in here but if its money then how do you know I'm really who I say I am. I mean you aint asked me for any identification.

"That won't be necessary; the man who introduced himself to you this morning is one of our best investigators. He has been looking into your whereabouts for several months and I might add, he has also been following you for several days. If Geoff says you are Thomas Reginald Mortimer then I have no doubt that is who you are. Now enjoy your windfall Sir but do take some time to let it sink in as this sort of thing can sometimes be quite a shock."

Leaving the office Tommy aimlessly walked along as he tried to take in what he'd just been told. Reaching Mansion House he entered Ye Olde Watling pub and after ordering a pint of bitter, took a seat at one of the corner tables and slowly opened the envelope. The first thing he pulled out was a handwritten letter from Henry Granger. The writing looked old and the paper
smelled musty but after scanning the first few lines Tommy discarded it. This bloke was claiming to be his father but it was of no interest to him now. Next he pulled out what appeared to be a cheque and when he saw the amount was for two hundred thousand pounds, a smile spread from one side of his face to the other. Stuffing the cheque into his pocket he swigged down the last of his drink and as he passed an open fire on his way out, threw the letter and envelope into the grate. He wasn't the least bit interested in some old fool wanting to clear his conscience or the fact that the letter may have revealed the identity of his mother. As far as Tommy was concerned it was too late, far too late for that.

From that day the market stall remained closed and

Acer Goldstein never again heard from the man he had given a life and an opportunity to. Tommy Mortimer was a free agent and he would never allow himself to grow close to anyone, that way no one could ever abandon him again. After a couple of weeks living the high life, Tommy decided he had to make the money start to work for him if he wanted to continue spending and living the lifestyle he had become accustom to. Purchasing a rundown drinking bar that was situated above several shops on Kingsland road in Hackney, Tommy set about turning it into the in place to be. Now rebranded the Den it was very successful for all of twelve months but in the late eighties when the recession really started to bite, things took a downward turn. Tommy went from earning a fortune every day to losing one on a weekly basis. He was in trouble and he needed help, help that would come in the form of one Taffy Jones a wannabe gangster. Taffy traded in any drug you could name and Tommy soon found that if drugs were offered for sale in the club, the place was packed most nights. Scared of getting closed down he quickly built up a client list outside of the Den that enabled him to run the place without risk and at the same time have a respectable business which would not bring any unwanted attention from the law. Tommy now saw himself as a ladies' man and in his own mind fantasized that women found him irresistible. He would invite girls from the club to come into his office on the pretence of giving them a job and then force himself on them but he was always sure to pick his mark. The girls had to look as if they were in desperate need of money, he didn't care if they were on the game or needed drugs as long as they kept their mouths shut. After the deed had been carried out, he would shove a handful of notes into their hand and no more would be said. It seemed to work for a long time but things would change one night in nineteen ninety six. Years later, events that had occurred that night would come back to haunt Tommy Mortimer.

CHAPTER ONE

December 1996

Peter Andre's 'Mysterious Girl' played loudly in the bedroom as Lizzie Chambers and her best friend Sonia were getting ready for a night out. It was still two weeks until Christmas but both girls were already in the festive spirit. The Chambers household on Ritchie Street Islington was never quiet but everyone seemed to muddle along just fine. Lizzie being the only girl in a house full of men had her own room and although it was really no more than a box room, she cherished her privacy. Her father Mike had the front bedroom and her brothers Joey, Steve and Dave had bunks in the middle room. Valerie Chambers had run off with the man from the provident when Lizzie was only four and although she had stayed in contact with her children for a few months, it had soon dwindled to just the odd birthday card and that was only when she was sober enough to remember. At first Mike had been heartbroken, Joey had only just turned ten years old and what with the three younger kids, his hands were full and it left little time for grieving. Six years later when the first of his son's left school, Mike decided to start up his own building business. He was a very capable brick layer and Joey was good with figures so Mike reasoned that once they got the hang of things and

1

if luck was on their side, they would do alright. As time passed, father and son did better than alright and they worked on sites all over England. There were times when they had to stay away and when that happened Iris Hutchins would be asked to look after the younger kids, for a fee of course. Steve, Dave and Lizzie hated Iris Hutchins more than anything. Dave said she smelled and there was always a fag hanging out of her mouth even when she was cooking their meals. Steve would wind his brother and sister up by saying that he saw fag ash fall into the food, he hadn't but in all probability it had happened. Iris was always dressed in a war time wrap around apron and her words seemed to sound like grunts to the children, so behind her back they called her the pig. The two boys were now teenagers and on many occasions they had wanted to give Iris a piece of their mind but the fear of a good thrashing from their father on his return made them behave with impeccable manners. Lizzie was only ten and Iris frightened her, she didn't know why but all the same she would curl up each night between her brothers and it made her feel safe. The years slowly passed and by the time Lizzie left school, Iris had passed away and her father and older brother now worked locally. Mike Chambers adored his children and none more so than his only girl. His son's, much to Mike's approval, were very protective of her but to Lizzie it seemed they were overly protective and it would sometimes make her feel as if she was being suffocated. After a particularly bad show down when someone had seen a boy kissing Lizzie, Joey had punched the lad in the mouth and Lizzie had finally exploded. A family meeting was called and she told them all, her father included, that unless they cut her a little slack she would leave. Reluctantly they agreed and now once a week Lizzie and Sonia got dressed up to the nines and headed out to one of the local clubs. Lizzie Chambers was now eighteen years old and was living life to the full. A very pretty girl, she wore the latest fashions and was the envy of all of her friends. One Saturday night, the girls had just finished getting ready and were giggling loudly as they reached the bottom of the stairs. The laughter instantly stopped when they saw Joey emerge from the kitchen.

"And where are you two off to tonight?"

Lizzie did a twirl in the hallway. Her leopard print mini skirt and white T-shirt hugged every curve and Joey raised his eyebrows in a disapproving manner. Lizzie giggled and lifting her leg showed him the massive platform boots that she had bought down Chapel Street market earlier that afternoon.

"What the fuck are they?"

"These lovely brother, are exactly the same as Baby Spice wears. Aint they great?"

Joey could only shake his head.

"You'll break your bleeding neck!"

Sonia was already out of the front door when she heard Joey call out to his sister.

"Lizzie you didn't answer my question. Where are you going tonight?"

Lizzie Chambers rolled her eyes upwards as she answered and Joey only heard 'Lady Gray's' before the front door slammed. The two girls walked a few yards before they spoke as they didn't want anyone to hear them.

"Why did you say we were going there?"

"Because Sonia, if I'd told him we were going over to Hackney one of my brothers would be made to follow me. They think I don't know but I've seen them plenty of times and it aint happening tonight I can tell you."

Lady Gray's was situated on Upper Street Islington and was a short walk from the family's home. Joey decided to give it an hour and then either he or Steve would wander down there just to keep an eye on what Lizzie was up to. Reaching the end of the road the girls hailed a cab and was soon on their way to 'The Den' on Kingsland Road Hackney. They hadn't been to this particular club before but Sonia had it on good authority that they played the latest tunes and the place could get a bit wild at times. As the cab pulled up outside, Sonia's face dropped, the club didn't look anything special and there were no neon lights or queues of people waiting to get inside. Still she didn't voice her disappointment and grabbing her friends arm

4

pushed open the door and walked into the ground floor foyer. Two doormen were leaning against the wall chatting and only gave the girls a passing glance before returning to their conversation. A brassy haired woman with scarlet red lipstick sat in a small booth behind a glass screen. Walking up, Sonia and Lizzie handed over their five pound entry fee and pushed their arms through a small gap so that the woman could rubber stamp the backs of their hands. Lizzie stared into the woman's hard face and the sight of the cigarette hanging from her mouth made Lizzie momentarily think of Iris Hutchins. The woman, whose name badge said Rita in bold black letters, looked up and seeing the distaste on Lizzie's face couldn't hold back from venting her anger.

"What the fucks up with you?"

Lizzie didn't answer and grabbing Sonia's arm the pair began their ascent up to the club. It was three flights of stairs to get to the top and by the time they arrived Sonia was puffing and panting. Pushing open the double swing doors the girls said in unison "You're joking." The place was all but deserted and it smelled heavily of old stale beer and cigarettes. The decor was tired and outdated and they both knew it had been a big mistake coming here.

"Now what do we do Sonia?"

"Well if we go back then we've wasted our entry fee and we'll have to pay again at Lady Gray's. Now I aint got that much money, so what say we stay here, get pissed and hope it livens up later?"

The girls linked arms and marched over to the bar.
"Two Martini and lemonade's please."

The barman looked them both up and down and
ran his tongue over his lips as he did so. Lizzie
could feel her face flush with embarrassment but
Sonia, who was a bit of a livewire, just giggled.
Glancing round the room the girls spied a group of
lads sitting around a low table on stools. There
were five or six local girls dancing beside their
handbags to Mark Morrison's 'Return of the Mack'
but they didn't look too friendly. By the time Lizzie
and Sonia were on their third drink they had started
to loosen up and when the Spice Girls 'Wannabe'
began to play Lizzie couldn't hold back any longer.
"Come on Sonia let's dance, I love this one."

Moving onto the dance floor, Lizzie began to sway
to the music and the dance steps she'd practised
from the telly night after night, now looked good.
The boys at the table all began to stare much to the
disapproval of the group of girls who now stood
further along the bar. Sonia knew there could be
trouble but her friend was having such a good time
that she didn't have the heart to tell Lizzie to stop.
When the song came to a close she pulled her friend
from the dance floor back over to the bar.
Whispering in Lizzie's ear she told her of the black
looks they had been getting. Lizzie Chambers
wasn't a fighter; in fact she hated any kind of
violence and would do anything she could to avoid

it.

"Let's just stand here and have a drink and keep our heads down for a while."

Things calmed down when the lads at the table lost interest and went back to their conversation and as the night wore on several more people entered the club. A group of eight girls from Shoreditch, who were out on a hen night, came in at just before eleven and straight away Lizzie could feel the tension begin to mount. At least she and Sonia were no longer of interest to the Bethnal Green girls but she didn't like how things felt as you could cut the atmosphere with a knife. Sonia who was by now feeling the effects of the alcohol and was in the process of draping herself all over the DJ, was oblivious to the volcano of female hormones that were about to erupt. Suddenly a girl by the name of Big Tracey and who was a member of the Bethnal Green girls Crew, as they liked to call themselves, threw a pint of larger over the bride to be. Tensions were running high and as another girl walked in the path of a woman carrying a tray of drinks she said she overheard a snide comment, though in all honesty Big Tracey had already fuelled the fire.

"What the fuck did you say?"

The girl with the tray of drinks looked slightly confused.

"I didn't say anything."

"Yes you did, you just called me a fat slag you fucking stick insect!"

With that all hell broke loose and the tray of drinks ended up all down the front of Big Tracey as she stood to the side of her friend. All of the girls were now going at it hammer and tongs, handbags were being smashed over heads and the dance floor was awash with brawling women. Scratching, kicking, biting and pulling hair was happening everywhere as the women really went for it. To Lizzie Chambers it always seemed so much more vicious when women got fighting. One particular girl was being dragged across the floor by her hair while another repeatedly kicked out at her. Skimpy designer dresses were being ripped from bodies and three of the girls were now semi naked. With breasts exposed, it all made for a good night out for the lads who stood watching with glee. Screaming and shouting went hand in hand with the ferocity of the fight. Two doormen were summoned from downstairs and as they tried to separate the girls, booing could be heard from the lads. It hadn't gone unnoticed by the boys that the bouncers were trying to separate the women who were semi naked first, the ones who were only left in their knickers and high heels. As they wrestled with each other, their body's looked somewhat erotic as the disco lights flashed and the lads weren't happy that their sideshow was being spoilt. One woman was still straddled over the bride to be and raining down blow after blow on her face. The girls top had been ripped off and her breasts were now exposed but

8

she could do little to cover her modesty as she tried
to protect her face with both hands. The group of
lads were still cheering and laughing and there was
no sign that things would calm down anytime soon,
in fact Lizzie thought that things were escalating
further out of control. The whole scene made her
begin to shake and running through the doors she
went into the first room she saw. Slamming the
door behind her she closed her eyes, lent backwards
and breathed out a sigh of relief. People fighting
actually made her feel physically sick but after a few
seconds of deep breathing she opened her eyes and
almost jumped out of her skin when she saw a man
staring back at her.
"Who are you?"
"I think I should be the one asking that question
sweetheart."
"There was a fight and I had to get away!"
Tommy Mortimer had owned The Den for the last
ten years and business was good. Door admissions
were reasonable but Tommy earned the majority of
his money by selling party drugs, come to that any
drugs that he could lay his hands on and all the
other club owners would regularly call in to get
their supplies. His main pastime was counting
money, second to that he liked young girls and the
one who had stumbled into his office by accident
was right up his street. Standing up he walked
around the desk and made his way over to where
Lizzie Chambers stood. He seemed to have a kind

face and strangely she wasn't scared. Tommy reached out and touched her shoulder.

"You're shaking, why don't you take a seat until it's all calmed down and we can have a drink."

Lizzie didn't resist when he held her elbow and guided her over to the velvet couch that was positioned along the far wall. When she was seated, Tommy went over to the filing cabinet and removed a bottle of scotch and two glasses. Pouring them both a liberal measure he handed Lizzie a glass and then took a seat beside her. Taking a large mouthful Lizzie suddenly started to cough, it was far too strong and not what she was used to. Slowly sipping it she began to get a really warn feeling in her chest and after he'd topped up her glass for a second time she found she now liked whisky.

When both of their glasses were empty, Tommy took the crystal tumbler out of her hand and placed the glasses onto the floor. As he looked at her he focused his eyes on the top of her slender legs and could see just a hint of her knickers peeping from under the fabric of her short skirt. Tommy leaned in and started to kiss her and to begin with Lizzie felt flattered. When his hand moved under her skirt she tried to push him away but Tommy Mortimer was too strong.

"Please don't, I have to get home my brothers will be worried."

"Don't start whining you know you want it."

"I don't, please please stop."

Tommy forcibly pulled down her underwear and the only words he said were 'Shush be quiet'. He used his knee to force her legs apart and when Lizzie tried to scream, Tommy placed one hand over her mouth while with the other he released his hard penis. As he entered her Lizzie let out a muffled scream but he didn't feel any pity as he began to move in and out. He was so forceful that the sofa started to bang against the wall. With one hand still over her mouth, he now placed the other onto the back of the settee to stop the noise. He continued for a further five minutes before he was finished and all the while silent tears streamed down Lizzie Chambers face as she thought of what her father and brothers would think. Rolling off of her and onto the sofa, Tommy Mortimer let out a groan of pleasure. He didn't speak another word and all Lizzie could do was scramble to her feet, rearrange her clothing and then run from the room as fast as she could. She didn't bother where Sonia was; the only thing on Lizzie's mind was getting as far away from this place as she could. Hailing a cab she tried to hold the tears inside. As soon as she reached home she ran up the stairs and made her way into the bathroom. Locking the door she sat on the side of the tub and sobbed her heart out. When her father tapped on the door and asked if she was alright, Lizzie stifled her tears and said that she wasn't feeling well and was going to take a bath. Mike Chambers had no reason to doubt his girl so

11

accepting her explanation, he went back downstairs to finish watching a cowboy that he'd been thoroughly enjoying. Lizzie filled the bath with water and it was as hot as she could stand. Wincing she lowered her body down and spent the next thirty minutes scrubbing as hard as she could. By the time she fell into bed her skin was red raw, the only problem was she still felt dirty but there was nothing more she could do.

The next few months passed without event. What had happened back on that fateful night in the Den had left Sonia in a strop and she still wasn't speaking to her friend and even though Lizzie had tried to explain it wasn't good enough. As far as Sonia was concerned her friend had abandoned her and it was unforgivable. Lizzie stopped going out at the weekends and it didn't go unnoticed by Joey but when he questioned his sister she would just say that she didn't fancy it. He soon gave up asking but a couple of months later something else began to play on Joey Chambers mind, his sister appeared to be gaining weight at an alarming rate. One Sunday morning when the family had enjoyed a cooked breakfast, he was alone in the kitchen with Lizzie helping her to wash up. Lizzie stood beside him tea towel in hand and waiting for Joey to pass her the first clean plate. Suddenly he stopped what he was doing and stared at her.

"What?"

"You're up the duff aint you?"

Lizzie burst into tears and Joey knew his fears were founded.

"Who's the father?"

Lizzie just shook her head and no matter how many times he asked her she wouldn't give him an answer. Taking the tea towel from her he dried his hands and then took his baby sister into his arms.

"You aint the first and you won't be the last. Now stop crying and come and sit down."

Lizzie explained that it had been a one night stand; she knew that if she told him she'd been raped then all three of her brothers would go after Tommy Mortimer and do him some real damage. There was no point as it wouldn't change things and besides she didn't want to risk any of her family getting locked up. Strangely and even though her child had been so violently conceived, she felt nothing but love for the baby growing inside her.

"So how far along are you?"

"I'm not really sure but I think I'm about six months"

"Fuck me Lizzie! When were you going to tell us, when you went into labour?"

Again she started to cry and he held her hand until the tears stopped.

"Would you like me to tell Dad?"

Lizzie Chambers began to panic at the thought of her father knowing and her eyes were open wide with fear but slowly she nodded her head..

"No time like the present then. You wait here and

I'll be back as soon as I've told him."

As Joey entered the front room, Lizzie remained in the kitchen and began to bite her nails with nerves. Mike Chambers was seated in his armchair reading the Sunday paper but stopped and looked up when his eldest son walked in.

"Dad there's something I need to tell you."

Mike removed his reading glasses and placed them down onto the arm of the chair.

"If you're going to tell me that our Lizzie has a bun in the oven then I already know."

"So why didn't you say anything?"

"I figured she'd tell us all when she was good and ready. Look son, it aint the end of the world. We've always managed and another mouth to feed aint exactly going to break the bank now is it? Beside I quite fancy having a kid around the place again, I've missed that since you lot grew up."

Joey was dumbfounded, he'd at least expected his father to fly into a rage and curse and scream. They all worshiped the ground Lizzie walked on and now she was about to become an unmarried mother, well to him at least, it was a shock.

"I thought you'd go mad."

"What would be the point of that? You can't undo what's already done, now where is she?"

'In the kitchen and crying her eyes out."

Mike was out of his chair in a second and heading to his daughter. When he opened the kitchen door and saw her beautiful tearstained face he held out his arms and Lizzie ran into them.

"You silly cow, whatever are you getting all teary for? Now we're all going to muck in and help bring this baby up. It might not have a dad but it will have plenty of uncles and a granddad who's going to adore it."

It was a further three months before Lizzie Chambers' waters broke and the house went into panic. The men were all seated around the table and Lizzie had been in the middle of dishing up the evening meal when they suddenly heard a gush of water. Following her gaze they all looked down to see a large puddle had formed on the kitchen floor. Mike took charge and barked in Steve's direction that he should go and phone for an ambulance. Dave and Joey took an arm each and helped their sister over to the table. By the time the ambulance arrived Lizzie was doubled over in pain and her father was stroking her back and talking softly to her. The female paramedic knelt on the floor and after a quick examination, informed all in the room that the baby wasn't far off being born and that they needed to get to the hospital as soon as possible. Mike travelled with his daughter in the ambulance and the boys followed behind in Joey's car. By the time he'd found a parking space and the brothers entered the materiality unit they were met by their father who was beaming from ear to ear.

"It's a boy, a beautiful baby boy."

And so little Michael Chambers had entered the

world to be greeted by more love than any child could ever hope for. He was doted on by his uncles who would nightly argue about whose turn it was to feed or bath Michael. Lizzie adored her son but although a happy little chap, Michael always seemed to be poorly. That fact only made his family love him even more and the next eighteen years passed happily.

CHAPTER TWO

Born in nineteen twenty nine, Dottie Stewart was known as a good time girl. Not a prostitute as such as she held down a full time job working on various stalls on Broadway Market but after eight hours of lugging and lifting Dottie liked a drink. It was something she openly admitted but not the fact that she would always get absolutely legless. The pub she frequented on a regular basis was situated on the corner of the market and is now known as the Cat & Mutton. Men would vie to buy her drinks, gin being her preferred tipple and the lucky bloke would then be treated to sex in the pubs rear yard. Over the years Dottie had more men than she could recall the names of but it didn't faze her, as far as she was concerned life was for living and anyone who had a problem with that could just go to hell. For a long time Dottie Stewart was lucky but finally the luck ran out when she found herself pregnant at the age of twenty five. She managed to hold onto her job for the whole nine months and her waters actually broke as she was serving a customer with two pounds of Jersey Royal potatoes. From the moment Blanche came kicking and screaming into this world Dottie had hated the very sight of her child. She had no maternal instincts and would palm the baby off on anyone who was willing to take her. Carrying on work at the market and drinking until the early hours meant that little

Blanche would be left alone for hours on end but back then people didn't seem to care if a baby was heard crying and there was no such thing as social workers. As Blanche grew she quickly learned to take care of herself and soon found her only comfort was food. By the time she started school she was well and truly overweight, her eye sight wasn't good and she was forced to wear thick round horn rimmed spectacles. All in all Blanche Stewart was a sad little girl to behold. Her mother never bothered if she was clean or had cleaned her teeth, her school uniform was stained and was straining at the seams. Friends weren't allowed in the flat but it didn't bother Blanche as in all honesty she didn't have any to speak of. Girls in her class were told to keep away from her by their own mothers, as Blanche was continually infected with head lice. By the time she left school at fifteen, Blanche's weight had soared but she had no money or interest in fashion so anything that would fit was always purchased at the churches monthly bring and buy sale. Tony Lanceman took pity on Blanche and offered her a job in the small cafe he ran on Duncan Road. It was a short distance from the market and mother and daughter would walk to work each day but there was hardly ever a word spoken them. In time Dottie's lifestyle started to catch up with her and she began to find stall work exhausting but she wouldn't change her ways or accept she had brought it on herself. As far as Dottie Stewart was concerned there was only one person to blame for her horrible life, her daughter Blanche. Years passed and when Dot reached fifty five she was forced to give up work due to ill health. Nights out drinking had to stop and instead she would spend all evening sitting in her armchair berating her daughter. As much as Dot hated Blanche, the feeling soon became mutual and they would each look for ways to wind the other up. Dottie still managed to make her way down to the market every day to have a catch up with all her old pals and would then head off to the cafe to have lunch courtesy of her daughter. She never missed an opportunity to embarrass Blanche and it didn't go unnoticed by all who knew the two women. Blanche had never bothered with men but in reality she wouldn't have stood much of a chance. Instead she indulged herself by going out to eat as often as she could. Pie and mash was her particular favourite but if the truth was told she didn't mind what she ate as long as the food was tasty and there was plenty of it.

Year of 2014

As retirement approached Blanche started to panic, all day in the flat with just her mother for company would drive her up the wall and then there were the finances to consider. It was hard enough for a pensioner to survive let alone one who constantly liked to eat. The owners of the cafe had been good enough to let her stay on until she was sixty five but even Blanche knew that she would soon have to call it a day. As luck would have it and as her very last shift was coming to an end, she heard some hopeful news. Lorraine Duggan, the cook and co owner of the cafe for the last twenty years and who had taken over when Tony retired, had always had a soft spot for Blanche Stewart. Being witness to the woman's bitch of a mother's past behaviour, she knew that Blanche must have led an awful life and over the past few weeks she could see a dramatic change in her.

"You alright Blanche darling, only you're very quiet today?"

Blanche began to cry and lifting her apron to wipe her eyes, she then went on to blow her nose on the fabric. Lorraine grimaced and quickly led the woman to the back of the cafe.

"Sit down love and tell me all about it."

"It's that old cow at home. When I finish here I'm going to have to look after her and I'm worried about the money and how we'll manage. As it is I have to pay everything, she's never got any money."

"How old is Dottie now?"

"Coming up ninety or she will be in a couple of months."

"And what about carers and mobility allowance?"

Blanche looked at her employer with a blank expression and Lorraine knew she didn't have a clue about what she was being asked.

"You mean to tell me that for all these years you aint

had any assistance? Bloody hell Blanche! First thing Monday morning you want to get yourself down the Social offices and ask for help. There are loads of benefits you can claim for and your mum could possibly warrant a career. If she does then there are loads of fridge benefits to be had.

"Mum would never allow a stranger in the flat."

"She doesn't have to; you can do it and get paid as well. Bloody hell girl you're already doing it now for nothing so you might as well get something out of it."

Blanche couldn't believe what she was hearing and as Lorraine continued to explain how things worked, she beamed from ear to ear. Just as she'd been told to do, Blanche Stewart was standing outside the Social Security office before they had even opened and she was the first person to be seen. Hauling her large frame into the interview room she flopped down onto the chair and explained everything to the kind looking young woman who sat behind the desk.

Deborah Jenkins had worked at the DHSS for the last five years and had also struggled with her weight. She felt empathy for Blanche and decided to do all she could to help the woman. Leaving thirty minutes later Blanche would have skipped if she'd been able to. Someone was coming to do a home visit and if everything was correct, Blanche would become her mother's full time carer. The seventy pounds a week would top up her state pension nicely and the added bonus of Dottie receiving fifty pounds a week in mobility allowance made it seem like all her Christmases had come at once. The home visit went well and Blanche was soon able to eat out two or three times a week. She didn't pass on the money she received for the mobility allowance when she cashed her mother's pension, Blanche reasoned that the old girl didn't even know that she was getting it and besides it was Blanche who had to do all the work. In reality she did very little and would feed her mother mostly things like beans on toast or bring her in sausage and chips, anything that was cheap and quick. Her home making skills were virtually none existent and the flat always had a strange stale smell about it. For the most part Blanche was content, Dottie hardly ever got out of bed so her daughter could do as she pleased but just lately things had started to change and it all came to a head early one Monday morning. Blanche was snuggled under the duvet when suddenly she heard her mother call out from the next room.

"Blanche! Blanche! I need to go to the toilet."

"For fucks sake Mum I'm coming! You'll just have to hang on for a minute."

Blanche Stewart sat up in bed and hauled her large legs over the side. At twenty six stone she found movement difficult and would have preferred to spend all of her time in bed as well. The only trouble was that now she was the chief carer for her ninety year old mother she had to at least show willing, social services were liable to do a spot check and she couldn't risk losing the benefits if she wasn't seen to be looking after her mother properly. Blanche knew that Dottie played on her illnesses and would do anything for attention. Again her mother's shrill voice could be heard.

"Too late, I warned you, I warned you but would you listen? Oh no you know best as usual!"

Pulling on her dressing gown and slippers, Blanche waddled out of the bedroom and along the hall to her mother's room. The council flat on Croston Street was only small but her bulk made it feel like she was on a two mile hike. Opening the door the smell hit Blanche Stewart's nostrils and she immediately brought her palm up to cover her mouth and nose. Dottie Stewart was sitting up in bed with her hands outstretched covered in shit.

"I called you but you didn't come so this is what happens."

"I was still in bed mother! Good God it stinks, whatever have you been eating?"

"You should know! All you ever give me is that cheap processed rubbish, it's no wonder me bowels are loose."

Blanche shook her head in despair.

"Give us a minute and I'll come back and get you cleaned up."

Before Dottie could complain further Blanche had left the room and was heading in the direction of

the kitchen. Placing the kettle on to boil she
breathed in deeply and counted to ten. Making
herself a cup of tea she used the remaining hot
water to fill the bowl in the sink. Adding a liberal
measure of bleach to the liquid she grinned to
herself and muttered under her breath 'that'll teach
the dirty old bitch'. After finishing her tea, she
carried the bowl along the hall but took her time
walking to her mother's room as she didn't want to
spill any of the liquid onto the carpet. Just walking
was hard enough for Blanche, let alone when she
was carrying something heavy. Dottie was still
sitting up in bed and she sneered as her daughter
entered.

"You took your fucking time!"

"The world don't revolve around you Mum, I do
have a life of me own you know."

"A life of your own? Who are you trying to kid you
big fat lump, no man worth his salt would give you
the time of day."

Her mother's words cut deeply and as she pulled
the bedclothes back Blanche pushed her mother
sharply.

"You want to thank your lucky stars and start being
a bit nicer to me. Who else would clean your shit
up and besides I'm thinking about putting you into
a home. You aint never been nice to me, lord above
knows you told me often enough that you wish I'd
never been born. Do you know something mother?
I often wish I really hadn't been born but that was

all down to you because you couldn't keep your
fucking legs together could you?"
Dottie Stewart had stopped listening when she
heard the words 'into a home', she didn't care about
Blanche's feelings but she was scared of being put
into an institution. Tenderly touching her
daughter's wrist, she forgot that her own hands
were covered in faeces. Blanche who had been in
the middle of washing her mother's backside,
pulled away sharply.
"Now look what you've done, you've covered me in
shit."
"Oooo! That's hurting me."
Blanched smiled to herself, her mother's bed sores
had been getting worse lately and the bleach water
must really be stinging.
"I can't do anything about that! If you weren't such
a dirty bitch I wouldn't have to wipe your arse."
Suddenly and for no real reason Blanche lashed out
and her fist made contact with her mother's temple.
Dottie could only stare open mouthed but Blanche
ignored her and concentrated on the task of wiping
the faeces from her mother's hands. Finally five
minutes later Dottie was once again clean and lying
back on the bed. Blanche closed the door and made
her way into the kitchen. Placing the soiled bed
linen into the washing machine she took a seat at
the table and watched as the soapy water swirled
around. Cleaning up her mother had really taken
its toll and she didn't know how much longer she

could carry on. It was becoming a daily occurrence and deep down she knew that her shallow threat of putting her mother into a nursing home was quickly turning into a distinct possibility. The rest of the day was spent in front of the television switching from channel to channel. Blanche loved watching Jeremy Kyle and any other chat shows that she could find on free view. Finally at four o'clock she was feeling peckish and decided to start preparing their evening meal. Walking into her mother's room she was about to ask what Dottie wanted to eat when she stopped in her tracks. Dottie Stewart was motionless and her eyes were staring wide, her mouth was slightly open and Blanche instinctively knew that she was dead. Thinking back to earlier when she had lashed out, Blanche became frightened when she realised that she might have killed her own mother. Quietly closing the door she made her way back to the front room desperate to think of a plausible story. Ten minutes later she dialled 999 and after informing the operator that her elderly mother had fallen out of bed she asked for an ambulance. As quickly as she could Blanche returned to her mother's room and grabbing the side of the bed sheet, proceeded to tip the old woman onto the floor. By the time any help arrived Dottie had been dead for some time but Blanche still feigned shock and cried at all the correct times. The next day an autopsy was carried out but due to her age it was accepted that Dottie Stewart died from a blow to the head caused by a fall. The funeral was a dismal affair paid for by the state. The only mourners were Blanche and Lorraine from the cafe. No one from the market bothered to attend and Dottie's numerous sexual conquests over the years, at least those who were still alive, would rather not be associated with a woman who had been little short of a slut. There was no wake or boiled ham and tea after gathering, instead Blanche returned to the flat alone and began going through her mother's personal belongings. She'd decided to do the decent thing and wait until after the funeral but now that it was over she set about the task like a woman possessed. After bagging up any clothes that were halfway decent she telephoned the local charity shop who said they would call in and collect them the following morning. Next there was a box of personal papers to go through but there was nothing of any value or interest so Blanche binned the lot. A small wooden box which sat at the back of the dresser drawer caught her attention and lifting it out she slowly opened the lid. Blanche gasped at the contents, three large bundles of bank notes were crammed inside and when she'd finished counting them out there was over five thousand pounds. She couldn't believe her mother had been squirreling away money unbeknown to her for so long. A large smile came over Blanche's face as she mouthed the words 'you crafty old cow'. After it finally sunk in that there was now plenty of

cash for treats, Blanche headed down the street to the all you could eat buffet on Paragon Road. After filling herself almost to bursting, she waddled home to the flat on Croston Street and started to make plans. She'd had her eye on a nice little second hand mobility scooter and there was now certainly enough money to pay for it. Blanche couldn't wait for her new life to begin, she knew that whatever happened in the future, it was now her turn to be looked after, her turn to be waited on hand and foot and as far as she was concerned, it couldn't come soon enough. True to herself she bought the bright red scooter and for a couple of months she really seemed to be enjoying life. Now Blanche ate out every day and the pizza delivery van was seen outside the flat most nights. She didn't miss her mother at all but the only problem, was the fact that she was getting larger and larger. Moving around the flat was becoming increasingly difficult and she now rocked from side to side as she walked. Finally and after purchasing an electric wheelchair to use indoors, she had to admit that the only option left was to get some help that or go on a diet and the word diet wasn't even in Blanche's vocabulary. Telephoning social services she asked to speak to Deborah Jenkins, the girl had been so helpful regarding Dottie that Blanche knew she would be a good place to start. Blanche tapped the side table nervously as she waited to be put through.
"Hello Miss Stewart, how can I help you?"

Blanche went into great detail about losing her mother and even added the odd sob for effect. "So you see Deborah I really can't manage all by myself. Do you know I've worked hard for my entire life and just when I retired and I thought me and mum could spend some quality time together, she goes and passes away. I know you helped me before and even though I hate asking, is there anything you can do for me sweetheart?"

"Well do you have any medical problems?"

"You only have to look at me sweetheart, I'm as big as a bleeding house so yes of course I do. I have arthritis in both knees and can hardly walk, the doc says I also have angina though I aint really got a clue what that means and, well is there any need for me to carry on?"

Deborah smiled and when Blanche at last finished talking, the young woman had a tear in her eye.

"You leave it with me Miss Stewart. I will put you down for a home visit as a matter of urgency."

Blanche thanked the young woman and when she replaced the receiver laughed to herself. She really was a good actress and maybe if Dottie hadn't have been such a demanding mother then Blanche could have been an actress. She spent the next few minutes daydreaming about being in one of the big shows up the west end, finally when she got bored she made her way into the kitchen to prepare herself some lunch.

CHAPTER THREE

Sue Hewitt had just reached her thirty eighth birthday and lived in Pitcairn House on St. Thomas's Square, Hackney. The address sounded posh like one of the big mansion houses in Chelsea or Knightsbridge but in all honesty it was just three blocks of local authority flats that had been built in the nineteen fifties. She had been resident in the same small two bedroom home since the day she was born and after marrying her husband John in a rushed ceremony eighteen years ago, he had moved in with Sue and her mother Barbara. The poor woman suffered with diabetes and within two years of her daughter's marriage she passed away. Sue and John took over the tenancy and with an eighteen month old child to care for things seemed to be working out well. When little Ian started school Sue got herself a job at Tesco's on Morning Lane in Homerton. She could walk it in five minutes so after dropping her son off at school it was perfect. With more money coming in Sue Hewitt dreamed of a family holiday and treats for her boy but it didn't work out that way. The more hours she took on at the supermarket, the fewer hours her husband did. John Hewitt had short arms and deep pockets and it had always been a struggle to get her weekly housekeeping out of him and things just got worse as the years rolled by. When Ian left school at sixteen Sue changed her hours and now worked the night shift stacking shelves. She offered to try and put a word in for her son but he had no intention of getting work and spent all day lounging around the flat with his father. The pair of them sponged from Sue, everything from beer money to cigarettes and there wasn't a thing she could do about it. Every morning before she went to bed she would hide her purse, it had only happened the once but when she had gotten up and every penny she had to her name had been taken and beer cans littered the front room floor, Sue had quickly learned a lesson. Still, meeting the rent and bills not to mention feeding the three of them was becoming harder by the week. Deciding that she had no alternative but to look for a second income she made her way to the local jobcentre. Just as she expected there wasn't much on offer but one vacancy did interest her slightly.

Personal help wanted to assist elderly lady in her home.

3 hours per day Monday to Friday. Above minimum wage paid.

Sue went straight to the counter to apply but was told that the interviews were being held by the lady herself and if she would like to leave her telephone number they would pass it on. Doing as she was asked, Sue Hewitt began to make her way home and kept crossing her fingers as she walked. About to enter the Square, she stopped when her mobile rang.

"Hello?"

Blanche Stewart put on the poshest voice she could manage; she'd never had staff before and wanted to get off on the right foot.

"Good afternoon my dear, I understand you wish to apply for the position of my assistant?"

Sue Hewitt screwed up her face, assistant? It was a carer's job, obviously the woman had delusions of grandeur but then again perhaps her hopeful employer was rich and lived in a large house. Ever the optimist she decided to go along with the woman on the other end of the line.

"That's right."

"Well if you'd like to call at my home tomorrow morning at nine sharp then perhaps we can discuss the matter further."

Sue quickly grabbed a notebook and pen from her bag and scribbled down Blanche's address. She wanted to explain that nine was a bit too early as she didn't come off shift until six in the morning and that she would like to go home to shower and rest first but she thought better of it. Making a sacrifice just this once would be well worth it if she got the job. Placing her phone back into her bag she studied the address and groaned when she realised where it was. Still beggars couldn't be choosers and if she landed the job then things at home would at least be a little easier financially. Reaching Pitcairn House she wearily placed her key in the lock and entering the hall could hear the television blearing out. After hanging up her coat she popped her head around the door to the front room. Her husband John was lounging in the recliner armchair and Ian laid spread out on the sofa. Sue's husband turned his eyes from the television long enough to look at her and smile.

"Put the kettle on love, there's a good girl."

Shaking her head she went into the kitchen to do as she'd been asked. The place was a mess, fish and chip papers lay open on the work surface and the sink contained dirty plates, mugs and cutlery. With every second that the kettle took to boil she became more and more angry. God she hadn't long finished an eight hour shift and she was absolutely knackered, it should be them waiting on her not the other way around. Pouring out two mugs of boiling water she went back into the front room and handed one mug to her husband and then the other to her son. As John Hewitt took a sip he yelled out in pain.

"Why you daft cow! This is bleeding boiling water, whatever are you playing at I could have been really hurt."

"Well that's the quickest you've bloody moved in years."

Walking over to the television she bent down and switched it off. Ian sat bolt upright and was about to complain but one look from his mother silenced him.

"Right you two, I've had just about as much as I can

take. Today I've hopefully landed myself a second job and all because you two lazy bastards don't lift a finger to help me. Well it stops from today do you hear?"

Staring at her husband, she shouted as she spoke. "John you are useless and a poor excuse for a husband. I work all the hours I can and all you do is take take take. Well not anymore, first thing in the morning you can get down that bleeding job centre and I don't want you back in this house until you find something. I don't care if it's part time as long as you get something do you hear me?"

Suddenly a snigger could be heard from Ian and Sue now directed her anger towards her son.

"And you don't want to sit there fucking laughing boy, because the same goes for you. I mean it Ian, if you aint got any work by the end of the week then you can sling your bleeding hook. And don't think I don't mean it the pair of you, because I'll change the bloody' locks if I have to. You've both pushed me just about as far as you can. Now I'm going to bed and god help the pair of you if that telly wakes me up."

At nine thirty that evening and after only managing to get a few hours sleep, Sue set off for work. After an eight hour shift of lugging boxes of vegetables from the warehouse onto the shop floor she was totally exhausted and all she really wanted was to do was go home, fall into bed and sleep. Unfortunately she didn't have much choice and after quickly making her way back to the flat, she grabbed a cuppa, showered and changed her clothes in readiness for her interview. At eight thirty she headed over to Croston Street. It was a bright sunny morning and Sue was now feeling optimistic or at least she was until her eyes settled on the building that Blanche Stewart called home. It looked even more dismal that her own flat, litter filled the stairwell and there was an overpowering stench of urine on each level. Stepping over a KFC bucket and strewn beer cans she surveyed the approach to the flat door. Pile upon pile of discarded pizza boxes, were stacked up under the kitchen window and Sue was starting to have her doubts. Still she was here now so she might as well go through with it. Knocking on the door, it seemed like an age before she could hear anything and then suddenly darkness filled the hallway. Through the frosted glass she couldn't quite make out what it was but she could definitely see something or someone approaching the front door. After hearing a lot of huffing and puffing, a voice finally spoke out.

"Who is it?"

"It's Sue Hewitt Miss Stewart; I've come for my interview."

Blanche lent up from the wheelchair and flicked the latch. As soon as the door opened, the smell hit Sue and she wanted to raise her hand to her nose but knew it would look rude. The paintwork and wallpaper were peeling and everything looked grimy and greasy.

"Come on in then before you let all the heat out." Blanche reversed the chair and went into the front room. As Sue followed she glanced all around her and immediately knew this was a bad idea. For starters the woman was huge and there was no way Sue would ever be able to lift her if she wanted a wash or a bath. She instantly dismissed the latter; there was no bath tub big enough in the world to hold this woman.

"Are you coming in or what?"

The posh accent of yesterday had disappeared and Sue wanted to giggle. Stopping herself she entered the room and almost gasped at the sight. If she thought the hall was bad, then nothing prepared her for this. There were even more pizza boxes stacked up beside the fireplace than there were outside. Newspapers, magazines and dirty crockery littered the floor but Blanche seemed oblivious to it all.

"Take a seat over there and we'll get started."

Lifting a tray of sandwiches from the sofa Sue looked around for somewhere to put them but it seemed that every flat surface was crammed full of stuff. Noticing that Blanche was staring at her in annoyance, she placed the tray onto the floor and took a seat.

"So what sort of care work have you done in the past?"

'Well none really but I know how to run a house as

I've been married for years and I've raised a son so it can't be that hard. The advert said that the pay was above the minimum wage?"

"Yes it is, six thirty two an hour."

"But that's only a penny above the minimum?" Blanche suddenly felt annoyed. She was in receipt of attendance and mobility allowance but she didn't want to give it all to her carer and being able to keep some for herself would allow her to buy even more treats.

"Look, you either want the job or you don't. Now what's it to be?"

Sue felt like she'd been well and truly trucked up but when it boiled down to it, she needed this job and didn't have any choice but to accept what was being offered.

"I would like to take the job please. What exactly will I be expected to do?"

"Well clear this shithole up for a start! Then there's my dinner to prepare and the washing to be done." Once again Sue surveyed the surroundings; she would need a lot more than three hours a day to get this place into shape.

"I can only give it a go but it will take a while before I get all of this mess sorted out."

"Mess! You cheeky cow, this is my home and you'd do well to remember that. Now when can you start? Tomorrow?"

Sue nodded her head.

"Good. Now I shall call you Sue but you must call

me Miss Stewart. Here's a key so that you can let yourself in and don't be late."
Sue couldn't believe the cheek of the woman and after a swift goodbye she let herself out and began the journey home to her flat and the hope of being able to fall into bed. Opening the front door she was surprised that no one replied when she called out. Entering the front room she almost gasped, it was tidy and there were no men lounging about watching television. Walking through to the kitchen it was the same, no washing up in the sink and the surfaces had all been wiped down. Maybe her stern words from last night had actually got through the thick sculls of the two men in her life. Walking through to the bedroom she collapsed onto the bed and didn't even have the energy to get undressed. It was six pm by the time she woke and it had been the best sleep she'd experienced in months. Taking off her uniform, Sue pulled on her dressing gown and slowly made her way down the hall. There was a really nice aroma coming from the kitchen and as she opened the door she was greeted by two smiling faces. John stood at the cooker stirring a Bolognese and Ian was seated at the table. "Hello love, come on take a seat its nearly ready." For a minute she was struck dumb, in all her married life John had never so much as boiled an egg so how he knew how to cook Italian she hadn't got a clue but she supposed spending all those years glued to the telly must have taught him something.

After placing three plates onto the table he took a seat and they all tucked in. Sue had to admit, if only to herself, that it was actually better than her own interpretation of the dish.

"Now I went down the job centre but in all honesty they didn't have much."

He could instantly see the look of disappointment on his wife's face.

"That said, they told me to go back at the end of the week as they were expecting several jobs to come in on Friday morning so at least that's something hey?"

Sue smiled but she still felt a bit sad, that was until Ian joined in.

"Well I got a job today Mum. It's only running errands for Tommy Mortimer but at least its work and the pay aint bad either."

Sue tenderly touched her sons arm but instead of the praise he was expecting to hear, he was taken aback by the look of worry on her face.

"I know I said you had to find a job love but Tommy Mortimer? I've heard he's really shady and that he deals in drugs at that nightclub of his."

Ian laid down his knife and fork and looked from his father to his mother.

"Maybe he does but it doesn't mean I will. As long as he pays me then I'll just keep me head down and do as I'm told, at least until something better comes up."

Sue smiled and nodded but his words did little to reassure her. The family finished their meal in silence, John and Ian were savouring the food and Sue was going over in her mind what her son had just told her. When the plates were cleared away and they were once more seated with a cup of tea the conversation resumed.

"Well neither of you have asked how I got on today at my interview. I got the job and I start tomorrow though lord above knows how long I'll be able to stick it. The old girl is as big as a house and a right narky cow. You should see her flat John, filth doesn't even begin to describe it but at least the extra cash will come in handy."

Both men nodded their approval and when the three had finished their drinks they made their way into the front room to watch a couple of hours of television before Sue had to head off for her shift at the supermarket. The thought of starting work the next day wasn't the least bit appealing and it was on her mind for most of the evening.

CHAPTER FOUR

It had been a long hard slog at work as there was a midnight delivery and they were three staff down. At six fifteen am the following morning Sue Hewitt placed her key into the lock and she had never been so glad to be home. Expecting her husband to still be in bed she was pleasantly surprised to find him sitting at the kitchen table with a fresh pot of tea.

"Come on love take the weight off your feet, you look done in."

Sue was still having trouble accepting the new man and wondered how long it would last.

"Thanks. I have to be out again by eight thirty to start at the old girls and I aint looking forward to it I can tell you."

John Hewitt reached across the table and grabbed his wife's hand.

"Maybe if I have a bit of luck down the job centre on Friday you can give it up."

Sue finished her tea and got up from the table.

"I aint holding my breath. I'm going to get me head down, don't let me oversleep."

As she closed the kitchen door Sue didn't see the look of hurt on her husband's face but he didn't blame her, after all he'd been nothing short of useless for most of their married life. Sitting at the table that had long since needed replacing as did the rest of the furniture in the flat, he swore to himself that he would prove her wrong and change and above all else he would get a job. An hour and a half later and without having to be woken, Sue reappeared in the kitchen. She was now showered and in a brighter mood than she'd been in earlier. After her second cup of tea that day she pulled on her coat and grabbing her bag, planted a kiss on the top of her husband's head.

"Wish me luck!"

"You don't need it darling and the old girl is lucky to have you."

"I don't know about that, the one thing I do know is that I don't want to be going there but I aint got much choice in the matter have I?"

Sue walked from the kitchen and didn't realise that her words had cut deeply. She wasn't a nasty person but she was just so very very tired. Stepping onto the concrete landing she glanced over the metal railings and sighed in a disheartened manner when she noticed that it had begun to rain. Pulling an umbrella from her bag she crossed the square and set off for Croston Street. It was less than a ten minutes walk but remembering Miss Stewarts warning yesterday, Sue didn't want to be late. She hadn't got far when the heavens had opened and by the time she arrived at her destination Sue's clothes and shoes were soaked through. The brolly she had bought down the pound shop a week ago was little more than useless and now she would have to work in wet clothes. Placing Blanche's key into the lock, she took a deep breath and called out as she opened the door.

"Only me!!!!"

Entering the hallway, the smell wasn't any easier to take than it had been yesterday and it made her feel nauseous. Unbeknown to Sue, Dottie Stewart had been a chain smoker and the once cream coloured walls were now a deep nicotine shade of yellow. Even though the woman had been dead for several weeks, you could still smell the stale tobacco. Sue didn't think Miss Stewart smoked but she'd been too scared to ask. As she entered the front room, Blanche sat in her armchair with a face like thunder.

"Morning, alright are we?"

There was no welcoming smile from Blanche and her tone was curt.

"Well at least you aint late, I suppose that's one thing you've got going for you. Now I'm bleeding starving so you can start by making my breakfast. I'll have two eggs, four rashers and a couple of them lovely juicy sausages."

Nodding, Sue turned around and was just about to walk into the kitchen when Blanche spoke again.

"Put a couple of slices of fried bread on the side as well, for some reason I'm overly hungry today."

Shaking her head, Sue entered the kitchen but when she saw the mess felt like screaming. The sink was overflowing with dirty pots and pans and there were several dead flies floating in a large puddle of cooking oil on the hob. Opening the window, she hoped that a nice breeze might help to take away some of the smells that was until Blanche's voice could be heard calling from the front room.

"Have you got that bloody window open? Shut it now, gawd above knows it's hard enough for pensioners to afford their heating without a silly cow like you letting in a force ten gale."

Sue sighed and closed up the window as she'd been ordered. Deciding to tackle the sink first, she washed up all the pots and then scrubbed the stainless steel bowl and drainer. It had taken twenty minutes but standing back to admire the gleaming sink, even she had to admit that she'd done a good job. About to start cleaning the cooker she nearly jumped out of her skin when Blanche's shrill voice boomed out again.

"Oi! You in there, is it nearly ready? My stomach thinks my bleeding throats been cut."

Walking into the front room Sue counted to ten under her breath and then nervously coughed.

"I'm afraid I haven't even started on your breakfast yet Miss Stewart."

"What the bloody hell have you been doing? I don't pay you to stand around doing nothing my girl."

Sue could feel her blood begin to boil and she'd been here less than half an hour. She didn't know if she could make it to the next hour let alone to the end of the week.

"Excuse me for being blunt but your home is absolutely filthy."

"Well of course it is, that's why I've got you."

Sue went back into the kitchen and put the pan on to heat, cleaning the cooker would just have to wait until later and if the old girl got food poisoning, well it was her own fault. By ten o'clock Blanche had at last been fed and as Sue went in to collect her tray and plate the woman was now tucking into a box of walnut whips. Cleaning the hob and worktops took ages but Sue managed to get it all done by twelve. Pulling on her coat to leave, she turned around and was stunned to see Blanche Stewart seated in her wheelchair in the doorway. "And where might I ask do you think you're off to?" "Well you said three hours a day and that's what I've done."

"What about my lunch?"

"But you've only just had your breakfast."

"And whose fault is that. If you're too slow at your job that aint my fault. You'll just have to work a bit longer today and don't think I'm paying you any extra because I'm not. Let this be a lesson to you, from now on you'll have to pull your finger out and get a move on. Now there's a nice bit of smoked yellow haddock in the fridge. I like it poached in milk and you can open up a tin of new potatoes and fry them up. Well come on then, what are you waiting for?"

With that the electric chair reversed and Blanche disappeared back into the front room. Shaking her head Sue removed her coat and hung it on the back of the door, at this rate she would still be here by the

45

time she should be leaving for her job at the supermarket. Thirty minutes later and Blanche was served her lunch. Picking up her coat and bag, Sue stood like a school girl and waited for her new employers' approval on the food but when none was forthcoming, she lost her patience and asked outright.

"Well is it alright?"

Blanche had already eaten half of the fish and on hearing the question prodded and poked the remainder with her knife.

"Not bad for a first attempt I suppose but if you want my honest opinion, it's a bit overdone for my liking. There you go, I'm an old woman so what choice do I have than to put up with it."

"So is it ok if I get off now?"

"Whose going to wash up my plate?"

By now Sue Hewitt was more than angry.

"You can do it and if you're not able to manage, you ll have to put it in the sink and I'll see to it tomorrow. I've gone well over my time, time you've already pointed out that you won't be paying for, so I think I'm being more than generous."

She didn't wait for Blanche to reply and walking out of the flat pulled her coat on as she swore under her breath. Her mornings work had brought on a bout of depression and as she walked along she looked at her surroundings more intently. Everywhere seemed rundown and unloved just like Sue Hewitt was feeling. Crossing the Square she waved at

Maureen and Derek Burrell who lived in the flat above her. Both in their early seventies, they always walked along hand in hand and Sue had never heard a cross word spoken between them. Maureen and Derek had lived in the flat for most of their lives and often spoke of how the area was years ago, when people looked out for one another and the good old London spirit was still going strong. Now it was everyone for themselves and people were afraid to go out after dark alone. Sue sighed as she began to climb the concrete steps and it was gone one o'clock when she at last arrived home. John was standing in the hall as she entered.

"Where on earth have you been, I was expecting you home ages ago."

Hanging up her coat, she was dog tired and really not in the mood for conversation but she could see the concern on his face.

"That woman is nothing but an old witch and eat; she could eat for bleeding England. I had to cook her breakfast after I'd cleared away all the dirty dishes in the kitchen. The place is rank; I tell you John I wouldn't let a dog live there let alone a human being. Anyway she'd no sooner wolfed down a full English and she was asking for even more food. By the time I'd got the kitchen in a liveable state I then had to turn round and cook her lunch. That's why I'm late and the old bitch said she aint paying me overtime as it's my fault I'm so slow."

John attempted to take his wife in his arms but it had been so long since they'd had any physical contact, the feeling was alien to her and she moved away.

"She's lucky to have someone like you. If it was me I'd tell her exactly where she could go, in fact I'd tell her to stick her poxy job right up her arse and then I'd be off."

"Yeh well you would do wouldn't you. You just don't get it do you, we need the bleeding money!"

One look from his wife told him not to say anything else about it. There was no way they could continue to manage with just one wage coming in. For years he'd plodded along and laid everything at his wife's door but since she'd given him a dressing down the other night, it was as if a fog had been lifted. When he looked into her tired drawn face he felt nothing but shame and guilt.

"Why don't you go and turn in and I'll bring you through a nice hot cuppa."

"That would be nice. Have you heard anything from our Ian?"

"Give him a chance love, he only started today."

"I know but I'm worried, I really don't like the thought of him working for that Tommy Mortimer."

"Enough about our Ian! You can't take the weight of the world on your shoulders love, now go on, off to bed with you and get your head down."

Doing as she'd been told she wearily walked down the hallway and on entering the bedroom was at least pleased to see that for once the bed had been made. Stepping out of her uniform she slowly pulled on her pyjamas. Turning back the bedclothes, Sue was about to climb in when her mobile started to ring. For a moment she contemplated not answering but then the thought that it might be her son entered her head. In the habit of keeping her handbag with her as she still didn't trust her husband or son, Sue lifted out her phone and answered.

"Hello?"

"Its Miss Stewart here."

Sue rolled her eyes upwards.

"What is it? I was just about to go to bed, I have a night shift to do later you know?"

"You young ones aint got any stamina, anyway I'm ringing because I want you to get me a lottery ticket on your way over in the morning. It's the big Friday roll over and I can't afford to miss it. Now I don't want any particular numbers, a lucky dip will do and if I win I'll treat you."

Sue was too tired to argue, her eyelids felt like lead weights and she knew that if she didn't get some sleep soon she was liable to collapse.

"Ok Miss Stewart but I really do need to go now, I'll see you tomorrow."

With that Sue hung up and hoped that the woman telephoning her wasn't going to become a regular occurrence. When John came in to bring her a cup of tea she was already snoring softly and he hadn't

49

the heart to wake her. Placing the drink on the bedside cabinet he crept quietly out of the room.

CHAPTER FIVE

For almost eighteen years Lizzie Chambers had raised her son as a single parent. She still lived on Ritchie Street with her father but her brothers had long since moved out. Dave now worked away in Scotland on the oil rigs and only came home a couple of times a year. Steve had decided to travel the world for twelve months after a failed relationship and Joey had been married for the past ten years but it wasn't a perfect union. The moment he met Sharon Jackson he had instantly fell in love and within a year they were married. She was tall, blonde and beautiful and every time they went out he felt as though he had a model on his arm. The only problem was that nothing was ever good enough and Sharon wanted more and more. An only child, her parents were comfortably off and as they'd given her everything her heart desired, she decided that any man she married would have to do the same. Since Mike Chamber's retirement ten years earlier Joey had taken over the building business and trade had soared when he moved into private house renovations. The majority of his work was carried out for private customers but occasionally he would do one off speck projects for himself. It was so profitable that Joey and Sharon were able to purchase a house on Lansdown Road in Notting Hill. They had started out in a first floor flat and after a couple of years the ground floor became available. Sharon nagged and nagged her husband and after mortgaging himself up to the hilt, they now owned the complete house. Sharon wasn't content and as the saying goes, patience definitely wasn't one of her virtues. They spent every penny that Joey earned and more besides. It always had to be the latest and most expensive style in furniture, his and hers top of the range motors, not to mention the thousands of pounds that she spent on the best in designer clothing. It got so bad that Joey was working a ten hour day seven days a week. He tried to pop over to Islington once a week to see his family but sometimes even that was difficult. His father and sister understood but it did nothing for family relations when it came down to what they thought of Sharon. The last time he had called in, Lizzie noticed how drawn he was and there were dark circles under his eyes. He almost flopped down onto the kitchen chair and Lizzie and her father looked at each other and they both had concern written all over their faces.

"You feeling alright Joey?"

"I'm just knackered Sis. No matter how hard I work or how much money I bring home it's never enough."

Mike muttered 'greedy bitch' under his breath but it wasn't quiet enough not to be heard by his son and daughter. Neither commented, Lizzie because she didn't want to get into an argument and Joey, well Joey couldn't argue as he knew that his father was speaking the truth.

"Let me make you a nice cup of rosie."

"Thanks sweetheart, where's the boy anyway?"

Lizzie laughed. They all referred to Michael as the boy even though he was only two months away from his eighteenth birthday.

"He's in bed bless his heart. He keeps saying he's not feeling well but I don't know if it's just a case of lazyitis."

"I'll pop up and see him before I go, give him a bit of a talking to."

Mike didn't like them speaking about Michael as if he was a good for nothing. The boy had brains, real brains and his grandfather knew that one day he would really amount to something. Michael had always been, what could only be described as a poorly kid. Over the years he seemed to come down with any manner of illnesses going but he was a happy soul and never complained. Mike Chambers was about to voice his opinion but was stopped when Joeys phone began to ring. Reaching into his pocket he sighed when he saw it was his wife calling.

"Hello babe, what's up?"

Joey had to pull the phone away from his ear as his wife screamed down the line at the top of her voice.

"Ok honey I'm just at me Dads I won't...."

Again he had to remove the phone and Lizzie felt embarrassed for her brother. For the life of her she couldn't work out what the hold her sister in law

53

had over Joey was but when she said jump he said how high. Lizzie hated it but she knew there was nothing she could do, Joey had to sort his own life out. A few seconds later and he pressed end call and stood up from the table.

"I best be off."

"But you haven't even finished your tea."

Joey bent down and kissed his sister tenderly on her cheek.

"I know Sis but if I don't get back they'll be murders and to be honest I'm way too tired for a row tonight. When Sharon has a mind too she can go on for hours and hours."

Joey nodded in his father's direction before disappearing into the hall. Only when they heard the front door close did Lizzie and her father discuss the situation.

"You know something Dad? It breaks my bleeding heart to see him being treated like that. Joey was always the strong one but now he's nothing more than a lap dog, I feel like slapping him sometimes."

"I know exactly how you feel darling but it aint him I want to slap, it's that cunt of a wife."

"Dad!"

"I know I know, it's a horrible word and I don't use it lightly but she really is one nasty horrible bitch. Anyway I aint going to waste anymore good air talking about that slag, now why don't you go check on that boy of yours and see how he's feeling."

Lizzie did as her father asked and as she climbed the stairs she couldn't help but smile at his words. In her entire life she had never heard him use the C word and knew that he must be really pissed off with Joey's wife.

Joey Sat outside for a few minutes. His Range Rover Evoke would be with him for another thirty six months before it was paid for and he hated the bloody thing already. Another of Sharon's must have purchases that he hadn't been able to say no to. He thought back to a time when he still lived here on Ritchie Street and the old escort van that he'd driven. He was happy then, really happy but now every day seemed to take more and more from him and sooner or later he knew he was going to explode. Until that day came he just had to carry on and keep his wife happy if he was ever to have a chance of any peace. As he pulled out into the road the traffic was starting to build and although it was only a five mile journey, it would take him over twenty minutes to get home. Walking up the steps to his beautiful home he was careful not to leave any fingerprints on the high gloss front door. The standard Bay trees that stood either side were immaculate and he knew Sharon could tell in an instant if anything was out of place. As he walked in the direction of the kitchen he could see his wife seated on a high leather stool at the breakfast bar. The kitchen had been hand crafted and all the work surfaces were made of solid black granite.

Everything gleamed and even though it was his home he always felt frightened to touch anything.
"You took your time. I wanted you to run me up West, there's a new boutique opened on Bond Street and I wanted to get something new to wear tonight."
"In case it's slipped your mind Sharon, you have got your own car!"
"Don't be bloody sarcastic. You know what the parking's like; I would have had murders trying to find a space. Well you've gone and spoiled that for me, they'll be shut soon and I aint rushing so there's no point now. You aint forgot that Lou and Steph are coming round tonight?"
Joey ran one hand through his hair and placed the other onto the worktop. Sharon was out of her seat in a second and pushing her husband to one side, she rubbed the surface vigorously with a duster.
"Now look what you've done! I wish you wouldn't do that!"
Joey walked back out into the hall and as he started to climb the stairs he called out to his wife.
"You can phone Steph and cancel, I aint in the mood."
Joey stood in the shower and let the hot water soothe his tired limbs. He felt like he could sleep for a week but would have to make do with only the weekend. Hearing the bathroom door open he saw Sharon enter and her doe eyes had a look in them that said she was feeling sorry for herself.

"Please Joey. I really want Steph to come round tonight. What can I do to make you change your mind baby?"

Sex was always her answer to everything. It solved her problems, got her anything she wanted but most of all it enabled her to twist her husband around her little finger.

"I'm too tired Sharon can't you see that?"

"But it's not even five o'clock yet! Why don't you come into the bedroom and I'll make you feel better?"

For once her magic wasn't working and inside she started to panic.

"What time are they due?"

"About eight."

Joey stepped from the shower and wrapped a towel around his lean waist. He was toned and handsome and even after ten years of marriage Sharon still found him irresistible.

"If you let me go to bed until they get here then they can come round, if not then you can just cancel Sharon and I aint arguing about it."

Slowly she nodded her head in agreement but when her husband ignored her and walked from the room without giving her so much as a peck on the cheek, her eyes opened wide with fear. Sex and her figure were the only bartering tools she'd ever had, without them she couldn't get her own way.

Staring into the full height mirror above one of the sinks she examined her face in great detail.

There were no wrinkles, her monthly Botox trip took care of that. Her clothes were expensive and smart and her makeup was meticulously applied and for the life of her Sharon couldn't see why he'd rejected her advances. Pouting her lips at the mirror she spoke to herself 'Gorgeous, absolutely gorgeous'.

At eight on the dot the bell rang out and Sharon Chambers flounced along the hallway to answer the door. Steph Mason was her oldest friend, in fact they had been buddies since their first day at school but their petty rivalry hadn't diminished as the years had passed. As the door opened both women looked each other up and down to see who was wearing the most expensive outfit, as usual it was Sharon who won. After double air kissing each other the women walked into the lounge leaving Lou to follow. Lou Mason was a strange character, he was always immaculately dressed and for years Sharon had a niggling suspicion that he was gay but she'd never had the guts to ask her friend. After pouring them both a glass of champagne she made her excuses and headed up to the bedroom. Joey lay on his back and was still sleeping soundly but seconds later was woken by a stirring in his loins. To begin with he thought it was a wet dream until he opened his eyes and looked downwards. Under the covers he could see the shape of his wife's head as it bobbed up and down. For a moment he thought about protesting but as his erection rapidly became harder he could only grip the bed sheets with his hands and groan with ecstasy. It didn't last long and a minute or two later Sharon's head appeared from under the sheet. Grinning, she gently wiped the corner of her mouth.

"Time to get up sleepy head, Steph and Lou are here."

Knowing that she had once again got her own way, Sharon walked out of the bedroom without another word and went down to join their guests. Joey slowly pulled himself from the bed and after a quick shower he entered the front room with a big smile on his face. Taking a glass of champagne from his wife he placed his arm around her waist and kissed her on the cheek. Joey Chambers couldn't deny that Sharon was a greedy, spoilt, manipulative cow; he also couldn't deny that he loved her deeply.

Over on Ritchie Street Lizzie had tapped lightly on Michael's bedroom door for the fifth time that day but this time there was no answer. For a moment she contemplated going back downstairs but she had a nagging doubt that maybe he really was ill. Coughing loudly just in case he was doing what all young men do in their bedrooms, she turned the handle and walked in. Michael was buried under two duvets and to begin with he didn't answer his mother when she spoke to him.

"How you feeling sweetheart?"

Walking over to the bed she slightly pulled the covers back so that she could see his face.

"I said how are you feeling?"

Michael's eyes were only half open and he was so drowsy that he looked like he'd been drugged.

"You aint taken anything have you love?"

This time he spoke and as he did so pulled back the duvets.

"Mum you know me better than that, I just can't seem to wake up and I feel so sick."

Glancing down Lizzie noticed that her son's arms, hands and feet were swollen and when she pressed her fingers onto his skin, could feel a build up of fluid.

"Dad! Dad! Can you come up here a minute?"

Mike Chambers was by his daughter's side in record time and when he saw the state that his grandson was in, he immediately called an ambulance. Mike knew that things were far from good, so staying with Michael he told Lizzie to go down stairs and phone Joey. Sharon was in the kitchen refilling the nuts and olives when the phone rang and she was annoyed that her evening was being interrupted. Snatching up the phone her words came out in a snappy manner as she was so annoyed.

"Yes! Who is it?"

"Its Lizzie, I need to speak to our Joey."

"I'm sorry but we have guests, if you'd like to call again tomorrow I'm......"

Lizzie didn't wait for her sister in law to finish and slamming down the receiver redialled her brother's mobile number. As Sharon walked into the front room she heard the phone ring and knew who it was. When Joey retrieved his mobile from his trouser pocket Sharon placed a hand on her husband's arm.

"Not tonight babe. It's probably a client and you know how customers can go on sometimes." Smiling at his wife, Joey pressed cancel without checking who the caller was but Lizzie wasn't about to give up and instantly redialled her brothers phone. This time Joey did check his phone and answered as soon as he saw who it was.

"Hi Sis!"

"That fucking bitch! This is the third time I've called, the first time she wouldn't let me speak to you."

Joey gave his wife a fixed stare and she knew she would be in the dog house when Steph and Lou had gone home.

"I'll deal with her later Sweetheart, now what's the problem?"

"It's Michael. He's just got worse throughout the day and now Dads called for an ambulance. They've just pulled up, oh Joey I'm so worried!"

"Where are they taking him?"

"I don't know Joey, give me five minutes and I'll call you back."

With that Lizzie Chambers hung up and went to let the paramedics in. Joey began to pace the floor and Sharon could see that something was really bothering her husband but every time she asked

what it was he tried to change the subject as he
didn't want to talk in front of Steph and Lou. If
they'd had any decency the couple would have said
their goodbyes and left but Steph was nosy and
loved a bit of drama so they both remained seated
on the sofa.
"Joey don't keep making me ask, now please tell me
what's wrong."
"Look our Michaels sick and they're taking him to
hospital."
"Well? Why don't you let your sister sort it out, you
can't go running every time she phones you."
Joey could feel his blood begin to boil but as they
had company he didn't want to get into a row. Over
on Ritchie Street Lizzie and her father watched as
the paramedics examined Michael but within a few
minutes it was obvious that the situation was
serious.
"We need to get him to hospital as soon as possible."
"Where are you taking him?"
"Bart's."
As the paramedics lifted Michael onto a stretcher,
Lizzie ran down the stairs and at the same time as
pulling on her coat she dialled Joey's number and
relayed which hospital it was. Telling his sister that
he'd meet her there, Joey snatched up his car keys
and left the house with no further explanation.
Twenty minutes later he ran into the emergency
department and spied his father sitting in the
waiting area. Mike Chambers suddenly looked old

and his face was ashen.

"Any news Dad?"

Mike could only shake his head and from the redness around his eyes Joey could see that his father was upset. From one of the side rooms the sound of a woman sobbing could be heard and moments later the door opened and Lizzie Chambers walked over to her brother and father.

"My boys got kidney failure; whatever am I going to do!"

Mike jumped to his feet and taking Lizzie into his arms led her over to the seating area. Joey joined them and with her brother on one side and her father on the other Lizzie began to cry again. A couple of minutes later and after blowing her nose she composed herself.

"So just explain this to me Sis, what does it all mean?"

"I'm not really sure yet. The doctor said they have to do some more tests but his kidney function is limited. I have to go home Joey and get him a few things, there wasn't time when we left, can you give me a lift?"

"Sure, I'll run you and Dad home then bring you back."

The three looked a sorry sight as they left the hospital and by the time they had gone back to Ritchie Street, returned to the hospital with Michael's things and after Joey dropped his sister back home for the second time; it was gone two am when he finally walked into his own house. Everywhere was in darkness and he couldn't believe that Sharon hadn't waited up for him. A bottle of Champagne and three empty bottles of red wine sat on the granite worktop and the thought that she was sitting here with her pals getting off her face while he'd been at the hospital, suddenly made Joey erupt with anger. With one swift move of his arm he smashed the bottles to the floor and walked up the stairs. The noise hadn't woken Sharon but she would be really pissed off in the morning when she came down and saw all the mess. For the first time in his married life, Joey Chambers didn't give a toss about what his wife would say.

CHAPTER SIX

Friday morning Sue Hewitt set off for Croston Street to do battle once more with Blanche or at least that's how she felt. Letting herself into the flat, the scenario was exactly the same as yesterday and entering the front room she immediately asked what the woman would like for her breakfast.
"Same as yesterday, there's a couple of them sausages left and I can't afford to let them go to waste. I did think about frying them up for me supper but changed my mind and ordered in a kebab. Jump to it what are you waiting for I'm starving."
Strangely after just one day Sue was getting used to Blanche and her rude ways and as long as she reminded herself that she was only here for the money, then she knew she'd be able to cope. Unlike yesterday Blanche was fed and watered by nine thirty and after washing up Sue still had a full two hours work ahead of her.
"What would you like me to do today?"
"You can start in my bedroom. The commode aint been emptied for two days and the sheets need a wash as I had a bit of an accident last night."
Blanche didn't say anything else and just stared at Sue with an expression that silently said 'get on with it then'. Going back into the hall Sue slowly opened the bedroom door. She had yet to go into this particular room and didn't know what would

be on the other side of the door. She was pleasantly surprised, there was hardly any mess; in fact there wasn't much of anything except a single bed, wardrobe, a commode and bedside cabinet. The floor covering was black Marley tiles that was standard in all council flats and a pair of large floral seventies curtains hung limply on either side of the window. It wouldn't take much cleaning and she was glad of that but there was still a rancid smell in the room. Pulling back the bedclothes Sue Hewitt let out a gasp. Positioned in the middle of the bed was a large turd. It was so meticulously placed that Sue couldn't help but think Blanche had done this on purpose, still she wasn't about to let the old woman get one over on her. Collecting a handful of toilet paper from the bathroom, she tentatively picked up the offending turd and lifting the lid of the commode, dropped it inside. Sue hadn't expected the bowl to be so full and as it hit the inside stale urine flowed over the rim. The liquid was dark yellow and it must have been at least a week's worth. Suddenly she began to wretch and running to the bathroom only just made it in time as the contents of her stomach went down the pan. Wiping her mouth she could hear the faintest chuckle of laughter coming from the front room but she didn't know if the woman was amused by something on the telly, or if she was laughing behind her back at the sound of Sue being sick. If she was a betting woman Sue would have placed her money on the latter. Plugging her nostrils with toilet paper so she couldn't smell anything she reluctantly went back into the bedroom and lifted the pot from the commode. Each step she took was slow as she had a vision of spilling the lot and having to clean it all up. With the sheets changed and the spilled urine cleared up, Sue without being asked, went into the kitchen and turned on the oven. Looking in the fridge she spotted two pork chops and pulling a bag of frozen chips from the freezer, began to fry it all up. Blanche was speechless when she was handed the tray of food and tucked in as if she hadn't eaten in days. Sue went into the kitchen so that the woman could eat in peace and glancing at her watch, noted that it was still only eleven forty five. She was pleased to see that after washing up in a few minutes time she would soon be on her way. A two day break would be enough rest for her to prepare herself for the ongoing saga on Monday morning. Hoping that the woman would be finished by now Sue went back into the front room but Blanche was still eating as she stared at the television.

"Is it alright?"

"Not bad but I would have liked to be asked what I wanted. I might not have fancied chops today."

Blanche Stewart talked as she ate and Sue could see mashed up food as it swirled around in her mouth. Blanche didn't even stop chewing as she talked and Sue found the sight disgusting.

"Sorry about that but there wasn't much else in the fridge. Now when I've cleaned up I'll be on my way."

"Hang on a minute, where's my lottery ticket?"

In her hurry to get here this morning it had completely slipped Sue's mind and she knew that she would now have to go to the corner shop before she finished but Blanche wasn't about to let her carer off that easily.

"You forgot it didn't you? I only asked you for one thing and you couldn't even do that for me, call yourself a carer?"

"I'll pop out and get it now Blanche alright!"

"Miss Stewart if you don't mind!"

Sue grabbed her coat and was about to open the front door when Blanche called out to her.

"Get a couple of bars of chocolate while you're down there and not the little ones either, they aint no good to man nor beast, I like the family size."

"You would!"

"What was that?"

"Nothing just talking to myself."

Sue quickly ran to the shop and back again. Glancing at her watch as she let herself into the flat, she knew that once again she would end up working later than she was supposed to. Placing the ticket and chocolate onto the small table beside Blanche Stewart's armchair she stood waiting to be paid.

"What are you hanging about for, you can go you

know?"

"Well I haven't been paid for the two days work I've done plus there's the lottery and chocolate that you owe me for."

Blanche waved her hand in dismissal.

"You'll have to wait until Monday now, I've spent all me pension money. Don't you worry you'll get it, I always pay my way, eventually!"

As Sue Hewitt walked home she felt deflated, she'd worked her socks off and had received nothing for it. She decided not to tell her husband and if the old girl was true to her word and settled up on Monday, then there was no need for him to ever find out. Realising that today her husband might be able to land a job gave her a swing in her step and suddenly she couldn't wait to get home and find out if it was good news for once.

Later that day Blanche was starting to get really excited about the lottery. It was a roll over and the jackpot was expected to be around fifty million. Sitting in her armchair she day dreamed about all that she could buy with the money. A big house would be first on her list and a huge bed that would be twice the size of a normal double and of course she would have to have one of those big American freezers maybe two if she felt like it. All that mind work was making her feel hungry so picking up the telephone she ordered a sixteen inch pizza topped with every extra that was available. After instructing the takeaway that the delivery time was crucial as she wanted to be tucking in when they called the numbers, she hung up and sat back to wait. At precisely seven forty five the door bell rang and Blanche Stewart hauled herself from the chair. Rocking her way along the hall it took over three minutes for Blanche to reach the door but the delivery lad had been here so many times before that he knew the routine well.

"Evening Miss Stewart. That'll be nine ninety nine please."

Blanche pulled a ten pound note from her purse and stood waiting for her penny change. The lad smiled as he handed it over and knew there wouldn't be a tip, there never was. Making her way into the front room took another three minutes and there were just nine left to countdown. With the large box sitting on her lap Blanche was now salivating and contemplated just nibbling a piece of the crust but for once she controlled herself as she thought for some silly reason it might be bad luck. Switching the television onto BBC she pressed the index and after choosing Lottery, Blanche sat back and waited for the numbers to appear on the teletext. She convinced herself that it would no longer be bad luck to start on her pizza and lifting the lid she wore a grin from ear to ear. She'd ordered so many toppings that the thing must have been two inches thick and pulling out a large slice she stuffed as much as she could into her mouth. By the time all the numbers appeared on the screen she was half

way through the supersize meal. Breaking off
another large slice she glanced down at her ticket
and saw that she had the first number. Her
chewing became quicker when she realised she had
not one but three numbers and by the time she saw
that she'd won the jackpot, Blanche was munching
in an almost frenzied way. Suddenly she began to
cough and couldn't get her breath. As the pizza box
fell to the floor a piece of pepperoni lodged itself in
her throat and Blanche Stewart slumped forward
clutching her chest. Her face was bright pink and
her eyes were bulging as she desperately fought for
air. Tears were streaming down Blanche's face and
as she gasped her last breath, she felt a massive pain
shoot through her chest.

Sue Hewitt didn't enjoy her weekend, John hadn't
been lucky down at the job centre and Ian was now
working until the early hours each morning which
she wasn't happy about. He was yet to bring home
any money and was becoming very secretive
regarding what his work involved; still Sue couldn't
dwell on it as she had too many other things on her
mind. The rent was due at the end of the week and
she was still thirty quid short not to mention not
having any money for the meagre groceries they
needed. If Blanche Stewart kept to her side of the
bargain today, then Sue could pay her bills and at
least it would be one less thing to worry about.
Monday morning soon came round and setting off
for Croston Street Sue hoped the old woman would

be in a better mood than she'd been in on Friday. It was strange how someone else's frame of mind could affect another person and today she didn't want anything to bring on her depression again. Climbing the concrete steps she placed her key in the lock and pushed open the door. She thought that by now she would be used to the smell but today it seemed even stronger. Sue could hear the television loudly blaring and called out but there was no answer. Walking into the front room she instantly stopped in her tracks. Blanche was doubled over in her armchair and Sue instinctively knew that the woman was dead. Kneeling on the floor she stared up at Blanche's face which was a deep shade of purple due to the fact that she'd been slumped over for so long. Beginning to panic she told herself to just breathe and think of what to do next. Standing up she grabbed the phone and dialled 999. At first Sue was confused and told the operator that she didn't know if she needed an ambulance or the police. The man on the other end said he would ask for both to attend, just to be on the safe side. Sue went and put the front door on the latch and then walked into the kitchen. Leaning against the sink to steady herself she slowly took in the enormity of the situation. She had now lost her job and to make matters worse, she hadn't even been paid. Deciding that it wouldn't be wrong, she went in search of Blanche's purse. Sue didn't see it as stealing as the money was hers fair and square.

Slowly going through each room of the flat, she didn't find it and could only imagine that the woman was sitting on it. If that was the case then she didn't have a chance of getting paid as there was no way she would ever be able to lift Blanche's huge bulk. Just as she heard someone knock on the door she spied the lottery ticket clamped in Blanche's hand, a shiver ran through her but it didn't stop her prising the old woman's fingers apart and taking the ticket. Quickly she placed it into her pocket, it was probably a loser but there was nothing else of any value so it was worth a chance. Two policemen who had entered with the paramedics began to ask Sue questions. After explaining that she was the carer and had only just arrived and that she hadn't seen Blanche since Friday, the policeman took her name and address and informed her she was free to go. As she went into the hall she heard the police and medics speaking.

"She's definitely dead then?"

"Stone cold."

"I wonder what it was; I mean she doesn't look that old."

The paramedic began to laugh at the policeman's words.

"You wonder what killed her? Bloody hell, just look at the size of her will you and judging by the remnants of what must have been a very large pizza, her diet was appalling. Believe me mate, when you get to that size there's only one place you're headed and pretty damn quick I can tell you."

For some strange reason Sue Hewitt could feel a tear in her eye. She hadn't taken to Blanche but it was still sad and the woman deserved a bit more respect than the men were showing her. Deep down Sue had a kind heart and she tried not to judge a person. She didn't know what kind of life Blanche had led but by her surroundings it must have been a miserable one. Yes the woman ate like a horse but then maybe eating was her only comfort. A shiver ran down Sue's spine at the thought of it and making the sign of the cross she prayed that her own life would never end up that way. She set off for Pitcairn House but didn't rush, the morning was bright and sunny and after what she had just witnessed Sue felt like being in the open air. Deciding to treat herself to a coffee from the upmarket cafe on Mare Street, a treat she couldn't really afford, she pushed on the door and entered. After what had happened Sue knew that she needed something to lift her spirits. Paying for a takeout she walked to St Agnes Gate, crossed the field and stood watching the deer's in the park. With every sip of her Latte she relaxed more and by the time she had finished her drink Sue just smiled and shrugged her shoulders, some things just weren't meant to be. It had now started to spit with rain so removing the pound shop brolly from her bag she set off for home. The flat was empty when she entered and crossing her fingers she hoped that John was having some luck for a change. Taking off her coat Sue remembered the lottery ticket in her pocket. Removing the crumpled piece of paper she smoothed it out and then went into the front room and put the television on to check the numbers. Anything would be nice and nothing ventured, nothing gained. As she slowly studied the screen she could feel her heart as it began to beat faster. Surely not, it couldn't be but finally when she'd checked the numbers at least twice more it at last began to sink in that she'd hit the jackpot. Picking up the telephone she was about to dial Camelot when she realised there was always a chance that her phone could be traced. Instead she removed her mobile, which was pay as you go and dialled the number. Reading off the serial numbers on the ticket she was informed that it was a winning claim and further more it was the only one for the fifty two million pound jackpot. The man at Camelot was about to ask for her details but Sue panicked and ended the call. Falling back onto the sofa her face was as white as a sheet. Questions began to invade her mind and her hands were visibly shaking. Suppose someone knew that Blanche had bought the ticket but that wouldn't matter as it was Sue who had purchased it from the shop. Suddenly she got up and began to jump around the room as she waved the ticket above her head but when the front door opened Sue quickly stuffed it into her trouser pocket. To be on the safe side she would wait, there was a one hundred and eighty day limit, so she had plenty of time to see if any questions would be asked.

What's all the noise about?"

"Oh it's just some stupid telly programme love."

looked forlorn. Sue instantly knew that her husband hadn't had any luck down at the job centre but for once she didn't care, it now didn't matter if he never worked again. Placing her arms around his neck she kissed him passionately on the lips.

"Whatever's got into you?"

"Nothing, I'm just happy for a change. By the look on you face I can tell that things didn't go well?"

"You can say that again."

It doesn't matter love, you'll find something sooner or later. Cuppa?"

Following his wife into the kitchen he couldn't for the life of him think what had got into her. Whatever it was he liked it and taking a seat at the table watched her as she made the tea. Sue was still a good looking woman and John could feel a stirring in his loins, a feeling he hadn't had for a very long time. For some reason and he didn't know why, he knew that if he made a move on her, his wife wouldn't reject him like she usually did. He was right and after the two of them had finished their tea, they went into the bedroom and had the best sex they'd experienced for several years. Since discovering she'd won Sue Hewitt felt like a new woman but just to be on the safe side she decided to keep the news of her win to herself, for the time being at least.

CHAPTER SEVEN

Ian Hewitt set out for work. He had begun working at the Den on the same day as Sue started her carer's job but he was far happier in his work than his mother had been in hers. He had to be at the club by ten am and after picking up a coffee and bacon roll for Tommy Mortimer's breakfast, he would do odd jobs such as collecting his boss's dry cleaning and tidying up the office until twelve thirty. Tommy always had a burger and fries for his lunch and once Ian had popped to the local cafe to collect it, he was then free to go home. His shift would begin again at ten in the evening and he had to stand and wait in the bar area, ready to do anything that was asked of him. When the Den closed at around three am he would finally be allowed to go home. The pay wasn't that good but for six days work he would take home three hundred which was still far more than the fifty seven pounds a week job seekers allowance he'd been claiming for the last month. Up until then Sue had been supporting her son as he wasn't entitled to any benefits until he turned eighteen. Ian was yet to receive his first pay packet from Tommy Mortimer but he had already decided to give his mum fifty for his keep and hoped that she wouldn't be expecting more. Ian Hewitt was a very quiet lad who had always kept himself to himself and never mixed with the others boys in the flats. That said he still knew them all by name and would nod on passing. Entering the Den Ian climbed the stairs and wrinkled his nose, in the daylight the place seemed really drab and stunk to high heavens. Old Joyce Lambert was the cleaner but even she couldn't work miracles. The woman would spray numerous cans of air freshener about but it made little difference. Ian preferred the place on his second shift of the day, when the flashing lights, loud music and punters all out for a good time, seemed to make the Den come alive. Knocking on the office door he waited until Tommy called out for him to enter. Ian had been told on his first day never to just go in as Tommy could be entertaining a woman at any time of the night or day.

"Morning Mr Mortimer. Ready for your breakfast?" Tommy grinned and pushed a ten pound note over the desk. Without another word Ian picked it up and disappeared from the room. Joe's cafe three doors down was bustling with cab drivers as he entered but Ian wouldn't have to wait. As soon as he saw the boy, Joe Parker beckoned him to the front and handed over a brown paper bag containing Tommy's bacon roll and coffee.

"Thanks Joe."

"Give my regards to Mr Mortimer."

"Will do."

Ian liked the special treatment and respect he received and decided that as soon as he had earned enough he would set up some kind of business.

He didn't know quite what yet but it would definitely be something where he would get the same kind of treatment as his boss. Again Ian knocked at the office door and waited until he heard the word 'Enter'.

"There you go Mr Mortimer, Joe said to give you his regards."

Tommy eagerly tucked into the food and his choice of diet showed on his frame. Eighteen years earlier when he had forced himself on Lizzie Chambers he had been toned, almost athletic in his build but now he sported a large belly, his hair was receding and all the late nights had caught up with him which showed by the bags under his eyes.

"So how are you finding it kid, how's the first week beer?"

"Great Mr Mortimer thanks. I think I could work for you for nothing, I love it that much."

"Careful kid I might hold you to that."

For a moment Ian didn't realise that his boss was joking and the scared look on his face made Tommy Mortimer burst out laughing. He liked Ian and could see the boy being in his employment for a long time to come, that was unless he did something wrong. It was common knowledge that Tommy's main income came from drug dealing but it was never mentioned and was taken as read that all his employees knew the score.

"I've got a delivery this morning so I want you to wait downstairs and let the man in. The blokes name is Taffy and he's a big cunt but don't let that scare you. He should be here in about half an hour and once you've shown him up you can get off. I'll sort me own lunch out today."

Handing Ian a couple of twenty pound notes he told the boy to get himself some food.

"It's not payday for a few days and what with the week in hand, you must be a bit brassic son?"

"Yeah I am Boss and thanks for this!"

Ian headed downstairs to wait and just as he'd been told, thirty minutes later there was a aloud banging on the front door. Releasing the bar Ian Hewitt pushed the door opened and was faced with a mountain of a man. Taffy Jones stood over six feet six tall and that was in his stocking feet. When he grinned Ian could see that his front teeth were capped in gold, not only were they gold but the two side fangs had been made extra long and looked like the teeth of a lion. Ian took a step back in fear but Taffy ignored the boy as he walked in and made his way upstairs. Ian Hewitt was glad to be going home; this was one man he didn't want to get to know. Deciding to use the same cafe as earlier as he liked the feeling of being the big man, Ian ordered a burger and fries to take away and began his walk home to St Thomas's Square. As he made his way up to the main entrance of the flats he was stopped by DD a local wannabe gang member. Real name Douglas Davidson, he had given himself the tag of DD as he thought it sounded the part. DD was a year younger than Ian and was desperate to get into the Hackney Crew, a gang of around ten lads who terrorised the area. DD screeched his BMX to a halt right beside Ian Hewitt.

"Hi Bro, how you doing man?"

Ian didn't like DD but he knew better than to show it as the Davidson's were renowned for violence and carrying knives.

"Alright DD."

"I heard you're working for Tommy Mortimer?"

"Yeah I just started."

"Wicked!"

DD flicked his wrist and his fingers made a clicking sound, something Ian had tried to do again and again but had never been able to manage it.

"Yeh it's alright, Mr Mortimer is an ok bloke."

DD laid down his bike and placed his arm around Ian's shoulders.

"I've got a proposition for you if you're interested, could make you a shit load of money man."

Suddenly Ian Hewitt was starting to warm to DD. If he could earn a good wedge, the sooner he could start up on his own.

"What do you have in mind?"

"Nah not here Bro, peoples always listening. You working tonight?"

"Yeh I'm on again at ten."

"Meet me in the Fox at nine; it's just past the club on Kingsland Road."

Ian nodded his head and began the climb up to his

parents flat. Only just legally allowed to drink he hadn't ever been in the Fox but he'd heard plenty about the place and what he'd heard wasn't good. Still Ian reasoned that if he didn't like it or felt threatened in any way he would just get up and leave. The rest of the day was spent lying on his bed making plans. This time next year Ian Hewitt was sure he would be a someone just like his boss. Sue called her son for his meal at six pm on the dot. Sitting at the table he couldn't help but notice how touchy feely his parents were and when his dad started to stroke his mother's hand he grimaced up his mouth in a look of distaste.

"Get a room you two!"

Sue and John giggled like teenagers and when Ian couldn't take anymore he got up from the table.

"Where are you off to?"

"For a shower, I said I'd meet a mate for a pint before I start my shift. Oh by the way Mum, I was thinking about when I get paid. Is fifty a week enough for me keep?"

Sue smiled at her son and was proud that he was thinking about someone other than himself for a change.

"You keep your money love. It's time for you to enjoy yourself; we've managed to get by so far aint we?"

Both father and son stared at Sue, Ian because he couldn't believe his luck and John because he didn't know about the win and he couldn't understand why his wife was turning down good money. Still he wasn't in a position to complain and as things were going so well between them for a change, he didn't want to go rocking the boat. At eight forty five Ian set off for his prearranged meeting with DD. Walking into the Fox he instantly felt uncomfortable. All eyes seemed to be on him and even though he recognised a few of the faces from the club, in different surroundings they didn't acknowledge him. DD was sitting in the back corner and waved when he saw his new mate enter. Two pints of larger had already been poured and were waiting on the table.

"Here you go Bro, I got you one in."

Ian Hewitt took a seat but he still didn't feel comfortable. There was plenty of time before his shift began but none the less he hoped DD would hurry up and tell him whatever it was that he'd got planned so that he could get out of the place. Ian sipped at the larger; he was still new to drinking and didn't want to arrive at work half cut.

"So what's with all the cloak and dagger stuff?"

"Too many people listening in on other people's conversations on that square, you get me Bro?"

"So? What did you want to talk to me about?"

DD looked from side to side to make sure no one was taking an interest in them.

"My cousin Bad Boy needs to buy some drugs and Tommy's the man. Only trouble is he don't sell to blacks see, so I thought if you asked the man for some and then Bad Boy sold them we all come out on top."

What DD didn't tell Ian was the fact that it had nothing to do with colour. Bad Boy hated Tommy Mortimer, had done for two years since he'd been forcibly ejected from the Den. Bad Boy was always saying how one day he would pay the man back and as DD was desperate to join the crew he saw it as a way in. Of course they would never pay for the drugs and it would drop Ian Hewitt in the shit right up to his neck but DD didn't give a toss.

"I don't know if he'd go for that, I mean I've only been there a few days and even if he did, what do I say when he asks who they're for."

DD turned his glance sideways and rolled his eyes in frustration.

"Just tell the man that they're for a friend of yours and don't tell him my name or that I'm black ok?"

"I need to think about this, I aint saying I won't do it as I need the cash but I just want to think about it ok?"

"No prob's Bro, take your time but there's some serious dough to be made here, you dig me?"

Ian finished the last of his drink and seeing that it was now half eight he decided to show willing and go into work early. As usual for midweek, the place was almost deserted. The DJ was playing all his favourite tunes from the eighties but there was hardly anyone in the club to complain. Those that were there were hardened drinkers who weren't the least bit interested in what music they were forced to listen to. Knocking on the office door Ian went in when he was called. Tommy Mortimer was seated on the sofa with a woman and by the look on his boss's face the dirty deed had already been done. "Ian this is Carol, Carol this is Ian my right hand man."

Ian Hewitt liked his new title, it made him feel like a man and nodding in Carol's direction he gave the woman a smile. Carol Warner was a regular and to Ian looked like she'd been around the block a few times. Her dress was low cut and he could see her saggy breasts that did nothing for the young man, although his lingering gaze didn't go unnoticed.

"I was just wondering if you need anything Boss." Tommy Mortimer slapped Carol's thigh and laughed as he spoke.

"Not now I don't! This little beauty has seen to all my needs, aint you darling?"

Carol giggled and Ian couldn't believe that his boss had just referred to her as a little beauty. For a start she must have been at least forty five and to Ian Hewitt that was ancient. As Tommy Mortimer had aged and his waist line expanded, he couldn't be as choosey as he once was. The younger girls weren't interested and he'd had to stop forcing himself onto women. Years ago very few of them would make a complaint and even those that did were seldom taken seriously by the Old Bill. It was different today, today you only had to smile at a young girl

and she would cry sexual harassment. No, Tommy
had long since realised that slappers like Carol were
the best way to get his satisfaction. Carol Warner
stood up and made her excuses. She didn't mind
Tommy Mortimer but time was money and the
night was young, so descending the stairs she set
out in the hope of finding another punter.
"Quiet out there?"
"Yeh really slow."
"Always is until eleven then all the old tarts start
coming in and the fun begins. Fancy a drink?"
Ian was surprised by the invitation but also pleased
as it might provide an opening for him to ask his
boss about doing a deal.
"Thanks Boss."
"So what did you reckon to Taffy Jones? Scary
bastard aint he?"
Ian sipped at the whisky; he didn't like the taste but
was frightened of offending Tommy if he'd said no.
"You don't see many blokes that big and them
teeth!"
Tommy started to laugh; he was warming to the boy
and was glad that he'd taken him on.
"Can I ask you a question Mr Mortimer?"
"You can ask but whether I'll answer is another
thing. Fire away and let's see where we end up."
Ian was embarrassed; he didn't really know where
to start and knew he had to be careful in his choice
of words.
"I would like to be more involved."

"How do you mean Son?"

"Please don't take offence Boss and this is probably all coming out wrong and I know that I aint been working for you more than five minutes but I...."

"For fucks sake just spit it out."

Tommy Mortimer was as sharp as a razor and already knew what the boy meant, he also enjoyed watching him squirm.

"Your other line of income, I'd like to be more involved."

"Would you now?"

Tommy thought for all of five seconds. The lad seemed trustworthy, he was likable and Tommy always needed fresh blood. It was a dangerous game and stabbings and beating were always happening to the runners. He didn't want to see the boy get hurt and he knew that he wasn't a scrapper but there were occasions when he required someone to do a drop or a collection to other villains and known faces and Ian would be perfect.

"Ok I'll give you a chance and we'll see how it goes."

True to form the Den livened up at just before eleven and although there wasn't much for Ian to do work wise, he counted seven fights through the course of the night and knew he would rather be doing the job that he had, than be one of the doormen. At ten past three he was told he could leave and zipping up his coat he headed home. The night was cold and misty and looking forward to his bed, hoped that his mum had put the electric

88

blanket on. Turning on to Mere Street Ian heard someone call his name but at this time of the morning he wasn't about to hang around and quickened his pace. Suddenly a BMX screeched to a halt beside him and Ian was surprised to see DD.
"Whatever are you doing out at this time of night?"
"Always am Bro, Hackney comes alive in the early hours, can't you feel it man?"
"No I can't and whatever you're on I don't want any.
DD began to laugh and getting off of his bike walked along with Ian.
"So have you thought anymore about what we were talking about Bro?"
"Yeh and I'm up for it but it might take a few days to sort out. I have to build up Mr Mortimer's trust before he'll let me loose with; well you know what we're talking about."
DD beamed from ear to ear as he imagined his initiation into the crew. He knew that a girl was given to new members to do exactly as they liked with and he couldn't wait.
"Keep me posted Bro, catch you later."
With that Douglas Davidson sped off down the street and Ian Hewitt was left to walk the remainder of the way home alone.

CHAPTER EIGHT

Sue Hewitt stood at the cooker frying eggs and bacon when her son entered. Her husband John was still asleep as the couple had enjoyed another amorous night in the bedroom and he was totally exhausted.

"Morning Son! I'm just frying up some breakfast, want some?"

Ian sat bleary eyed at the table. He was tired even though he hadn't worked the previous night. It had been hard to sleep what with his mother and father going at it hammer and tongs in the next room and no matter how hard he tried he couldn't stop thinking about DD and what he'd agreed to do.

Dishing up the food Sue laid the plates onto the table and sat down to join her son.

"So how are things going with you?"

"Good Mum. Mr Mortimer is a great bloke to work for and he's already promoted me to his right hand man."

Sue Hewitt narrowed her eyes, she still wasn't happy with the set up but she supposed if Ian was happy then she didn't want to burst his bubble by saying anything.

"I've been meaning to have a chat with you. I was out on the balcony yesterday afternoon having a fag when old Derek from upstairs walked by. He said he'd seen you the other night in the Fox with

Douglas Davidson?"

"So!"

"Don't take that tone with me Ian. You know well enough what I'm on about; the Davidson's are no good."

"Look Mum, it was just a pint nothing more now please stop worrying. I'm eighteen now and you can't keep wrapping me up in bleeding cotton wool."

Sue stared at her son for a few seconds and then smiled. In just a few days he seemed to have really grown up and looking at him now her heart was filled with pride.

"Ok, I won't mention it again. What are you up to today?"

"Work of course!"

"Well, when you finish I wondered if you wanted to meet me for lunch, my treat."

Ian Hewitt pulled a face, meet his mother for lunch? He'd never heard anything like it.

"Why? What's this all about?"

Sue leaned forward just in case her husband was lurking behind the door listening.

"I've come into a bit of money, well a lot of money actually but I can't claim it for a few weeks. Your dad doesn't know yet and I want it to stay that way."

"Fine by me but how much are we talking about Mum."

Sue got up from the table to clear the plates.

"Enough so that I don't have to work anymore! Anyway, never you mind about how much it is but I am handing in me notice today."

"Ian stood up and walking over to where his mother now stood at the sink, kissed her on the cheek.

"Well I'm really pleased for you and yes I would like to have lunch with you later."

Mother and son arranged to meet up around twelve fifteen at Nando's on Kingsland High Street. Within the hour and just as Ian was entering the Den to begin his morning shift, Sue was already on Hackney High Street waiting for the shops to open. Always short of money, Sue only had one credit card to her name and she watched it like a hawk. Anything she spent, which wasn't very much or very often, was always paid off by the end of the month so she didn't accrue any interest. Now she felt like going on a spree, reasoning that she could clear any debt as soon as she cashed in her ticket, the ticket that she took everywhere she went just for safe keeping. Entering the Kingsland Shopping Centre she headed into The Perfume shop. Never having owned any high end scent, she felt like treating herself. The shop assistant, Lydia Overson, who worked on bonus related pay, snootily looked Sue up and down. The anorak and jeans were a dead giveaway that there wouldn't be much commission to earn from this customer. The girl's manner wasn't overly friendly and when Sue asked to sample five different fragrances, Lydia huffed under her breath as she unlocked the glass cabinets. Removing the tester bottles she placed them onto the counter then walked over to her colleague and began chatting but she never took her eyes from Sue as she looked the type to walk out with the testers which was a common problem. Sue Hewitt took her time and gently sprayed each scent onto her wrist and took in the beautiful floral aromas. They were all gorgeous and she couldn't decide which one to have. Waving in the direction of the assistant she had to wait for the girl to finish her conversation before she was served. Normally Sue would have gotten angry but not today, today was for self indulgence and she wanted to be in a happy frame of mind while she shopped.

"I'll take one of each please."

For a second Lydia Overson stood with her mouth wide open and Sue wanted to laugh.

"Will that be 50ml or 100?"

"Oh 100 definitely, I find the smaller bottles don't last very long."

Sue handed over her credit card and by the time she'd left the shop had spent over three hundred pounds. This shopping lark felt good and she knew as soon as the big money came through she was going to go up west and shop until she dropped. Her credit limit was only two thousand pounds so before she continued she decided to apply for more cards. Trawling the High Street she called in at every available bank. In the past she would have been reluctant to use a foreign bank but now she even tried the Turkish one and ended up with twenty five thousand pounds worth of credit because she had always been so careful not to get into debt. Happy with the result of being accepted, Sue was slightly disappointed when she was informed that the cards would take five working days to be processed. Still there was plenty left on her original card and it would be enough to see her alright until the new cards came through. She was really enjoying her day and glancing at her watch saw that she had a good hour before she had to meet Ian. Store cards were instant and heading into Marks and Spencer's she opened an account. Her three thousand pound limit was a lot to spend on clothes but Sue didn't have a problem finding plenty of items she liked. After fitting on an array of clothing, she purchased three quarters of them and on leaving the store had spent almost nine hundred pounds. Making her way back to the shopping centre she called into Matalan and bought a canvas shopping trolley as she knew she wouldn't be able to carry much more. It was then on to Sainsbury's to fill up the fridge. Three of the best fillet steaks, fresh vegetables and a couple of bottles of wine were purchased as Sue had decided to cook a celebration meal tonight. Now more than a little tired she felt like a rest from all the shopping, so headed off to meet her son. As his mother walked into Nando's Ian couldn't believe what he was seeing. She was laden down with bags and looked totally exhausted. Luckily Ian had chosen a booth or there wouldn't have been any room for the bags and trolley. Flopping down onto the soft leather seat Sue let out a loud sigh.

"I'm bleeding knackered! I reckon all those rich people must feel like this all the time."

"Well it certainly looks like you've had a bit of a spend up Mum."

"I aint even started yet, shall we order? Pick anything you want, it's all on me. I fancy a beer as well."

Ian waved to the waiter who minced over to take their order. He liked the look of Ian and decided to chance his arm and flirt a little. Gino was Italian and had worked at Nando's since arriving in England two years earlier. His accent as he spoke was Pidgin English at its worst and staring at Ian Hewitt he gave a lingering wink.

"What canna I geta fa yew 'andsome?"

Sue wanted to burst out laughing but was able to control herself. It wasn't just that the waiter was flirting with her son but the fact that Ian's face had turned a scarlet red. When Gino left the table and minced in the direction of the kitchen, Ian started to kick off.

"Bleeding bender, they make my fucking skin crawl."

"Ian!"

"Well they do. Where does he get off coming onto

me like that."

"Darling there aint no harm done and anyway you should take it as a compliment. Now I've got you a little present."

Sue fished about in one of the bags and handed Ian a bottle of Armani eau de cologne. Old spice for John and Lynx for her son was about as much as she'd ever been able to afford but now it was nothing but the best for all of them. The meal was good and they both cleared their plates and ordered another beer.

"You're not shooting off after this are you?"

"No."

"Good because you can help your old mum home with this little lot?"

"Yeh of course I will and anyway after two beers I'm going to need a lay down before my next shift. Are you going into work Mum or are you going to hand in your notice over the phone?"

Sue hadn't really thought about it. She didn't feel like turning out tonight and she had no intention of working anymore after today but there were still her work pals to consider. Sheila on cold meats would be heartbroken not to mention Val on fresh produce. It was only right that she should actually go in and say goodbye in person.

"I think I'll pop in because there are a couple of the girls I'd like to see. Maybe I'll stop off on the way home and get them both a little gift.

"If you start giving it away Mum it won't last five

minutes."

"Believe you me it will. There's only one problem and that's how to get this little lot into the flat without your dad seeing them."

"I don't understand all the cloak and dagger stuff, why don't you just tell him?"

Sue thought for a second, would it be so bad if John knew? It wasn't as if he could start spending straight away and in any case it was her money. Maybe tonight would be as good a time as any and they had got a couple of bottles of wine to share after Ian went to work.

"Ok, I'll do it tonight when we're alone."

On their way home Sue asked Ian to wait with the bags while she went back and purchased another two bottles of perfume for her work mates. Lydia Overson was surprised to see the woman back so soon and nearly fell over herself to serve Sue. Asking for the perfumes to be gift wrapped, Sue smiled when they were handed over, her work mates would really love them. Entering the flat, Ian went straight through to his parents' bedroom and crammed all the bags into the bottom of the wardrobe. Wheeling the trolley through to the kitchen he began to unload the food. John Hewitt was making tea for them all and his wife was in the middle of telling him about lunch with her son.

"Alright for some I must say!"

"You can come next time."

"Oh so there's going to be a next time is there, won

the lottery have you and that looks new."

He was staring at the shopping trolley and Sue smiled and winked at her son.

"I bought it off Sandra at work, it's hardly been used and she only wanted three quid for it. I'm fed up with carting bags of groceries home; it's a real strain on my arms."

John placed the tea on the table and sat down. He was so engrossed with watching his son unload the food without having to be asked, that he didn't take any notice of what his wife had actually bought.

"I thought I'd do us all some egg on toast for our dinner tonight?"

"No need love, I'm cooking us a special meal."

"What's that in aid of?"

"Never you mind, all will be revealed later."

John Hewitt smiled, for once his wife was happy so whatever she was going to tell him wouldn't be bad. When he'd finished unloading Ian yawned loudly.

"I'm off for a couple of hours shut eye, see you both later."

"You know that aint a bad idea, I think I'll do the same. Wake me up about five will you love?"

"Sure you don't want any company?"

"I'd love some but sleep is what I need and I know if you get in that bed and start your shenanigans, well that's the last thing I'll get."

John laughed and as his wife headed in the direction of their bedroom, he decided to see what afternoon programmes were on the telly. Within a few days they had started to get on better than ever and his life seemed to be going in a good direction. For once he felt happy, he didn't know if it would last but he was going to enjoy it for as long as it did. John must have fallen asleep in front of the television because suddenly he could hear laughter and smell something mouth watering coming from the kitchen. Glancing at the mantle clock he saw that it was twenty past five and stretching out his arms, went to see what was going on. Pushing open the door he saw his son sitting at the table and his wife about to dish up what looked like the best steak he had ever laid his eyes on.

"Hi Darling, I was just about to call you. Now sit down and tuck in before it gets cold."

John Hewitt did exactly as he was told and the food was so good that there wasn't any conversation during the meal. When the kitchen was once again tidy Ian said he was heading off to work early and after kissing his mother gave her a sly wink. Sue removed the wine from the fridge and picked up two glasses.

"You coming or what? I've bought a new DVD to watch tonight."

John was out of his chair in a second and after Sue had poured them both a glass of wine, they cuddled up to watch the movie. She couldn't really concentrate as she kept thinking about the bomb shell she would drop as soon as the film had finished. It was a good bomb shell but all the same she didn't know how John would react. When the credits began to roll Sue sat up and turned both the DVD player and the television off. Her face was serious as she looked at her husband and for a moment he felt concerned. They'd had such a lovely night that he didn't want it spoiled but then he remembered that Sue had to go to work and it was probably the reason she'd turned the telly off.

"You going to work early tonight?"

"No but I do need to talk about something and I want you to hear every word I'm saying to you."

"This is serious aint it?"

"Yes but in a good way darling so don't look so worried. When I finished work at the old girls last Friday she wanted me to go to the shop and get her a lottery ticket which I did. Anyway, I gave it to her and waited to be reimbursed for the money and my wages. The cheeky old cow said I'd have to wait until Monday."

"Bloody hell Sue! You mean the old girl had you work like a slave and then died before she'd paid you? Fuck me! As if you don't work hard enough already and then don't get paid well I ..."

Sue Hewitt placed her hand tenderly onto her husband s arm.

"You haven't let me finish what I was saying. When I went in on Monday morning and found her dead I looked around for her purse to take my wages, well it wasn't as if I was stealing, I mean I'd worked my socks off for her. I searched every room but it wasn't there and I realised she was probably sitting on it. Remember I told you she was a big woman and I mean big. Just as the paramedics arrived I saw the lottery ticket still in her hand so I took it and shoved it into my pocket."

"And?"

"Remember when you came home and asked what all the noise was and I said it was the television? Well I suppose it was but it was also me jumping round the room for joy."

John Hewitt still hadn't fully grasped what his wife was talking about and she laughed out loud.

"We've only gone and won the bloody jackpot. John are you alright? You don't half look pale love."

Flopping down onto the sofa he just stared blankly ahead. His lips felt dry and he was in dire need of a drink. If this was true then all their problems were over, they could move, buy a big house, a car, and travel all over the world. Within a few seconds he had mentally spent at least a couple of million pounds and it was exactly what Sue had been worried about and why she'd been so reluctant to tell him.

"You got anymore of that wine?"

"Another bottle, I'll go and get it."

When Sue returned and their glasses were replenished John turned to face his wife.

"So how much are we talking about?"

"Fifty two million and it's the only winning ticket. I've applied for a load of credit cards and they

101

should be here by Saturday morning, at least that's what they told me. I don't want to place my claim yet, I just want to be careful John in case the old woman had told anyone. I really don't think she did but you never know. There's several months until its void so we can take our time."

"Where is it?"

"Why?"

"No reason, I just want to see it."

Sue reached into her bra and pulled out the small piece of pink paper that was going to change their lives forever. Her husband went to take it from her but Sue quickly pushed it back down her top.

"This little baby aint leaving me until my claim is in."

"But what if you lose it? You're always losing things, why don't you let me look after it?"

Sue was now suspicious and was suddenly in doubt regarding her revelation.

"It's fine John. Now I need to head off to work, I'm going to hand in my notice tonight. When the credit cards come through in a few days you can have a bit of fun as I've had you added as a second card holder. Her words cheered her husband up and he now couldn't wait until the weekend, William Hill and Ladbrokes wouldn't know what had hit them.

CHAPTER NINE

Over in Islington and unlike in Hackney, things
were far from good. Between them Lizzie and her
father had been at the hospital constantly. Mike
Chambers had covered the afternoons and Lizzie
had swapped with him each night. She wouldn't
leave her son until he was asleep so most nights she
didn't get home until almost midnight. The same
night that Sue and John Hewitt were celebrating
their win, Lizzie had been sitting at Michael's
bedside watching him sleep. About to call it a day,
she was surprised when the door opened and her
son's consultant entered.
"Could I have a word with you Miss Chambers?"
"Certainly, what's wrong?"
"I think it would be better if we discussed the matter
in one of the side rooms."
Finn Armstrong was forty years of age and had
been a consultant in nephrology for the last five
years. He was tall and athletic looking and if Lizzie
Chambers hadn't have been here for her son, she
may well have flirted with the man as he was just
her type. It had been years since she'd gone on a
date and every evening at the hospital would be
spent fantasising about the man. Two doors down
from Michael's room was a small area that was
sectioned off by screens.
"Please take a seat. Now we've been studying
Michaels test results today and I'm afraid that his

condition is far more serious than we first thought. I would go as far as to say that his kidney function is almost nonexistent, obviously there is dialysis but it's not a cure. In the short term it will keep him alive but his mental state will be tested to the limit as Michael will have to spend many hours each week connected to the machine. The only real hope he has is to undergo a transplant."

"Only real hope?"

"Of survival, I really am very sorry."

Lizzie sat in the chair and softly began to cry. Her face was ashen in colour and it felt with his last word of 'sorry' that all the stuffing had been knocked out of her. She knew her son was sick but not once had she imagined he was so ill that he might not survive. Finn Armstrong sat next to Lizzie and placed an arm on her shoulder, there was nothing untoward, he was purely trying to comfort her but she shrugged him away. Standing up she wiped her eyes and pulled her handbag onto her shoulder.

"So where do we get a donor from?"

"Well Michael has already been placed onto the register but that can be a very long wait. His best chance is a family member but that's only if they are a match. Anyone can offer to donate, family or otherwise and we will happily test them for compatibility."

With that Lizzie left the hospital and hailed a cab over to Notting Hill. Knocking hard on the front door it was a couple of minutes before it was answered and much to Lizzie's disappointment it was her sister in law that opened up.

"I need to see Joey."

Sharon could feel her whole body tense up, she really disliked the Chambers clan and none more so than Lizzie and her spoilt brat of a son Michael. In reality Michael was anything but spoilt, what Sharon couldn't stand was the fact that he received so much attention and the love they all showered on him. Jealousy is a terrible thing but Sharon Chambers could never see, or if she did, would never admit that she was eaten up with it.

"He's asleep you'll have to come back later. He does work for a living you know."

Lizzie was in no frame of mind to be fobbed off. Using her forearm she forcibly pushed her sister in law sideways causing the door to open to its maximum and Sharon Chambers fell backwards onto it. Marching into Joey's front room she saw her brother lying full out on the sumptuous sofa. Walking over she roughly shook him awake just as Sharon came running into the room.

"I told her you was asleep but she just barged right in, bloody cheek. Joey you need to teach...."

"Just shut your fucking mouth for once will you."

Joey Chamber adored his sister and he knew for her to just turn up, then it must be something serious. Standing up, he was about to hug her when she suddenly burst into tears. Sharon rolled her eyes

105

upwards and it didn't go unnoticed by her husband. Placing his arm around her shoulder Joey guided her down onto the sofa.

"Sharon make some tea!"

His wife stood with a look of defiance on her face.

"Now!"

Walking into the kitchen her blood was beginning to boil. In the past her husband had always treated her like a princess but just lately he was always having a go at her. To begin with she had put his moods down to tiredness but now she had a niggling thought that perhaps he was getting fed up with her and the idea worried her more than anything. She loved Joey but it wasn't just down to emotional feelings, without him she couldn't afford her lavish lifestyle and if he was to leave her then she would have to find a job. The thought of that frightened the life out of her, Sharon Chambers had never worked a day in her life and now if she wasn't careful it could become a distinct possibility. Joey stood up and closed the front room door so that his wife couldn't hear what was being discussed. Taking hold of Lizzie's hand he stared deep into her face as he spoke.

"So what's all this about sweetheart?"

Lizzie took in a deep lungful of air and blew her nose on a tissue.

"I've just come from the hospital. The consultant asked to speak to me and told me Michael is far worse than they thought. Oh Joey, without a kidney transplant there's a good chance that he's going to die."

His sister's words shocked Joey Chambers to the core. He knew Michael was ill but this, well this was far worse than he could ever have imagined.

"And what's the chance of him getting a transplant?"

"Pretty slim. Mr Armstrong said it would need to be a match and waiting for someone else to die who was suitable was clutching at straws. He said he could test family members, anyone in fact even if they aren't related. I know it's a lot to ask Joey but would you consider it?"

"Honey you don't even have to ask, of course I will. I'll also contact Dave; I know he'll be home in a shot. Steve might be a bit more difficult to track down but I'll do my best. Then there's Dad of course and you and..."

They were interrupted when the door opened and Sharon appeared with a tray containing three mugs of steaming tea. She was wearing her best smile as she was only too aware that she had well and truly over stepped the mark and was skating on thin ice as far as her husband was concerned.

"Sharon our Michael has to have a kidney transplant and we're all going to be tested. It's a long shot but are you up for it?"

The look of terror on her face was evident to both Joey and Lizzie and they waited with baited breath.

"I'm not being funny but can I have a minute to

think about it, it's a big decision."

Lizzie was surprised to say the least and for once she genuinely smiled at her sister in law as she spoke.

"You're right Sharon it is a big decision and of course you should think about it."

Sharon nodded her head and after handing them their drinks, took her own tea back into the kitchen. Perching herself on one of the bar stools she held her head in her hands as she thought. Sharon Chambers didn't give a damn about Michael but if she agreed to do this it would tie Joey to her. The only thing that really worried her was the fact that she could be a match. Sharon couldn't bear the thought of her perfect body having a huge scar on it but then again the chances of her being suitable must be very remote. Joey was an honourable man and just by her offering it would make him see her in a different light. By this one act, he would be forever grateful and never leave her. Walking back into the front room she stopped and looked at them both.

"I'll do it!"

Joey couldn't believe his ears and standing up he hugged his wife and showered her cheeks in kisses. Lizzie now stood and embraced her and even though Sharon didn't like being touched by her sister in law, she didn't say a word and smiled sweetly. Joey broke away and took hold of Lizzie's hand.

"So when can all this be done?"

"As early as tomorrow but I aint told Dad yet."

"Give me a minute to get hold of Dave and I'll drive you home, the sooner the old man knows the better."

Picking up his mobile Joey dialled his brothers' number. It only took a couple of minutes to explain things and then he hung up.

"He's catching the first train in the morning, should be here by early afternoon. I'll try and get hold of Stevie when I get back but I aint got the foggiest where he is at the moment."

Lizzie started to cry again and once more her brother, much to his wife's silent annoyance, took his sister in his arms.

"Come on honey don't cry. I promise we'll sort all this out and Michael will be home before you know it. Now let's head over to Dads and break the news."

On the journey over to Ritchie Street both brother and sister discussed how to tell their father and they were dreading what he was going to say. Mike Chambers adored the ground Michael walked upon and they knew he would be devastated. They agreed that for the time being at least, it would be best to play things down. As Lizzie opened the front door she at first thought her father had gone to bed but then she noticed a light shining from the bottom of the kitchen door. The radio was playing a gentle tune as they entered but the volume was turned so low that it might as well not have been on. As head of the family Mike had always taken care of everyone but now he felt helpless. He wasn't sure what was wrong with his grandson but he'd been on this earth long enough to know that it wasn't going to be good news. For the first time in his life Mike Chambers had been thinking about what it would be like to lose a member of his family and he felt nothing but pure grief at the thought. As his son and daughter entered the room Mike looked up and smiled and Lizzie could immediately see that her father had been crying.

"You alright Dad?"

Mike Chambers was about to answer but stopped when his oldest son appeared in the doorway. He was momentarily filled with panic and as Lizzie sat down and took hold of his hands, Mike's eyes were pleading as they welled up with tears.

"Something's wrong aint it? Please don't tell me it's Michael."

"Dad I don't want you to panic but yes there is something wrong. Michael needs a kidney transplant and we're all going to be tested, even Dave is coming back tomorrow to see if he's a match."

"Well I hope I'm included?"

"Don't be daft Dad, of course you are, even Sharon's agreed to do the test."

Mike Chambers was about to come out with a sarcastic remark regarding his daughter in law but thought better of it. If she was good enough to offer to help Michael then he had no right to slag her off. "A parent never expects to bury their own child let alone their grandchild."

Joey couldn't believe what he'd just heard and before Lizzie had time to say anything her brother almost shouted as he spoke.

"Dad! No one's burying anyone alright? We are all going to do our best for Michael and don't let me hear you talk like that again; it's the last thing Lizzie needs. Now I suggest we all get some sleep as tomorrows going to be a long day."

The following morning the family congregated at the Ritchie Street address and their moods were sombre. Just after lunch Mike set off for his afternoon visit to see his grandson. It had been agreed that Michael should know as little as possible until there was good news, something they were all praying for. Sharon sat at the kitchen table filing her nails while Joey and Lizzie just sat in silence holding hands. An appointment had been made for them all to see Mr Armstrong at three that day. Joey was on tender hooks in case Dave wasn't back in time but he needn't have worried as the door opened at just after one.

"Fuck me Bro you made good time."

"As soon as my company heard what was going on they flew me into City airport on a private helicopter."

Walking over to Lizzie, Dave embraced his baby

111

sister and the tears started all over again. Sharon let out a loud sigh and Joey glared daggers at his wife. At two thirty Joey Chambers drove his family over to Bart's hospital to an appointment that would hopefully save Michaels life. There was nothing high and mighty about Finn Armstrong and after Mike had come down from the ward to join them; Mr Armstrong invited them all into his office. Five chairs had been strategically placed in front of the consultant's desk and they all took a seat.

"Thank you all for coming today. Now firstly I will explain the procedure. The next step is for everyone to have a blood test, this can be done today and we will have the results within the hour. It's to see if any of you have a suitable blood group so it's nothing to worry about. As there are so many members of the same family it does look hopeful. After that, the most suitable donor will go through medical, surgical and psychological assessments. Lizzie was the first to speak.

"Suppose one of us is a match, how long will all of this take?"

"On average three months."

"What! My boy could be dead by then."

"Lizzie we are doing all that we can. Michael is on a cocktail of drugs and with his dialysis it should keep him stable. Now if you would all like to go down to the Path lab and give blood, I'll see you back here at four o'clock."

Finn Armstrong walked over to the door and held it

open. Everyone went outside except Joey.

"I have another brother doctor but he's travelling around Asia at the moment and we're having trouble locating him. Would he be able to be tested?"

"I can't see why not although we would need to carry out further tests in case he has contracted anything on his travels. Let's just see what happens today and then we can take it from there."

After all the blood samples had been taken, Joey drove Sharon home and then returned to the hospital to wait for the results. At five past four Mr Armstrong called the family into his office and waited until they were all seated before he spoke. Finn Armstrong loved his work but regarding this particular part of his job, he would be happy if he never had to do it again.

"Right, I won't beat about the bush, it isn't good news I'm afraid. It seems you are all blood group B positive except for Mrs Sharon Chambers who is B negative."

Lizzie's eyes began to well up with tears and it was Joey who took control and asked the doctor to explain further.

"What does that mean?"

"Michael is blood group O Rh minus and therefore can only receive blood from anyone of the same."

Finn Armstrong turned his attention to Lizzie Chambers. Apart from your brother who you say that you are not able to contact, you have never mentioned Michael's father."

Suddenly all eyes were on Lizzie and she immediately stood up and walked from the room. Mike looked at Joey.

"Go after her son."

Joey ran out into the corridor and grabbing his sister's arm, swung her round to face him.

"I have never pushed you regarding Michael's father but you have to reveal him now. There's no telling how long it will take to track down our Steve. If we manage it at all, it's more than likely that he'll be the same blood group as us. I've realised over the years that you have your reasons but now is not the time for secrets Sis. The only thing that matters is saving Michael's life."

Lizzie flopped down onto one of the chairs that lined the corridor on either side. Her eyes filled with tears and it broke her brother's heart. The secret of Michael's dad had been kept buried deep inside his sister for years and Joey didn't know why, but he could only assume that it wasn't a happy memory. Sitting down he placed his arm tenderly around her shoulder.

"Take your time sweetheart."

Lizzie Chambers sighed heavily and at the same time ran her hands through her hair.

"One night me and Sonia went to a club over in Hackney called the Den. I'd told you I was going to Lady Greys but it was a lie. I just wanted a night out without you, Steve or Dave watching me like a hawk. The place was rough and after Sonia got off her face on Martini, a fight broke out. You know how I am around any kind of violence Joey? Anyway I ran but there wasn't really anywhere to run to except outside so I just went into the first room I came across. It happened to be the owners office and he was nice to me, remember I was so scared Joey not to mention young and naive. He gave me a couple of drinks and before I knew it he was on top of me. I tried to fight him of but I couldn't. Don't get me wrong it wasn't really violent although I did plead with him to let me go. When it was all over I ran outside and jumped in a cab. The rest so they say is history and nine months later my Michael was the result."

"So the cunt doesn't even know he has a son?"

"No and that's the way I wanted it to stay but I suppose now I don't have any choice in the matter do I?"

"No you don't. I'll tell you this for nothing Lizzie, if I had have found out back then I would have killed the bastard with me own bare hands."

"I know you would and that's the reason I never said anything about it."

Joey pulled his sister in close and gently squeezed her to him.

"What's his name?"

"Tommy, Tommy Mortimer. I've heard a few things over the years and they're not good. Seems I wasn't the first and no doubt I wasn't the last. For all I know he could have twenty illegitimate kids that he knows nothing about."

"Do you want me to go and explain to him?"

"No, if it comes down to it then I'll go but it really will be, only if we need to! I think we should still give it a few days just in case we hear from our Steve."

"Whatever you want darling, I'll go and get Dad and Dave and then run you all home. Are you coming back tonight to visit?"

"Well of course I am, my boy needs me to be here as much as possible. Joey please don't say anything about this to Michael, as far as he's concerned there's no change in his condition and that's the way I want it to stay."

Twenty minutes later Joey dropped his father, brother and sister off at home and told Lizzie that he would call back in a couple of hours to give her a lift to the hospital. Waiting until they had all gone inside he removed his mobile and dialled his home number.

"Sharon it's me. I'm gutted; none of us were a match. I know, I know but at least you offered. I won't be long, see you in a bit."

His wife had really shocked him regarding taking the test and even though she wasn't a match he felt so proud of her. Joey Chambers was totally exhausted and pulling away from the curb was looking forward to a couple of hours rest. The traffic was light and he made it home in no time at all. Opening the front door he could hear Sharon on the telephone talking.

"Oh I know Steph and thank god I wasn't a match for the little brat because there's no way I would ever have gone through with it. I love Joey but as for the rest of the Chambers family, well to be honest I can't stand them. The old man makes my skin crawl and that bitch of a sister-in-law well she...."

Joey didn't hang around to hear anymore. Climbing the stairs he pulled a holdall from the top of the wardrobe and threw in enough clothes for a couple of days. Opening the safe he took out all of their cash and every piece of expensive jewellery that he'd ever bought his wife. Tomorrow he would cancel all her credit cards and he was thankful that he'd never allowed her access to his business account. Running down the stairs he was almost at the front door when his wife emerged from the front room.

"Hi babe, that was quick."

Sharon looked down and noticed the holdall but Joey didn't give her time to ask what was going on. With one last look of disgust, he slammed the door, got in to his car and drove away.

CHAPTER TEN

Ian Hewitt had been working at the Den for just over a week and as he walked to work was thinking about what he could spend his wages on the following day. Out of the corner of his eye Ian spotted DD on the other side of the road and when he realised the boy had seen him, he let out a groan.

"Hey Bro, chill out man!"

Ian was forced to stop while he waited for DD to cross the road.

"How you doing man?"

"Fine thanks DD but I really can't stop or I'll be late for work."

"Cool Bro, I'll walk along with you. Any news on that deal that's going to make us all rich?"

Ian knew the question would be asked and deep down he wished that he'd never agreed to it. If it wasn't for the money he would make which would enable him to set up a little business of his own, he would pull out.

"I asked the boss for more responsibility so I think it's going to be soon. I need to have your phone number DD so that you can collect straight away. How much did you say we'd make?"

"Double, though my cousin said you should have a bigger share as you're doing all the work."

Ian raised his eyebrows; he hadn't been expecting this so it was an added bonus. He didn't feel quite as bad now and after DD had punched his number into Ian's phone, the pair went their separate ways. When Ian was out of sight, DD stopped to phone his cousin Big Boy and give him an update on things. Ian continued in the direction of the Den and after collecting Tommy's breakfast, climbed the stairs and knocking on the office door waited to be invited in. Tommy Mortimer must have been especially hungry today as he instantly called out for him to enter.

"Morning Mr Mortimer, breakfast is served." Tommy laughed, the boy could be a right comic at times and he was growing fond of Ian. The lad was young and a bit wet behind the ears but that only made him pliable which would allow Tommy to mould the youngster into his way of thinking.

"You know you asked to be more involved, well I need a collection done today."

"Brilliant and thanks Mr Mortimer."

"Don't thank me, now you need to be on your guard at all times. Make sure no one's watching or following you. You can get a cab there and back so you shouldn't get into any bother."

Tommy instructed Ian to go over to Soho and collect a holdall from Taffy Jones. When the man's name was mentioned, Ian's face paled and again Tommy laughed.

"Don't let him scare you it's just business. Now here's your cab fare and his address, he's expecting you in about half an hour."

Ian took the cash and was about to leave when he

119

was stopped by his boss's next sentence.

"I'm giving you my trust so make sure you look after my merchandise boy. There will be over twenty grand's worth of coke in that holdall and if anything happens to it, well let's just say Taffy wouldn't be very pleased and you definitely don't want to get on the wrong side of him."

For the entire journey Ian tried to weigh up the pros and cons of doing what DD wanted. If it all went as planned then surely his boss would be pleased with him but if it went wrong, well Ian didn't even dare contemplate that scenario. The cab driver wasn't overly chatty and Ian thought the man kept looking in his rear view mirror and it unnerved him. In reality he was just driving but for some reason Ian was feeling paranoid. Stopping on Charing Cross road at the top of Old Compton street, the cabbie was feeling generous or so he told himself and instructed Ian that this was the best route and that if he walked straight down, Lexington Street could be found running horizontally. In all honesty the streets were narrow and he didn't feel like getting stuck as he had an airport run in just over an hour and couldn't afford to miss it. Doing as he was Instructed, Ian began to walk. It was a nice sunny morning and in no real rush, he took in the sights and sounds of Soho. Reaching Lexington he walked along looking for a boutique with a gold tiled facade. Tommy had said that next door was a small second hand furniture shop that was painted all in black. It only took Ian Hewitt a couple of minutes to find the place. Pushing open the door he made his way to the back of the shop and began to climb a flight of stairs. The woman sitting behind the downstairs counter hadn't even looked up when he entered. Reaching the top landing he rang the bell and stood waiting outside a steel plated door. There was a small spy hole in the centre and even though Ian couldn't see anything, he knew he was being watched. Seconds later the door opened and Taffy Jones's body almost filled the doorway. Ian felt just as intimidated as he had been on their last encounter.

"Morning Mr Jones, Tommy sent me and he...." Taffy turned and walked into the room before Ian had finished talking and he now felt even more nervous. Closing the door Ian followed the mountain of a man into the next room and was surprised by what he saw. The room could only be described as a very classy library or it was as far as Ian Hewitt was concerned. The walls were lined with mahogany bookcases and in the middle of the room sat an antique partner's desk and leather chair. Taffy Jones walked over to a highly polished cupboard and removed a small holdall just as Ian was about to take down a book from one of the shelves.

"Touch it and your fucking dead kid!" Ian immediately dropped his hand back to his side and mouthed the word 'sorry'. As the sun shone through the window it momentarily bounced off of Taffy's gold front teeth and the glint sent a shiver down Ian's spine. He mentally imagined being bitten by them and the agony it would cause. Ian had a good imagination but what he didn't know was that particular sadistic act had happened many times; in fact it was a personal favourite of Taffy Jones whenever he was forced to administer any punishment. Taffy threw the holdall to the ground and Ian stooped to pick it up.

"Oi! Did I say you could touch that, you cunt?" Ian instantly stood up and frantically shook his head, his eyes were wide open with fear and he could feel his heart beating faster as his hands began to shake. This was all turning into a nightmare and he wished that he'd never gotten involved. Still he couldn't blame anyone but himself, if he hadn't have been so greedy then he wouldn't be in this situation.

"Now you can pick it up."

Ian did as he was told. The bag wasn't that heavy and after he placed the straps onto his right shoulder, waited to be given further instructions but there weren't any. The cold hard stare of Taffy Jones's eyes seemed to bore into him for an age but still he didn't move. Taffy studied the boy for several seconds and wondered why Tommy Mortimer had entrusted such an expensive cargo to someone so young and so green.

"Right you can go now but remember one thing you

little cunt, you're responsible for that lot until you deliver it safely to your Boss understood?"

Again Ian nodded his head vigorously.

"Well what you waiting for? Go on fuck off out of it then."

As Ian walked through the door he heard Taffy cough and hawk up what he could only imagine was a large amount of phlegm and descending the stairs as quickly as he could, Ian was out of the shop like greased lightning. Megan Jones, Taffy's mother and business partner, was still seated behind the counter and suddenly burst out laughing. Her son had a knack of putting the fear of god into people and even though it happened on a regular basis, it still tickled her. His father had been a weakling so heaven knows how they had raised a man like Taffy between them; still she was glad that they had. No one crossed her boy without paying and the fear he instilled had brought the Jones's a lavish and lucrative life style. Outside and before he walked to get a cab, Ian called DD. He was nervous and the palms of his hands were sweating badly as he tapped in the number. He breathed a sigh of relief when the call was answered after a couple of rings.

"Yo?"

"DD it's Ian, I've got the gear! When can you meet me?"

"Wo good going man, I'm on my way."

"I ain't in Hackney at the minute but I'm now about to jump into a cab. Meet me in the cafe a few doors

down from the club in say twenty minutes ok?"
Ian hung up and after a short walk was able to hail
a taxi. As the black hackney drove a long Ian
removed a small canvas shopping bag from the
inside pocket of his jacket. Opening the holdall he
found four packets of what he knew could only be
cocaine. Tommy had told him there was twenty
grand's worth so carefully removing two of the
packets he placed them into the shopping bag and
zipped up the holdall. All the while he kept
glancing up to make sure that the cabbie hadn't
seen what he'd been doing, he hadn't as the traffic
was heavy and it forced the driver to concentrate
hard on the road ahead. Stopping outside the cafe,
Ian paid his fare and was about to go inside when
DD came screeching to a halt on his BMX. Ian
handed over the bag and naively waited for DD to
pay him but as he cycled away he shouted over his
shoulder 'Big Boy say's thanks'. Ian began to panic,
was this some kind of joke or did DD plan on
paying him later? Removing his phone Ian dialled
DD's number but it just kept ringing. After what
seemed like an age he hung up when he realised
he'd been well and truly shafted. Ian Hewitt was in
turmoil. he knew he had to return to the club but
what Tommy would say or do was another matter.
Pushing open the door he entered and slowly began
to climb the stairs. Ian was aware he was being
watched and wondered if the fear he now felt was
evident on his face. After knocking on the office

door and as he waited to be invited inside, Ian placed the holdall onto the floor and vigorously rubbed his wet palms down the side of his trousers. "Enter."

Tommy was alone and sat behind his desk with a broad smile on his face.

"Everything go alright boy?"

Ian again placed the holdall onto the floor and as he began to speak he could feel the onset of tears as they began to well up in his eyes.

"Yes and no Boss."

"What'd that cunt Taffy give you a hard time? Take no notice of him he's always like that. Don't get me wrong, the blokes got a Fucking mean streak that I wouldn't want to get on the wrong side of but as long as everything's going his way then he's alright."

"It aint that Mr Mortimer though I aint going to deny he scared the shit out of me. I suppose there's no easy way to put this so I might as well just come right out with it."

Tommy sat back in his leather swivel chair, crossed his arms and now wore a stern look on his face. He knew he wasn't going to like what he was about to hear but he still had to let the boy have his say and explain things.

"Get on with it then!"

"I live on a square surrounded by blocks of flats. I generally keep myself to myself, always have but I was propositioned the other day by a bloke called

125

DD."

"DD?"

"His real names Douglas Davidson."

"He aint nothing to do with that fucking tosser Big Boy is he?"

"Yeh he's his cousin anyway..."

"You're telling me you mix with that scum bag Big Boy Davidson?"

"Well not exactly, I only know him because I've seen him hanging about with DD."

"Come on then, finish what you was saying before I really get pissed off."

"Well DD said if I got some drugs he would double the money. I thought you'd be really pleased so I gave him half of what was in the bag, only he shot off without paying for them. I keep phoning him but he aint answering my calls."

"You fucking little twat! He's mugged you off good and proper. Ain't answering your calls? Did you really think he would, this is exactly the kind of thing Big Boy would do."

"DD said you hated blacks and that's why you fell out with his cousin."

"Hate blacks! They really have fucking sucked you in. The reason Big Boy hates me is because I had him thrown out if this place and a couple of the doormen got a bit fucking heavy with him. It aint like the cunt didn't deserve it. He came in here late one Saturday night and kicked off because his girl was dancing with another bloke. Mind you she was a tasty little piece and I wouldn't have said no. Anyway the black fucker started smashing up the bar and I had to eject him and have him slapped."

"So you mean DD lied to me?"

Tommy stood up and walked over to where Ian now stood. Opening up the bag he peered inside and shook his head from side to side as he did so. Tommy Mortimer wasn't what you would call an out and out hard man but none the less he'd been around for long enough to know the score. As Tommy spoke he was feeling partly responsible as he'd allowed the kid to be the go between but there was no way he'd ever let Ian know that.

"You my son, have put me in a very awkward situation! Half of me is saying you need to be punished and the other half is saying give the lad another chance! Believe you me, when Taffy finds out, he won't be so fucking understanding."

"Please Tommy! I'll go and get it all back or the money they're worth."

"Personally I can't see how you're going to do that. For a start the street value of that little lot far outweighs the double your money you was going to get from this DD bloke. Didn't you realise that you soppy twat?"

"No I didn't, I just wanted to please you and be a part of it all."

Tommy shook his head at the boy's naivety.

"If you play with fire son, sooner or later you're going to get burnt. I'll tell you what I'm going to do,

127

you've got forty eight hours to sort this but after that I don't know what will happen."

"Thank you and I won't let you down Mr Mortimer."

"You'd better not, for your sake."

Ian Hewitt now stood with his mouth open wide. He hadn't known what to expect but this definitely wasn't it. Taffy Jones would annihilate him and Ian knew he wouldn't stand a chance in hell of even landing a punch. He supposed he had hoped that Tommy would bail him out but what Ian didn't know was the fact that every penny Tommy Mortimer made was spent straight away. The club had been running at a loss for years and any cash left over from his deals went on prostitutes, funding his next purchase of drugs and of course his gambling addiction.

"Remember, two days and if you aint sorted it out by then, I aint going to have any choice but to call the big man. I really thought you'd be ok Ian but I suppose that's what I get for hiring a fucking naive kid that's still wet behind the fucking ears. Get off home and sort this mess out and I hope for your sake that the next time I see you, you've got the fucking money or the gear back."

It was just before noon when Ian entered the square and glanced in the direction of his mothers flat. He toyed with the idea of asking her for the money but knew she hadn't cashed her ticket yet and even if she did it today there was no way the money would be through in time. The flats covered three sides of St Thomas's Square and the Davidson block was on the opposite side to Ian's home. For once he had to be a man and be responsible for his own actions, so climbing the concrete steps he walked up to the third floor landing. Five or six children were playing and as he wove his way in between them, one boy who couldn't have been any more than seven years of age and who was seated on a bicycle, spat onto Ian's shoes.

"What you doing up here Honkey?"

Ian ignored the remark and made his way to the very last flat on the landing. The kitchen window was open and a strong smell of ganja was drifting outside. Knocking on the steel plate he quickly heard voices and the door opened a few inches. It wasn't much but it was enough for Ian to see that the person on the other side was DD. With members of his family inside the flat Douglas Davidson was full of bravado. Opening the door wider he grinned at Ian.

"Hi there Bro, how you doing man?"

Ian couldn't believe what he was hearing and he could feel his blood begin to boil.

"How am I doing? Are you having a fucking laugh or what?"

DD stepped outside of the flat and pulled the door as far as it would close without locking himself out.

"Look man, it was never personal but you don't want to be messing with Big Boy or the others.

129

Tommy had it coming to him and he's just going to have to suck it up and take the loss."

"But it aint Tommy whose going to lose out in all of this. That gear wasn't paid for and now Taffy Jones is going to be baying for my blood."

"Sorry to hear that Bro, that man is one mean son of a bitch, get me. Anyways I need to get back inside so see you around maybe."

Ian grabbed hold of DD's shoulder as he was about to disappear back inside the flat. In a flash he swivelled round and had Ian Hewitt up against the wall. Ian was no fighter and he knew he was in for a beating if he pushed things any further.

"Look you're a good bloke Ian but your shit aint my shit, you got me? You're such a soft pussy, you was all but asking for it. If you want to run with the big boys then you got to learn to stick up for yourself man."

"Run with the big boys? That's a fucking laugh coming from you DD, the only reason you're running with the big boys apart from the fact that you lick their arses, is because you conned a, what was it you said? Oh yeh a soft pussy like me. You aint no man DD, you're the fucking scum of the earth."

With that Ian turned and walked away. There was no point arguing further as he knew he wouldn't get anywhere and now he had to face Tommy and Taffy Jones alone. As he walked along the landing the boy that had insulted him a few minutes earlier

130

got ready for a second round of abuse but before he could open his mouth, Ian viciously kicked out at the child's bicycle and it went from underneath him leaving the boy in a heap on the floor. Crying out in pain, the boy's mother was outside her flat in a few seconds and just as Ian reached ground level she began to curse and swear over the balcony.

"You cruel fucking bastard, he's just a kid! I'm gonna get Big Boy to sort you out you fucking nonce."

Ian looked up at the woman and simply said.

"Too late Bitch he already has!"

As Ian crossed the square he dejectedly hung his head. The only option open to him was to plead with his mother for help but he had to pick the right moment.

CHAPTER ELEVEN

Over in Islington things were going from bad to worse. Joey had spent the night on the family sofa, Lizzie had begged him to use his old room but he wouldn't. Even though he was as mad as hell with his wife, going upstairs to sleep would somehow feel like the final nail in the coffin as far as his marriage was concerned. After the second night and still not having heard from his wife, Joey knew that she would soon be getting desperate. There was no way she would run to her parents for help as she would then have to admit what she had done. Tidying up the pillows and after folding the blanket, Joey Chambers walked towards the kitchen. His hair stuck out in all directions, he hadn't had a shave for forty eight hours and his mouth, choosing a phrase his father always used, felt like the inside of a Turkish wrestler's jockstrap. All in all he looked a real mess and he knew it. His wife was a selfish spoilt bitch but without her he was nothing. The rest of the family were still asleep and as he placed the kettle on to boil he heard the faintest knock at the front door. Seeing her silhouette through the frosted glass, Joey instantly recognised the form of his wife. It was only seven o'clock and it must have taken real effort for her to be here this early. Joey clicked the Yale, opened the door and then turned and walked back into the kitchen. He didn't speak and Sharon wasn't sure what reception she was going to receive but with no other alternative, she stepped into the hall and closed the door. Placing a bag of clean clothes onto the floor she glanced around the hallway. The house was clean but run down and she hated being here, even when she and Joey had been going out together he always had to call for her. She had only ever been to the Ritchie Street address a handful of times and even then it had only been at Christmas time or on the odd birthday but it was always under duress and never willingly. Sharon prayed that the rest of the family weren't about as she didn't feel like having them all gang up against her which was a distinct possibility taking into account how close they all were. Entering the kitchen she saw her husband sitting at the table with two mugs of tea. He looked a complete mess and she never would have allowed him downstairs looking in such a state. Taking a seat without being invited, Sharon clasped his hand and began to cry. Joey studied her trying to work out if the tears were real or not. It was difficult reading her, even after all these years his wife knew how to play him.

"I thought you'd have turned up sooner, money run out has it?"

"Don't be like that Joey. I've come to see you and nothing more, honest. I want you to come home; the house is cold and lonely without you."

"And whose fault is that?"

"I know, I know."

133

Sharon began to sob and it wasn't something Joey had seen before. Oh she could turn on the crocodile tears at the drop of a hat but this was different. She'd either upped her game or she was genuinely remorseful but whether she was sorry for her behaviour or just sorry for herself was another matter. Joey couldn't help but feel pity for her, couldn't help but love her and he caressed her hand as he spoke.

"If I come home, things are going to have to change Sharon..."

"They will I swear they will Joey."

"I haven't finished! You will have to make the effort to get on with my family, I aint having no more of your snooty ways and spending money like it's going out of fashion it's got to stop. I aint being mean but you're bleeding me dry and I can't keep working like I have been just so you can buy anything and everything your heart desires. Fuck me girl! Half the stuff in our house we don't need and I think you only do it because you're bored. You need to get some friends, get out more, get a fucking dog; I don't care what it is but shopping aint the answer. You're so fucking uptight all the time and it's wearing me out, a bit of mess now and again doesn't hurt anyone. Sometimes Sharon I feel like I'm living in a show home."

Sharon looked around the dated kitchen and he instantly knew what she was thinking.

"Yeh it aint much is it but I'll tell you one thing, it's a

home."

It was going to be hard but she knew she had no choice, not if she wanted to keep him. The idea of a dog had started to fill her mind, not a big slobbering dog but a little designer Chihuahua like the ones celebrities have and there was so many designer bags that you could buy to carry them in. Maybe it wouldn't be such a bad idea after all. Sharon Chambers dried her eyes and smiled at her husband.

"Ok I promise I'll change but please come home."

"I need a few days longer. We've all taken Michael's illness hard and the family need me now more than ever."

"But I need you Joey!"

"Don't push your fucking luck Sharon."

"Ok ok I'm sorry, I won't mention it again. I've brought you a complete change of clothes, they're in the hall. If you go and get washed and dressed I can take your dirty stuff back with me."

Joey stood up and kissed his wife tenderly on the cheek. Walking into the hall he picked up the bag and made his way upstairs. About to enter the bathroom he saw his sister's bedroom door open. Lizzie was bleary eyed and yawning as she stepped out onto the landing.

"Morning Joey sleep well?"

"Not too bad thanks. Lizzie I need to tell you something, Sharon's downstairs please don't give her a hard time."

Lizzie Chambers didn't reply to her brother and quickly descending the stairs, went straight into the kitchen. Joey quietly followed, he knew his sister well and there was no way she would let Sharon get away with what she'd done, at least not before Lizzie had said her piece. He wanted to hear how his wife would handle it, in fact he needed to know how she would handle it and see if she really was willing to change.

"You've got a fucking cheek showing your face around here you old cow!"

"I didn't come to argue Lizzie I came to see my husband."

"Came to see your husband! Don't make me fucking laugh. Joey told me what you did and I think it's disgusting. My poor baby is lying in the hospital so sick that he might die and you used that to get on my brothers good side. Whatever sort of a woman are you?"

Sharon stood up and walked over to her sister in law. She had to make the peace and after realising that Joey had eaves dropped the other day, she had a feeling he might be doing it again.

"Look I know you are all angry with me and I can't say I blame you but I am really sorry. Maybe you don't believe me but I'll prove it to you and my husband that a leopard can change. Now I really hope you reach Steve and that he's a match and if you need anything Lizzie please call me. We aint never been what you'd call bosom buddies but I

136

aim to change all that. I have to go now, can you tell Joey I'll pop back for his washing later."
Sharon knew that if her husband was listening then it was his cue to disappear and just as she imagined, the hall was empty as she walked to the front door.
Lizzie Chambers was still standing with her mouth wide open as Joey reappeared in the kitchen. She hadn't believed a word that had come out of Sharon's mouth and she was still in shock at the cheek of the bitch.
"So how was she?"
Lizzie didn't want to cause her brother any more upset and as she smiled at him, had already made her mind up to play her sister in law at her own game.
"Surprisingly polite and she did apologise."
"So what do you think?"
"About what? Are you talking about me or the state of your marriage?"
"Don't be like that Lizzie. I know you're going through a tough time but this isn't just affecting you, its hit us all hard and the last thing we need is to be at each other's throats all the time."
Lizzie Chambers smiled warmly at her brother, he really was a lovely bloke and she idolised the ground he walked on. He could have done far better than Sharon Jackson and Lizzie wished with all her heart that he had.
"Ok I'll call a truce, now have you had any luck contacting Steve?"

"No and I really don't think we should keep trying, time is moving on and we need to think about the boy's father. I know you don't want this Lizzie but what other choice do we have?"

"I know you're right but there's no way I could face him again. I've thought about little else and I just can't do it Joey."

"You don't have to darling."

Lizzie knew there was no other option and reluctantly she nodded her head giving her brother the signal to do whatever he had to do. Joey smiled and running up the stairs got showered and changed. At eleven o'clock he set off and after driving over to Hackney, parked behind Iceland in the Kingsland shopping centre. Joey then walked along Kingsland road looking for the Den. It was on the opposite side of the road and he stood looking up at the place for a few seconds. The first thought to cross his mind was that this was where Michael had been conceived and where his sister had been raped. Joey could feel anger beginning to build up inside him and he tried hard to calm himself, he needed to be able to think straight when he met this Tommy bloke and if he was full of rage it wouldn't help matters. Crossing the road he tried the door but it was locked and after ringing the bell and waiting for a couple of minutes he decided to try around the back. A long alleyway ran behind all of the shops and businesses and as far as he could see none of them were covered by CCTV. A small open yard led up to a fire exit and beside that was a normal looking door. Joey tried the handle, never in a million years expecting it to be open but much to his surprise it was. Quietly he let himself inside into the rear hall that led through to the front reception area and the stairs up to the club. Out of the corner of his eye Joey saw the camera follow him as he climbed the stairs and knew he was being watched. He didn't know who or what would greet him at the top but right at this moment he didn't have a choice, getting Michael well again was all that mattered and he would do whatever it took to make that happen. The smell of the place hit his nostrils as he reached the top landing and it brought back memories of when he was younger and spent his weekends in places like this. Joey saw a door with the word 'OFFICE' emblazed across the front and knocking firmly he walked inside. The room was empty which disappointed him but he decided to wait it out. Spying the digital recorder he realised that the camera must have had a motion sensor. Pressing the eject button he removed the disc from inside and slipped it into his pocket, at least now there wouldn't be any evidence that he'd been here. About to take a seat he froze when he heard someone cough and standing behind the door waited nervously to see who would come in. Tommy Mortimer, after the aggravation this morning had let Ian go early and had been forced to collect his own lunch. Climbing the three flights of

139

stairs had taken its toll on Tommy and he was puffing and panting when he reached the top. Walking straight past Joey he flopped into his chair and began to unwrap his burger. Licking his lips, Tommy was just about to take a bite when he saw the stranger standing in the corner of the room.

"Who the fuck are you?"

"My names Joey Chambers."

"Well if you've come to rob me sunshine you're out of luck as there's no cash kept on the premises."

Joey laughed and took a step forward.

"I aint come to rob you I've come to ask for your help."

Tommy's brow furrowed, he didn't have the first clue what the man was on about and by the look on his face it was evident to Joey that he didn't recognise the surname but then why should he, Lizzie was just another of his victims, another innocent young girl who had never got any justice for what he'd done to her.

"Nineteen years ago well almost nineteen right in this very office you raped my sister."

Tommy Mortimer was about to protest but was stopped when Joey held up his hand.

"The result of that rape was my nephew Michael. Now our Mikey is a good boy but he's always been a bit sickly. What we didn't know was the fact that he had a progressive kidney disease. He's in the hospital at this very moment on the transplant list but the chances of that happening are pretty slim.

My family have all been tested but none of us are a match, seems you not only gave my sister a baby but you also gave your son a rare blood group. Now I've come here to ask you to be a donor, you've given the poor little fucker nothing in his life and this is the least you can do don't you think?"

By the time he had finished Joeys heart was pounding as he waited to hear the outcome of his speech. Tommy placed the burger back into its wrapper and stared long and hard at his visitor.

"So I've got a boy have I? That's the fifth or six that I know of. Look I'm afraid you've had a wasted journey because there aint no way I'm being cut open to help some kid that I aint never met. Now fuck off out of here, I'm a busy man and I aint had me lunch yet."

Joey went to take a step further but as quick as a flash Tommy opened the desk drawer and before he knew what was happening Joey Chambers was looking down the barrel of a pistol. Backing his way towards the door, he held up his hands in submission.

"I'll give you time to think about it and call back in the next few days."

Tommy raised the gun and Joey ran out of the office and slammed the door as he went. He had never gone down so many steps in such a short time and he was also breathless when he reached the bottom but not because he was out of shape. Walking back towards his car he ran through everything in his

mind. He wasn't naive and hadn't expected
Tommy Mortimer to agree for a second but he had
to see who the man was and gauge his reaction.
Ever since Lizzie had revealed the name of the
culprit, Joey had been hatching a plan, it was a long
shot but at the moment he had little choice but to
take a chance. It would mean going against all he
believed in but if it saved Michael then it would be
well worth the effort.

CHAPTER TWELVE

Ian Hewitt had decided to leave it a day before he asked his mother for help. The previous night he had kept out of Tommy's way in the club but now it was D day and he was worried sick. He'd spent a restless night tossing and turning and when his alarm burst into life at seven he was up and dressed within minutes. Normally his mother had to call him several times before he hauled his backside out of bed but not today. Walking into the kitchen he saw her standing at the sink washing up and his father had his arms around her waist and was nuzzling her neck.

"For God's sake you two!"

Sue turned and smiled but John Hewitt gave his son a quizzical look that said 'what are you on about'. Sue dried her hands and walking over to the hob placed the kettle on to boil.

"I'm glad that's done; I tell you when I cash my ticket the first thing on the list will be a dishwasher."

"Don't you think you've spent enough already love?"

Sue Hewitt fiercely turned to face her husband.

"Don't you ever bloody tell me what to spend my money on, I've slaved for bleeding years while you sat on your arse doing nothing. It's my ticket, my winnings and my money alright?"

"Calm down I was only saying so don't get your

knickers in a twist."

After his mothers outburst Ian knew it definitely wasn't the right time to ask her for any money. Deciding to do his morning shift, he would wait and see what sort of mood she was in at lunch time. Ian carried on with his usual routine and the first thing was to collect Tommy's breakfast. He wasn't looking forward to seeing his boss today but knew that he had no choice in the matter. When he entered the office Tommy Mortimer didn't even look up from his newspaper. Ian placed the bacon roll down and was about to leave when his boss spoke.

"You know what day it is today?"

"Yes Mr Mortimer."

"Good and you'd better make sure you have the cash because Taffy Jones will be here tonight and you don't want to get on the wrong side of him!"

Ian closed the door and he could feel his whole body tremble. He respected Tommy but wasn't frightened of him, Taffy Jones on the other hand put the fear of God into Ian Hewitt and that was just at the mention of his name. He prayed that by the time his evening shift began the man would have been and gone. The morning flew past as there was a delivery from the brewery and Ian had to check the order and fill up the stockroom. After fetching Tommy's lunch he headed home and hoped that his mother would be there. Opening the door he couldn't hear anyone and when he walked into the front room his eyes nearly popped out of their sockets. Two, large expensive looking oversized sofas almost filled the room. A fifty Inch plasma television was perched on a glass stand and underneath was a Bang and Olufsen sound system. Two wall units were filled with ornaments and to Ian they looked trashy but had probably cost the earth. The kitchen was the same with a new washer, dryer, cooker and American style fridge freezer. Everything was still packaged and he could hardly get in the room. The work tops were filled with boxes containing everything from a kettle to a food mixer and all the items were the best that money could buy. Ian smiled and at the same time hoped that somehow his mother had cashed in her ticket but then he reasoned it could never happen that quickly. Making his way to the bedroom, he laid on the bed in the hope that sleep would help him to forget what he had done, at least for a few hours. Staring up at the ceiling for what felt like an age, he must have finally drifted off as just after seven he was woke by the sound of groaning and the noise of the head board in his parents room banging against the wall. Ian rolled his eyes and getting up went to go into the kitchen. Nothing had been moved and he wasn't even able to make a cup of tea. He decided to watch television for a while but as he opened the front room door, saw his parents clothing scattered around the room. Deciding to set off for work early and get a bite to eat on the way, he was stopped when out of the corner of his eye he spied his mother's bra. Normally he wouldn't have given it a second thought but for some strange reason he was drawn to it. Lifting it by the strap his jaw dropped when the lottery ticket fell to the ground. Puffing out his cheeks in shock, Ian knew to take it would be very wrong but it was now about self preservation and when it boiled down to it, he was far more frightened of what Taffy and Tommy would do to him than he was of his mother. Snatching it from the floor he ran from the flat and didn't stop until he was two streets away. Maybe he could do a deal with the men and split the cash, at least that way his mother would at least get some money. Whatever the outcome, Ian felt as if he'd been thrown a life line. Quickening his step and just as he was about to cross the road, Ian spied DD approaching on his BMX. Expecting and more than ready for another row, he was surprised when DD rode straight past him. Somehow that action was worse for Ian than if he'd stopped and they had ended up fighting. Douglas Davidson and his cousin had well and truly stitched him up, not only had they stitched him up but hung him out to dry.

Sue and John Hewitt had enjoyed another session of great sex and they both felt as though all of their Christmases had come at once. As Sue pulled on one of her new dresses, John handed her a bottle of

expensive perfume that he'd picked up on his way
to the bookies.

"Try this one love."

Sue giggled as she applied a liberal amount to her
neck and arms. They had decided to go out to
dinner to celebrate the win and hadn't given a
second thought to Ian or where he was. It felt as
though they were both in the best dream possible
and were getting swept along on a wave of
spending as much as they could as fast as they
could. John held open the front door as his wife
passed through. He had ordered a mini cab to take
them up west to one of the fanciest restaurants he
could think of. It was only a steak house but as far
as Sue and John Hewitt were concerned it was fine
dining. They ordered prawn cocktails and steak
and chatted about what they were going to do with
all the money. Moving was the first thing they
wanted to do and Sue asked her husband where he
fancied living.

"I've always thought I'd like somewhere really
rural."

"I've always quite fancied Essex myself, there's some
bloody fabulous houses there."

"Yeh I know but I'd like some land, a bit of peace
and quiet for a change. I was grateful to your old
lady for taking us in and without her we wouldn't
have had a home but those flats craze me.
Screaming and shouting at all hours and you can't
get away from it. Fucking noise does my head in

love; anyway we won't have to put up with it for much longer."

Sue smiled and tenderly stroked his hand and John couldn't remember the last time he'd felt this happy.

"How are we doing on the money front love?"

"Well I've maxed out three of the cards and there's about four hundred left on the last one. All the stuff for the house I got doesn't come cheap. What about the card I gave to you?"

John Hewitt lowered his eyes and wore a sheepish expression.

"John?"

"Well I got a bit carried away down the bookies."

"You've been gambling! Oh John how much this time?"

"All of it."

"All of it! But there was five grand on that card. You promised me years ago when you got into trouble and I bailed you out that it wouldn't happen again."

"I know I did and I'm sorry but I knew when you cashed in the ticket we'd be rolling in it. I'm sorry and I swear on our Ian's life that it won't happen again."

Suddenly Sue sat bolt upright and her eyes were wide with fear.

"What's the matter darling?"

"The ticket, I haven't got the ticket! It's still in my bra on the front room floor. Oh John we need to get back there."

After quickly paying for the meal, with the few pounds that she still had in her purse there was just enough left over to get a cab back home. The couple didn't speak on the journey, John because he was still ashamed of his gambling habit and Sue because she had a gut feeling about the ticket and it wasn't a good one. Racing up to the flat Sue's hands shook and she struggled to get the key into the front door. Finally she managed and they both burst into the front room. Their clothes were still strewn around and bending down she rummaged through each piece of her clothing but it wasn't there.

"It's gone, oh my god John someone's taken it!"

"Don't be daft; it's got to be there."

"I tell you it isn't; here take a look for yourself."

John knelt on the floor and slowly picked up each item. Meticulously he examined the pieces and then looked up into his wife's face. Sue was instantly suspicious and narrowed her eyes.

"You didn't take it did you?"

"You silly cow, of course I didn't. I aint left your side since this morning, how the fuck could I have taken it?"

"Then we must have been burgled."

"We aint been fucking burgled soppy, the place is still exactly the same as we left it. It must be Ian."

"He wouldn't do that to us, I know he wouldn't."

"Then what other explanation do you have?"

Suddenly Sue burst into tears. Her dream of a life of luxury had gone down the pan in a matter of hours. Instantly reality hit her, if they didn't get it back they would be in so much debt that they would never be able to pay it off. John stood up and took his wife in his arms.

"Come on darling it aint as bad as all that. Hopefully when Ian comes home tonight he will still have it and we will have been worrying for nothing."

"I hope you're right because all this will bankrupt us if not. Do you think we should go to where he works and get it back?"

John Hewitt didn't answer his wife straight away as he was still thinking about how much they had spent in the last couple of days. It had run into thousands and all on credit cards.

"John? Did you hear what I said; shall we go and find him?"

"No I think we should just stay here and wait until he gets back. There's no point in causing a scene and he wouldn't thank us for going to his place of work. Just wait and see, you are really worrying over nothing. I bet he came in, saw the ticket and took it for safe keeping. He's a good boy Sue, you know he is."

"I just hope for our sakes you're right, if not we're in a shit load of trouble with no way to get out of it."

John made them both tea and they took their seats on the sofa and began to wait. They must have drifted off to sleep because Sue was jolted awake by a load of screaming outside at just after four in the morning.

"John! John wake up."

"What's going on?"

"I don't know but it's gone four and he aint back yet, something's wrong I just know it. He's always home by now."

"Let's give it a bit longer and if he aint back in the next few hours I'll go and look for him in the morning?"

"Promise?"

"Cross me heart and hope to die. Now I know it won't be easy but let's try and get some sleep."

John curled up on the new sofa and was soon snoring softly but it was a different story for Sue. She was worried about the money and the racket outside was horrendous. There was always music blearing out and shouting but usually by this time it had quietened down. The sound of police cars screeching to a halt and the loud noise of an ambulance siren made her get up and take a look from behind the net curtains. It must be serious as there were hoards of people gathered in the square below. Whatever it was, she was glad that none of her family were involved.

CHAPTER THIRTEEN

Earlier that evening as Sue and John Hewitt had been tucking into their meal, Ian was climbing the stairs up to the club. Never in his life had he been so nervous and he continually tapped his trouser pocket that contained the ticket. Deciding not to go into the office until he was called he made his way to the bar area. As usual the place was almost deserted and walking over he ordered a whisky to calm his nerves. Dicky Stinton was on duty behind the bar and as he poured the drink, studied the young man's face. The boy had only been working here for a few days but the stress of the place was already beginning to show. Dicky was time served and had been a part time barman at the Den for over ten years. He didn't particularly like the place or Tommy Mortimer come to that but the extra income topped up his day job and allowed him to live just above the breadline.

"You ok Ian?"

"Nah not really."

"Want to talk about it, you know a problem shared and all that, besides I aint exactly rushed off me feet now am I?"

Ian didn't really know Dicky and although he would have loved to unburden his troubles, he wasn't going to bandy his boss's business about to just anyone.

"I wish I could but it's a bit personal. Thank you for

offering though."

"Any time. Been in to see the boss yet?"

"Not yet but I've got a feeling that'll change pretty soon."

"Not too soon I hope. That wanker Taffy Jones is in there with him, I fucking hate that bloke."

Ian wanted to say 'me too' but didn't voice his opinion. Seconds later the phone behind the bar began to ring. Dicky answered and as he spoke looked in Ian Hewitt's direction.

"Seems you've been summoned. Good luck."

"Thanks, I think I'm going to need it."

Ian gulped down the remainder of his drink and headed in the direction of the office. Waiting to be told to enter he again tapped the pocket of his trousers and said a silent prayer in the hope that the little piece of pink paper would get him out of the scrape that he knew could turn very ugly very soon. Walking inside he'd tried to focus his attention on Tommy and not look in Taffy's direction. The man with the golden teeth was sitting on the sofa, the same sofa that Lizzie Chambers had been raped on all those years ago but Taffy wasn't aware of that fact and definitely wouldn't have cared even if he was.

"Take a seat Ian."

Doing as he was asked Ian Hewitt sat on the chair that had been placed in front of the desk. It wasn't normally there and he suddenly felt very vulnerable.

"Now then son, I know you've done wrong and I accept you was acting in the best of interests just to please me. That said, you took a fucking liberty and there are consequences. Now did you manage to get my money from the Davidson's?"

Ian shook his head and could feel the onset of tears. "I have got this though and me mum said it's a winner. Will it help?"

Ian placed the ticket onto the desk and both Tommy Mortimer and Taffy Jones looked at each other and began to shake their heads.

"I'm afraid not sunshine."

"But it's a winner, I don't know how much but mum said it's a lot."

"Ian I like you and I'm glad I took you on but we're talking about ten grand plus here, not a poxy little win on the lottery. I'm right fucking sad it's come to this but Taffy here wants his money and unless you've got ten big ones on you then it's out of my hands."

Ian may have been eighteen but this was a whole different world to the one he was used to. Men like Taffy Jones killed people without a second thought and it scared the hell out of him. When Taffy stood up Ian could feel his legs turn to jelly. Walking around the office he looked at the pictures that adorned the walls, Taffy knew exactly what he was doing and all the while Ian was becoming more and more frightened. Tommy Mortimer also didn't feel that brave and he was hoping that whatever was going to happen, would just happen so they could all get back to normal. You could feel the tension building in the room and when Taffy Jones made his way over to the chair and leaned in close Ian gasped. The man was now only a couple of inches away from Ian's face and smiling he revealed his gold teeth. Up close they appeared even more frightening.

"Who the fuck are the Davidson's?"

Tommy began to speak but was silenced by one look from Taffy Jones.

"I want to hear it from the boys own mouth. Now cunt, are you going to tell me or do I have to beat it out of you?"

His words scared Ian so much that he began to talk so quickly that even Tommy Mortimer had a job to keep up and understand what his employee was saying.

"They live on the same square as me. There's a whole load of them, brothers, cousins you name it and they all live between each other's flats but mostly they're in the block directly opposite mine. They formed a gang about three years ago and will do anything for money and respect. You know what them gangs are like, it's all about kudos. The head man is called Big Boy and..."

"Fucking Big Boy! Whatever sort of a name is that?"

Ian just stared at the man standing in front of him and Taffy prodded Ian hard in the face with his index finger before he continued.

"I'm warning you boy! You'd better spill your fucking guts!"

"One of the younger cousins approached me a week ago and asked if I could get some drugs. He told me that Tommy wouldn't deal with them because he was a racist."

"Black cunts are they?"

Now Tommy Mortimer was going to speak up with or without Taffy's permission.

"For the last time, I aint no fucking racist. I told you before Ian, Big Boy caused me a lot of aggro and I banned him. It didn't have anything to do with the colour of his skin, so I don't know why he's saying any different."

Taffy Jones couldn't believe what he was hearing and looked from Ian to Tommy.

"What the fuck! You two sound like fucking old women, I don't give a shit what it was over I just want to know who they are and where they are. Now start talking boy because I'm fast beginning to lose my fucking patience."

Ian knew better than to ignore the request. Taffy had begun to pace up and down and as naive as he was, Ian really didn't like how things were progressing. The atmosphere was extremely tense and he could sense that the man was liable to snap at any moment.

"As I said they are in a gang and DD is desperate to join but he has to do something to get in. He told me that if I could get them some gear they will double the value and I wanted to prove myself to Mr Mortimer. On my way back from your place Mr Jones, I handed over half of the contents of the bag but instead of DD giving me the cash he fucked off leaving me with nothing. Of course I went round there but I was told to sling me hook. I aint no fighter Mr Jones so there was little more I could do. They really are a bunch of nasty bastards."

"Where did you say they lived?"

"St Thomas's Square right opposite me in Colony House, number twenty five on the second floor but it's like fort Knox in there. They've got a steel door and they don't answer it unless they know you. I went round there and ...."

Tommy had been watching Taffy and he could visibly see the colour drain from the man's face. It was a look he'd seen often enough when Taffy was about to erupt into violence and Tommy half closed his eyes and slowly shook his head. He didn't know what was going to happen but either way he didn't fancy Ian's chances. Suddenly and before either Ian or Tommy noticed what he was doing, Taffy grabbed the onyx ashtray that sat on the top of the desk and with as much force as he could muster, smashed it into the side of Ian's head. The force of the impact knocked Ian to the floor, blood sprayed from his temple and a line of claret liquid hit the wall. Taffy Jones immediately straddled his victim and violently repeated his assault a further four times. Taffy was like a man crazed with pure anger

as the solid lump of onyx again made contact with
the side of Ian's head. It had all happened so
quickly and now Ian's body lay dead on the office
floor. Tommy sat in the chair with his mouth open
holding his breath and was unable to take in what
he'd just been witness too. He was used to seeing
violence on a regular basis but this was a kid, a kid
who had just been trying to do the right thing and
look good in the eyes of his boss. Now that the
pressure had been released the blood flow
diminished to a trickle rather than a spray and for a
moment Tommy Mortimer hoped his young
employee was going to be alright but deep down he
knew it was wishful thinking His eyes were fixed
on Ian's lifeless body but he quickly pulled himself
together and went over to where the boy lay.
Bending down, Tommy placed his fingers onto Ian's
neck and he felt for a pulse but there wasn't one.
"Fuck me Taffy; you've killed the poor little sod!"
"You twat, that was my intention, anyway he was
apathetic little cunt so it aint as if it's any loss to you
now is it?"
"That aint the point. He was a good kid who made
the wrong decision; he didn't deserve to die for it."
Taffy hawked up a mouthful of phlegm and spat it
onto Ian's body.
"No cunt robs me and gets away with it and you'd
be fucking wise to remember that!"
As Taffy passed Tommy he used his shoulder to
slightly knock into the man and it was a move that

158

silently told Tommy not to continue with this or he might just be next.

"So now what do we do?"

"We? There aint no we pal, you're on your own. I'm going after the slags what've got my gear and god help the cunts because I'm going to fucking annihilate them."

"But what about the boy, what do I do with him?"

Taffy Jones rested his hand on the door handle and turned to face Tommy as he did so.

"You really have gone soft in your old age. I can remember a time when you would have disposed of a stiff without a second thought, aint as if you aint done it in the past now is it?"

With that Taffy Jones walked out of the office leaving Tommy to clear up the mess but he wasn't able to do anything at the moment as he had to wait for the club to empty. Closing the office door he locked it and made his way into the bar.

"Give us a double scotch Dicky."

"Everything alright boss?"

Suddenly Tommy was on his guard and his eyes narrowed as he spoke.

"Yeh, why do you ask?"

"No reason, I just saw young Ian earlier and he looked like he had the weight of the world on his shoulders, poor little fucker."

The barman's choice of words only made Tommy feel worse. He knew Ian didn't deserve what had happened to him and he would have loved to see

Taffy Jones get his comeuppance but men like that seldom did. Tommy wasn't disillusioned and he knew he'd done plenty of bad things himself over the years and yes Taffy was probably right and he was going soft. Thinking about it some more he came to realise that he didn't mind in the least. Being soft wasn't so bad and maybe he should think about retiring, the only problem was the fact that he needed money to fund his lifestyle. Although he had a good amount of cash stashed away, it wouldn't last long, well not the way he liked to indulge himself.

"I had to let him go tonight, just wasn't pulling his weight. It's a shame because he was a nice lad but there you go that's life. I'm off home Dicky, lock up and I'll see you tomorrow."

With that Tommy Mortimer went home for a few hours. He was confident that no one would come across Ian Hewitt's body as there was only one key to the office and Tommy never let it out of his grasp.

After collecting a few items from the boot of his car and placing them in a holdall, Taffy Jones set off for St Thomas's Square. He was already in a bad mood which wouldn't bode well for the Davidson's. Stopping at a Cost Cutter shop he purchased a box of cream cakes and a pack of paper plates. It had been a while since he'd been active but after disposing of Ian, his adrenalin was starting to pump through his veins. A couple of times he had to stop and ask a passerby if he was going in the right direction but not once did he offer any thanks when they either told him yes or redirected him. The last person he asked was a young bloke who was in his early twenties and out with his girlfriend, when Taffy just walked away after they had helped him and didn't even say thank you, the young man shouted out 'ungrateful tosser'. For a nano second Taffy stopped dead in his tracks, he would have normally gone back and beat the man black and blue but for once he contained his anger; tonight he had more pressing business than dealing with a rude mannered cunt that didn't have the first clue who Taffy Jones was. Entering the square he spent several minutes surveying the layout of the buildings. Ascending the concrete stairwell, he took every step slow and steady so as not to create any noise. Reaching the second floor he pressed his back against the wall and peered around the corner. It was ten thirty at night and a couple of kids were still running about on the landing. One of the front doors was propped open and Taffy guessed this was where the kids lived. Loud reggae music boomed out into the corridor and the sweet smell of cannabis filled the air. Taking out the cakes and paper plates that he'd bought earlier, Taffy proceeded to place a couple of cakes onto one of the plates. He threw the rest on the floor and after taking one more look along the landing, began to walk along towards number twenty five. When he reached the kids he stopped and turning his attention to a half cast boy by the name of Jay Jay and who was no more than eight years old, he spoke.

"Do you want to play a game Son?"

The boy looked Taffy up and down and didn't flinch an inch when he saw the array of glinting gold teeth.

"Fuck off you pervert before I get me bruvver onto you. He hates kiddie fiddlers and he'll knock them teeth down your fucking throat!"

It had been a long time since Taffy Jones had any dealings with children and he'd forgotten how fast they grew up nowadays. Putting a hand in his trouser pocket he pulled out a five pound note.

"Fair enough. Do you fancy making a fiver, no funny business I promise."

The boy eyed him up. He had seen many things, things no child of eight should ever have to be witness to and he knew the score.

"If you've come after the Davidson's it's going to cost you a lot more than five lousy quid mister."

"How much?"

"Fifty."

"You're having a laugh aint you!"

"Take it or leave it."

Jay Jay was about to walk off, at such a young age he was already adept in the art of negotiation. His mother had taught him that if someone wanted something badly enough then they would pay your price and if not, then you should just walk away. Jay Jay's mother, who went by the name of Carmen to her punters, didn't practice what she preached and would often bring men back to her flat for as little as a tenner if trade was slow. Taffy knew the kid had his balls in a vice and as much as it went against the grain, he had to give in to Jay Jay's demands.

"OK ok, here's your money but if you try and shaft me I'll come looking for you."

"That wouldn't be good business mister and you never know when you might require my services again, now what do you want me to do."

It was now Taffy's turn to laugh and at the same time he showed Jay Jay the cakes on a plate.

"I want you to knock on the door and when they answer tell them your mum has some cakes left over."

Jay Jay burst out laughing, his mother did a lot of things but giving away food wasn't one of them. Taffy ignored the laughter and continued with his instructions.

"When they've taken the plate I want you to run, because what's going to happen won't be pleasant. Now are you ok with all of that?"

Jay Jay nodded and wasn't fazed in the least, he'd seen enough violence in his short life that it would have to be pretty bad to bother him but he'd never met anyone like Taffy Jones before and what he would be witness to in the next few minutes would scar him for life. After knocking as hard as he could Jay Jay waited for someone to open up. DD could be heard behind the door but when he looked through the spy hole he couldn't see anyone as Jay Jay was too short.

"Who's there?"

"It's me Jay Jay, me mums got you a couple of cakes."

Bolts could be heard sliding and as Douglas Davidson, with a smile on his face, opened the door and reached out to take the cakes, Taffy Jones raised the machete and brought it down with force severing DD's right hand. The dismembered hand fell to the floor still holding the plate with the cakes intact. It all seemed to happen in slow motion and as DD's eyes were open wide with fear, Taffy raised the machete again and struck it low into his victim's right leg, smashing through DD's shin bone. The wound had been inflicted deliberately to stop DD leaving the flat and running for help. Douglas Davidson fell to the floor with blood pouring from his wounds and Taffy casually stepped over him as DD screamed out in agony. Many residents in the flats heard the terrible sounds but not one person came to help. In this area you kept your head down and your nose out of anyone else's business. Jay Jay ran to his own home and slammed the door shut, he'd never seen anything like this before and he was utterly terrified. Leaning back on the cold paintwork, he looked down and could see his little hands shaking with fear. Back in the flat, Taffy slowed down and cautiously walked from room to room. All were empty until he reached the front room. Big Boy was on the sofa with his arm around some girl and they were both completely stoned. "Where's my drugs you scheming cunt?" Big boy held out his hands and shrugged his shoulders as if to say 'aint got a clue what you're on about' and then he began to giggle. Taffy raised the machete and brought it down square onto Big Boys head splitting it in two. As he lay spread-eagled with his arms and legs outstretched and with the machete wedged deep in his skull like an axe in a timber log, the girl screamed and tried to stand from the sofa. Taffy Jones's large hand loomed in and grabbed a handful of her hair pulling her head backwards. Forcefully he dragged her across the carpet and finally let her go in the corner of the room where she huddled in a foetal position sobbing uncontrollably. Taffy walked back over to Big Boy and placing his foot on the man's chest, un-wedged the machete from his skull. For a second he studied his handiwork and then coughing loudly, spat out a mouthful of phlegm onto the corpse. It was now time to make a decision regarding the girl. She hadn't once made eye contact with him and she was so spaced out with the amount of drugs she had consumed that he reasoned she wasn't a threat and probably wouldn't be able to tell what was real and what she had hallucinated. Scanning the room

165

Taffy Jones saw the two white plastic bags he'd been looking for   They were slightly light in weight but at least he had most of it back and there was still Tommy to sort out. Unaware of Taffy's success, Tommy Mortimer was still under the impression that he owed the man big time for the stolen merchandise. Taffy would make sure that he was paid in full, so all in all it could end up being a win win situation for Taffy Jones, albeit a messy one. Outside he placed the drugs and his weapon into the holdall and then beat a hasty retreat. Jay Jay watched the stranger disappear and then made his way into the Davidson's flat. His pal had gone home as soon as Taffy showed his teeth and now alone Jay Jay wasn't so full of bravado. Stepping over DD who was groaning in pain on the floor, he walked into the front room and his eyes opened wide when he saw the carnage. The police would be here soon and Jay Jay knew he couldn't hang around, so he quickly frisked Big Boys pockets in the hope of finding some cash. The girl was still huddled in the corner sobbing but Jay Jay ignored her. With the fifty Taffy had given him and the cash he'd just robbed from Big Boy, rounded off the night with five hundred reddies to swell his small pockets. In the opposite block of flats, Sue Hewitt was on tender hooks as she waited for news of her son.

CHAPTER FOURTEEN

At six the following morning Tommy once again let himself into the club. As he made his way through to the foyer and into the back yard he could feel his nerves start to kick in. He hadn't worked out how to dispose of Ian's body yet and was wracking his brains to come up with a plan. Tommy didn't drive and there was definitely no one he could ask for help. Walking along the back alley he stopped when he saw the commercial wheelie bin at the rear of the opticians shop two buildings along. Luckily it was almost empty and grabbing the handle he pulled hard as he wheeled it into the clubs yard and positioned it outside the back door. At least he had found a way to get rid of the problem but disposing of Ian's corpse still wasn't going to be easy. Accepting that he had no option but to get on with things, Tommy climbed the three flights of stairs up to the club. Time was moving fast and he had to get a grip and sort things out before the cleaner arrived. Old Joyce was as sharp as a razor and would know there was trouble as soon as she looked into Tommy Mortimer's eyes. As he stood outside the office he mentally relived all that had happened last night and was now nervous about going inside. Unlocking the door he slowly pushed it open to see Ian's body still lying on the floor. There was a bad smell in the room as the corpse had released its bodily fluids and Tommy had to concentrate hard to stop himself from retching. What he hadn't bargained on was the fact that three or four hours after death rigor mortis had begun to set in. As Tommy tried to place his arms under Ian's he found that the boy was as stiff as a board. Tommy began to sweat and now knew he had a real problem. Crossing the dance floor he made his way over to the clubs kitchen and after rummaging around in several cupboards, found an extra large table cloth that he could use. Laying the fabric out onto the office floor, he rolled Ian's lifeless body onto it. Tommy surveyed the situation for a few seconds and was now worried that he wouldn't be able to fit the corpse into the wheelie bin; still he'd cross that bridge when he came to it. For now he was more concerned about getting Ian downstairs. Wrapping the corners of the tablecloth over the body as best he could, Tommy then knotted it in the middle and hauled it over his shoulders. Thankfully Ian Hewitt was a thin boy but even though he didn't weigh that much, he was still a dead weight and difficult to lift. With each step Tommy could feel the sweat as it began to drip down his face. When it came to the stairs it was another story and Tommy had visions of falling and being found later by the cleaner with the body of Ian Hewitt at his side. He decide the best way to go about the task and limit his risk of tripping was to go down backwards and haul the cloth down one step at a time. It worked but took Tommy Mortimer over ten minutes to achieve his goal. Out in the yard he stopped for a moment to catch his breath before laying the wheelie bin onto its side. Tommy removed a couple of bags of rubbish and placed them against the wall. Grabbing hold of the tablecloth he dragged the body outside and slowly began to push it inside the bin. It was touch and go but he finally managed it and using every bit of strength he had left, lifted the bin back onto its wheels. Placing the rubbish bags on top of Ian's body, Tommy then pushed it to the clubs boundary. After checking that there was no one in the rear ally he wheeled the bin back to its original position outside the opticians and then made a hasty retreat back inside the club. Closing the door he lent back against the wood and gasped for breath. He was too old and overweight to be dealing with this sort of thing and right at this moment he cursed Taffy Jones to hell and back. Regaining his composure Tommy again climbed the stairs up to the club. As he entered the office, the smell hit him full on and this time he threw up. Now there was even more mess but he couldn't leave it to Joyce to clean up as she would ask too many questions, so Tommy set about washing everything down. With bleach, it wasn't too difficult to clean the blood from the walls but the carpet was a different matter. Disinfectant masked the smell but that was about as much as he could hope for. He decided that later that day when the carpet was dry he would tip the contents of an

169

ashtray onto it; at least it would satisfy Joyce's curiosity regarding the stain. Ian's lottery ticket still sat on the desk and it did momentarily catch Tommy's eye but he was far too busy to pay any attention to it. By the time he'd finished he was totally exhausted, he also didn't smell too good so he decided to go home and get changed but not before he'd removed the disc from the close circuit television recorder.

Madeline Dumont or Mad Maddy as most people knew her had lived in Hackney for over sixty years. Her flat on Ellington Road was once part of her original family home. It had long since been divided into two apartments and renting out one of the flats gave her a decent income each month. Maddy had been born into wealthy stock but the family fortune had long since dwindled. She still received a small allowance each month from a trust fund setup by her grandfather and along with her pension, Madeline Dumont wanted for little. She could have dined out and dressed well but instead she led a frugal existence, preferring to use any spare money she had to buy clothes for the homeless. Her neighbours found it hilarious as they watched her set out early each morning laden down with shopping bags and her faithful old trolley as she went on her hunt for unwanted items. Maddy walked for miles each day and most of the charity shops in London knew her on first name terms and would often put aside clothes that they knew she would want. Madeline Dumont had a heart as big as the ocean and could see no wrong in people, even when she was sometimes verbally abused by the wino's who camped out around Victoria station. Maddy got immense enjoyment when she handed clothes over to the down and outs and always shopped to suit the season. When April arrived short sleeved shirts were the order of the day and as soon as the clocks went back she would try and stock pile all the warmest coats and jumpers she could get her hands on. Sometimes she would hunt through the bins to see if anyone had thrown anything away and that was how she came to be in the back alley of Kingsland road on the day that Ian Hewitt's body had been disposed of in a wheelie bin. Maddy often talked to herself, it wasn't that she was mad as people referred to her but just that she was lonely. Sometimes she would sing or ask herself what was the best piece of clothing to buy and then she would answer which gave people the notion that she was stark raving bonkers but nothing was further from the truth. Making her way along the alley, she had already checked four bins and found nothing of interest when she reached the rear of the opticians shop. There was a strange smell and wrinkling up her nose she was about to continue on her way when curiosity got the better of her. Slowly lifting the lid Maddy stood on her tip toes and peered inside. Moving the rubbish bags from side to side, her experienced hands could tell by the feel that there was nothing of interest. When she had moved the last bag, the sight that greeted her made her drop the bins lid and she had to support herself on the wall as she feared she was going to pass out. After several deep breaths she took another look just to make sure she hadn't imagined it. Again she dropped the lid only this time she made the sign of the cross and mouthed the words' heaven help the poor soul'. Walking onto the high street as quickly as her legs would carry her, she didn't have to go far before she spotted a policeman. Running over she began to rapidly talk and PC Larry Claymore had to gently touch her arm and ask her to slow down. In this area he got approached on a daily basis with stories made up by the winos and down and outs.

"I'm sorry my love but I can't understand what you're saying. Now take a deep breath, relax and start again."

"There's a body over there."

"Where?"

"In the back alley, it's been stuffed into a wheelie bin."

Larry Clayman didn't know Maddy but by the look of her dishevelled clothing she could easily have been a vagrant. That said he didn't want to appear rude, so removing his note pad and pencil he made out that he was taking notes but in reality nothing was written down.

"Have you been drinking today love?"

"I beg your pardon! How dare you speak to me like that?"

"So what time did you find this alleged body?"

Madeline Dumont was well educated and spoke the Queen's English perfectly; she also knew when she was being patronized.

"You may find this all highly amusing officer and if you choose not to investigate that's your prerogative but when that poor man is found, it will be you that is hauled over the coals for ignoring me."

"Alright alright! If it will make you feel better I'll have a quick look but if you're winding me up and wasting my time, I aint going to be happy."

Maddy made a huffing sound but didn't argue with the man. Turning, she walked back towards the alleyway and stopping beside the bin, she held out her arm and pointed. The officer made his way over and sighed heavily, he could really do without time wasters this early on in the day. As soon as PC Claymore lifted the lid to the wheelie bin he recoiled backwards. He recognised the smell of a dead body without even looking inside. Calling for backup and an ambulance he led Maddy to the opposite side of the alley. All of a sudden he was taking her seriously and it really made her angry, too many people judged others before they knew anything about them and she was fed up with being the butt of peoples jokes.

"So Miss?"

173

"Dumont, Madeline Dumont."

"So Miss Dumont do you have any idea who the person in the bin is?"

"Good God if this is the best that the Metropolitan police can offer then God help us all. Of course I don't know who it is, why should I?"

"Well what were you doing snooping about in rubbish bins in the first place. Identity theft is a criminal offence you know."

Maddy shook her head, she was fast running out of patience and this particular policeman seemed to be as thick as two short planks.

"I was not trying to commit identity theft as you so eloquently put it, for your information I wasn't snooping either. I happen to help out people that are homeless by providing them with fresh clothing. Mostly I get what I need from the charity shops but sometimes I look through bins, you would really be surprised at what others class as rubbish and throw away. Now if you don't mind I need to get on my way as I've wasted the best part of an hour already."

"I'm sorry Madam but you will need to remain here. We will need to take a statement in due course but for now could you please give me your address."

"Its flat A Elrington Road in Notting hill."

The policeman raised his eyebrows in surprise.

"Very nice area if I do say so myself."

When the ambulance and patrol car at last turned up, the area was cordoned off to the general public. The place was teeming with people and Maddy was able to sneak off without being noticed. Madeleine saw herself as a good citizen but there was nothing more she could tell the police so she headed towards the High street as quickly as she could. Ian Hewitt's body was removed from the bin and the paramedics inspected the corpse and told the police to call the undertaker. After scene of crimes officers had scoured the area and come up with nothing, a policeman checked Ian's pockets for identification but they were empty. Ian's finger prints and DNA would be taken in due course but if he'd never been in trouble with the law, then his identification for now would remain a mystery. Hopefully a family member would report him missing but it wasn't unheard of for bodies never to be claimed. Just as the ambulance was about to pull away, the blacked out undertakers van arrived to transport Ian to the local morgue. At exactly the same time a reporter turned up from the Evening Standard and began to ask questions.

"So what's going on here Officer? I heard a body had been found."

Larry Claymore hated the press as much as he hated time wasters and it didn't go unnoticed by Cynthia Fallington. Cynthia had worked at the evening standard for the last five years and she was dreaming of joining one of the big tabloids like the Mail. All she needed was that one big story that could see her career escalate.

"Look you know the score love; there won't be any

news until we know more so stop prying ok? I'm sure a statement will be issued by the press officer in due course, until then you will just have to wait."
"Come on Officer give a girl a break, I'm only trying to do my job. There's a drink in it for you."
Larry Claymore didn't like the way she was looking down her nose at him and still feeling as if he'd failed in his duty earlier, lashed out his frustration at the reporter.
"If I have to tell you again, I will arrest you for attempting to bribe an officer of the law. Now on your way and don't come back!"
"Ok ok, I'm only doing my job the same as you, so there's no need to have an attitude."
As Cynthia Fallington walked away from the scene, PC Claymore was now well and truly pissed off. The fact that he hadn't believed Madeline Dumont was playing on his mind and deep down he was worried that she might put in a formal complaint. His record was as yet untarnished and the idea that after today that could change bothered him.

CHAPTER FIFTEEN

By nine o'clock in the morning Sue Hewitt was almost frantic with worry. Ian still wasn't home and what with all the commotion outside in the early hours, her nerves were in shreds. John came into the front room with to mugs of tea and found his wife pacing up and down.

"Here drink this, you're working yourself up and getting in a right state."

Sue spun round and the words that escaped from her mouth were spoken in pure anger.

"What the fuck do you expect? My son is missing and I've lost a ticket worth millions of pounds and it could have changed our lives forever. I don't think you have grasped the fact that without it we are well and truly up the creek without a fucking paddle!"

Placing the mugs onto the new coffee table, John tried to take his wife in his arms but she roughly pushed him away.

"You always think things will just sort themselves out, well I've got news for you, they don't. I tell you John, I feel like strangling that son of ours with my bare hands. God help him when he does come home, is all I can say."

Again Sue began to pace the floor and every few seconds she would peer out onto the square from behind the net curtains. There were still a lot of people congregated down on the ground and old mother Davidson was sobbing her heart out. The woman had raised her family, albeit very badly, single handed and as old and young members of her clan surrounded her, she was inconsolable.

"Whatever happened last night must have been pretty bad John, looks like the whole of the Davidson's are outside. There were coppers and ambulances here this morning."

"Shall I go and have a nose and see what's gone on?"

"Don't you think we have enough of our own problems to worry about without anyone else's?" John picked up his tea and as he sipped the sweet liquid thought of what to say. His wife was doing his head in and he had to get out of the flat for a bit. He had a feeling that today was going to be a bad one and he needed to gather his thoughts and be alone for a while.

"Someone might have seen our Ian; I don't suppose it would hurt to ask around."

The mention of her sons name changed things and Sue stared at her husband.

"Well go on then, what are you standing about waiting for?"

John pulled on his coat and went down to the square. Mingling in with the neighbours he casually asked what had happened. Derek, the Hewitt's neighbour from the flat above moved closer to John so that he wouldn't be over heard. Speaking in an almost whisper he began to explain what had occurred last night.

"So Big Boy is dead and DD is in hospital minus his right hand. Apparently they tried to sew it back on but it was too badly damaged. I tell you John, I really don't know what this world is coming to. When me and my Mrs first came here many moons ago, it was a really nice place to live. Everyone took pride in their gaffs and if your front step wasn't polished to within an inch of your life you would be the gossip of all the women in the block. Now look at things, people killing each other and over what? If I could get out of here I would, a nice little bungalow on Canvey Island would do me and the Mrs just fine."

John Hewitt shook his head and after saying his goodbyes made his way back up to the flat. His wife stood nervously looking out of the window and her face was pleading as he entered the front room.

"So?"

"Well there wasn't really anyone that I could ask regarding our Ian but old Derek from upstairs reckons there's been a murder at the Davidson's and that young Douglas has had his arm chopped off. Now have I got that wrong, did Derek say his hand, either way he won't be using it again. I'm glad Ian wasn't involved in any of it, I really wasn't happy when he started hanging around with that DD and maybe after all this he won't. I think we should perhaps go to that Den place and ask a few questions, don't you?"

Sue smiled, she knew she had a short fuse sometimes when it came to her husband but deep down he was a decent man and Sue knew she could have done a lot worse than marry someone like John Hewitt.

"Let me have a quick wash and then we'll get going. I don't fancy meeting that Tommy bloke but then we aint got much choice I suppose."

"I think we should give him a chance and not judge him, I mean our Ian thinks very highly of him and he seems to treat him alright."

Sue smiled; maybe she had listened to too many rumours regarding Tommy Mortimer and his club. Tommy had showered and changed and been back at the club within an hour of disposing of Ian's body. He now didn't know why he'd even bothered to come back and when he'd heard all the commotion in the rear alley, he wished he hadn't. Walking outside he was shocked to see the amount of police. He hadn't expected the body to be found for a few days and had hoped that it wouldn't be here but at the rubbish tip. PC Claymore made his way over and informed Tommy that the area would be cordoned off to the general public for the next couple of hours at least.

"What's occurred officer?"

After his lack of a response earlier regarding Madeline Dumont and then the hassle with the reporter, Larry Claymore didn't want any more trouble laid at his feet so his reply was friendly and informative.

"Sadly Sir a body was found this morning and we are in the process of an investigation."

Tommy shook his head and looked as shocked as he could.

"Any idea who it is?"

"Not at the moment Sir but we're working on it. I think it's best if you go back inside, we'll inform you as soon as we've finished."

"I don't know, whatever is the world coming to Officer?"

PC Claymore wearily nodded his head and then walked back over to the taped off area. Back inside Tommy could feel the rise of vomit in the back of his throat again and panted hard in the hope of halting its reappearance. This was all getting out of hand thanks to Taffy and he could sense a whole shit load of trouble landing on his doorstep pretty soon.

It had taken Sue just a short while to change and fifteen minutes later, the couple left their flat and set out for Kingsland road. Knocking hard on the front door, they waited for what seemed like ages until they finally heard huffing and puffing coming from behind the door. A few second later Joyce Lambert's head appeared through a small gap.

."What do you want?"

Sue pushed her husband forward and as she did so the stale smell of the club began to filter through the gap in the door and out onto the street.

"Hi. I'm Ian's dad, I wondered if you'd seen him today only the little bleeder didn't come home last night."

Joyce shook her head.

"Aint seen him since yesterday love. Why don't you come on in, the Guv'nor's upstairs and he might know more."

Sue and John stepped inside and Joyce Lambert slammed the door shut making Sue jump. The foyer lights were dim and it took a few seconds for the Hewitt's to focus their eyes properly.

"Follow me and mind your step, this bleeding carpet is as dodgy as fuck. I keep telling him upstairs but he don't do nothing about it. He'll soon shift his arse when someone falls down and breaks something you mark my words."

As they followed the old woman up the stairs John and Sue looked at each other but didn't speak. Like all members of staff had been instructed over the years, Joyce tapped on the door and waited to be told to enter.

When he heard the knock, Tommy silently mouthed the words 'fuck me, now what'.

"Come in!"

"I'm sorry to trouble you Tommy but Ian's parents are here and they're a bit concerned about him. I told them to come and have a word with you."

Tommy Mortimer could physically feel the colour drain from his face but it went unnoticed by Sue and John. Standing up he walked around the desk

182

and holding out his hand gave the best smile he could muster. John Hewitt shook the hand of his son's boss but Sue just stared at the man. On her way over here she had decided to give him the benefit of the doubt regarding all the stories she'd heard but one look into his face had told her all that she needed to know.

"So you're Ian's Mum and Dad? Well I'm pleased to meet you and that boy is a credit to you both, lovely lad is Ian."

John didn't know how much to tell Tommy so he kept to the bare minimum.

"He didn't come home last night and we've been out of our minds with worry. It's just not like him, not without letting us know. What time did he leave here last night?"

"He didn't? Ian came in for his morning shift and said he was leaving as he didn't think he was nightclub material. Reluctantly we parted ways but it's a shame really as I thought he had a bright future here at the Den. He left on friendly terms and I haven't heard from him since but then there aint no reason why I should have. He's young and I'm sure he'll come home with his tail between his legs. You know what it's like, they meet a girl, think only with their cock's and all sense goes out of the bleeding window."

Sue narrowed her eyes, she could tell the man was lying but she didn't know why. They were fretting so much about Ian that neither of them noticed the lottery ticket that had been sitting on the desk since yesterday and was underneath the very object that had caused Ian's demise. Turning to her husband she spoke in a confident tone.

"Come on John we're not getting anywhere standing here, I think we need to go and see the Old Bill."

Terror filled Tommy and his voice had a slight quiver as he spoke.

"I really don't think there's any need for that Mrs Hewitt. Don't you think it would be best to just wait, I mean it's only been a few hours."

"Look! I aint seen my son since yesterday morning now that might not mean much to you but it does to me."

"Well that aint exactly true love, we know he came home yesterday at some point and...."

The look Sue gave her husband instantly stopped him going any further and she could see that Tommy Mortimer was about to ask what he meant but she didn't give him the chance and turning around she walked out of the office door. Tommy rubbed his mouth with the palm of his hand and he could feel the sweat under his armpits again. He didn't know whether to contact Taffy, sit it out and wait or just make a run for it. Deciding to wait he closed the office door but this time he locked it. The one thing he was grateful for was the fact that the Hewitt's were not aware of what was going on in the back alley. Once they were back on the street, Sue began to march off and John had to grab her

184

arm to stop her.

"Now where are you going?"

"The police station but we'll have to go over to Stoke Newington, I read in the paper that the station in Hackney don't deal in anything serious anymore."

"Serious? Don't you think you're going a bit over the top?"

Sue quickly turned around and the look on her face made him wish he hadn't said anything.

Swallowing hard he tried to appease her.

"Shall we get a cab?"

"Get a fucking cab! It's only a couple of miles away and if we don't find that son of ours and get my ticket back then we're going to need every bleeding penny we can lay our hands on, so no John, we will not be getting a fucking cab!"

"What about the tube then?"

"No! Besides by the time we've waited around on the underground, we can walk there quicker."

When they reached their destination John Hewitt was totally knackered but he didn't dare complain to his wife. Sue had been like a woman on a mission and had almost frogmarched her husband along the road. Now standing outside the imposing building she suddenly stopped.

"What's the matter?"

"I'm scared John, scared of what we're going to find out."

John Hewitt climbed the front steps and gave his wife a look of disbelief as he did so.

"For fucks sake whatever's got into you. Ian didn't come home last night that's all, now I wish you'd get a bleeding grip and stop being so sodding melodramatic."

Entering Stoke Newington police station they came to a small area with a counter that was screened off by a reinforced glass panel. Bob Franks the desk sergeant was about to go off duty but his replacement was yet to arrive. Eager to get home as his wife Rose was cooking his favourite steak for lunch, he huffed out loud as the couple walked in. Sue approached the desk and leaning forward spoke into the microphone.

"I'd like to report a missing person please."

Bob was less than happy as there were three forms to fill in and he knew he was now going to be late clocking off. Trying to get out of it he asked how long it had been since the person had last been seen.

"Twenty four hours."

Sue prayed that John wouldn't pipe up that Ian had been home in that time and luckily he didn't. Bob Franks huffed again and picking up his pen began to fill in the forms. After giving Ian's name, address and medical history, Sue was asked for a photograph of her son which luckily she always carried around in her handbag. Slowly she handed it over; it was one of her favourites and had been taken the previous Christmas. Ian looked so happy and the memory made her momentarily smile. Bob then asked about any distinguishing marks, where

186

Ian worked and his known associates.

"Until last night he worked at the Den on Kingsland road. He's got a small birthmark on his right shoulder in the shape of a shamrock; well that's what I always thought it looked like anyway. My boy doesn't really have any friends but just recently he's been hanging around with DD, I mean Douglas Davidson who lives on the same square as us."

When Bob Franks had finished his report he informed Sue Hewitt that they would circulate a description and as soon as they had any news they would contact her. In all honesty Bob wasn't going to process the form until the morning, only then would it be passed onto the missing persons department. Sue and John set off for home and although she was still worried sick about Ian, she felt a little better that at least the police would now be looking for him. As they approached St Thomas's square John placed his arm around his wife and pulled her close.

"Come on darling let's get you inside and I'll put the kettle on."

There were still plenty of people milling around in the square, all gossiping about the earlier events. It was an everyday occurrence for someone in the flats to be kicking off about something but what had happened at the Davidson's flat was not the norm and people would feast on it for weeks to come. Jay Jay Bevan hadn't said a word to anyone and he wasn't about to as for all his bravado, the man with the golden teeth had really frightened him. His mother was turning a trick inside the flat and he had been told to wait outside. Peering over the balcony wall he watched Sue and John as they climbed the steps to their own block. Jay Jay didn't really know them but he wondered why they didn't join all the other residents who now seemed to be having a bit of a party. Someone had bought a case of larger and fat Jilly from the ground floor was in the middle of rigging up her boom box. Within minutes Bob Marley's 'No woman no cry' began to blare out and a few of the women started to dance. Jay Jay turned around when the door to his flat opened. The punter Carmen Bevan had been servicing emerged and was zipping up his trousers as he exited the flat. To Jay Jay he looked old but in reality he was only in his early forties, to the boy that was ancient. Carmen wasn't particular and some of the men looked disgusting to her son, at least this one was clean. He didn't make any eye contact with Jay Jay and the boy was just thankful that the bloke hadn't taken too long as he was hungry and his television programme was about to start. Opening the door he went inside and didn't give the Hewitt's another thought. In her own flat Sue was pacing the floor and no matter what her husband said to her she just couldn't relax. John made them both tea and then sat down on the new sofa beside his wife.

"Darling you really need to calm yourself. It aint

going to do you any good pacing up and down and biting your nails to the quick. You're really starting to worry me and there aint no point fretting until we know something, now is there?"

Sue turned to face him but instead of the mouthful of abuse that he was expecting, he was shocked to see her eyes were full of tears.

"John he's my baby, he might be eighteen but he's still my baby and he always will be. Call it a mother's intuition but I just know that something really bad has happened."

John Hewitt didn't know what to say, Sue was always the strong one and seeing her like this, well it scared him and he was beginning to think that she might be right after all. He couldn't and didn't want to imagine how she would be if things turned out badly. He had always known that she loved him but there was a bond between mother and son that had always been strong since the day that Ian had been born. John Hewitt wasn't jealous; in fact he was proud that his wife loved their only child as much as she did. There were plenty of kids out there who led terrible lives and some of them lived right here on St Thomas's square.

"I aint saying you're wrong but if you carry on like this you're going to make yourself ill. Hopefully the police will have some news soon enough and then we will deal with things as and when we know. Ok?"

Sue sipped at her tea but she didn't reply, inside her

stomach was churning and she felt as though her heart was breaking but she didn't really know why.

CHAPTER SIXTEEN

Chief Detective Sonny Warren wearily entered his office. The previous night he'd had a heavy session of drinking with friends and was now suffering the ill effects of overindulging. To make matters worse Sonny had been put in charge of the Hackney murder inquiries of Big Boy Davidson and the unknown body of a young boy and in a short while he was due to address his team in the incident room. Pouring a glass of water he removed two pain killers from his drawer and taking a seat hoped they would kick in before it was time to make an appearance. Scanning his desk Sonny noticed a file that hadn't been there yesterday and opening it up he began to read the missing person report. Normally he wouldn't deal with this sort of inquiry but as there were no new leads regarding the victim's identity, he had asked that any reports such as this be handed to his team. Sonny studied the details and something struck a chord, the age of the missing person, was in his estimation, similar to that of the body and the fact that he'd worked at the Den and the body was found close to that building aroused suspicion. The desk sergeant had mislaid the photograph Sue Hewitt had given him, so until the autopsy report came through there wasn't much else to go on. Hopefully the pathologist would have carried out his tests last night and the report should be with the team in the next few hours. Making his way to the incident room, Sonny rubbed the back of his neck, the headache was getting worse and if it hadn't have been for this case he would definitely have called in sick. Pushing open the swing doors he was momentarily stopped by a WPC who handed him the autopsy report. Entering the incident room he sighed heavily at the level of noise, his headache was getting worse and all he really wanted to do was go home and crawl into bed.

"Quieten down you lot, now the autopsy report has just this second come in. Take a ten minute break while I go through it and Chilvers don't pull the piss; I said ten minutes and not half an hour like you usually take."

The rest of the team all sniggered and detective Chilvers had a face the colour of beetroot, though he didn't answer his superior back. In the quiet of his office Sonny began to read the report that had just been handed to him. Death was due to blood loss, a fractured skull caused by a blunt force trauma to the side of the head and there were also signs of severe brain damage. When he reached the photographs something suddenly made him sit up and take notice. A small birthmark on the victim's right shoulder had alarm bells ringing and picking up the missing persons report Sonny compared the two. Quickly returning back to the incident room he made his way to the front where two wipe boards had been set up. The team were back from their break and already seated as he turned to face them. "Right there's been a breakthrough regarding the unknown victim. It looks like we may now have an identification."

Running through both reports he began to make notes on the boards and the room was silent as the team watched and waited to see what emerged.

"I think this case may turn out to be far more involved than we first thought. I have a gut instinct that this one is not gang related but linked to the crime underworld."

Nicky Chilvers held up his hand to ask a question and Sonny nodded for him to go ahead.

"What makes you think that Boss?"

"The club that backs onto the alleyway is run by one Tommy Mortimer. We've been after Mortimer for a long time now, too long if you ask me. There's been someone reported missing who coincidently worked at the club, a young lad by the name of Ian Hewitt. The ages match and there's also an identical birthmark on the victims right shoulder."

Again Nicky Chilvers held up his hand and the rest of the team began to grumble and moan. Sonny wished that the man would work as hard on his cases as he did in the incident room. Chilvers liked the theory work but when it came down to the practical and having to walk the streets, the man was about as lazy as they came.

"I still don't see the link."

"No you wouldn't Chilvers. It's too much of a coincidence and I've come to learn over the years that coincidences rarely happen, beside the poor bastard didn't crawl into the bin by himself now did he?"

Again the team laughed out loud and again Nicky Chilvers faced turned scarlet.

"Mason, Brewer, I want you to visit the parents of the missing boy. Tell them the bare minimum and ask them to identify the body. If it's a match then at least we have something to go on. Delve into his associates and find out who he mixed with but handle it with kid gloves and you'd better take a W.P.C along as well. Well what are you waiting for? Jump to it. Chilvers you'll come with me, I think it's time to pay a visit to the Den to see Mr Mortimer. The rest of you pair up into your usual teams and hit the nearby streets. I want every door knocked on and every business visited. Don't stop digging and make sure you keep in regular contact, any details no matter how small, get straight back to me. Remember the early stages of a murder inquiry are the most vital while anyone connected is still vulnerable and nervous. Let's make sure this trail doesn't go cold, now on your way and good luck."

"Sir?"

"Yes Chilvers!"

"So what about the murder at the flats, is that getting put onto the back burner?"

"No Chilvers it is not. I have plods doing door to door as we speak but so far no one saw or heard anything. We still need to show willing and after I've been to see this Mortimer character, I'm going over to the flats and then onto the hospital to see the surviving Davidson boy. We still have the DNA reports to come in and hopefully they will show something but it's going to be a few days before they we get them. Now is there anything else?" Nicky Chilvers was now slightly embarrassed and shook his head. Graham Mason and Charlie Brewer had been detectives for over five years and part of the murder squad for the last four. They both loved their jobs and had excelled within the department, what they didn't like was informing relatives of someone's demise. Standing up they made their way down the stairs into the reception area where W.P.C Karen Hall had just exited the canteen.

"Hall, tell your sergeant that you are needed to attend a home visit and then meet us out in the car park."

Karen only nodded her head and moments later she joined Graham and Charlie out in the yard. The unmarked Astra was parked in the corner and Graham Mason slowly shook his head as he threw the keys to his partner.

"I aint looking forward to this one little bit!"

"Well none of us like giving bad news Graham but it goes with the territory."

"I aint on about that you soppy twat, I mean going

to St Thomas's square. It's where those Davidson boys got set on and I've heard that their family are baying for blood. With a bit of luck we can be in and out pretty sharpish without being seen. I'm just glad that it's the Chief going to see the Davidson family and not us."

Charlie Brewer didn't reply but he did think about what his partner had said. Just lately it felt as if the police were losing control and the gangs were one step higher up the ladder. A lot of the time Hackney could be a good place to work but it could also be one of the meanest and most dangerous.

Changing his plan, Sonny Warren decided to call at the Davidson's before he went to see Tommy Mortimer and as his car, along with a squad car pulled into the square, Bobbies could be seen on every landing going from door to door. Sonny and Chilvers, accompanied by two uniformed police officers, climbed the steps to the flat that was situated five doors before DD's. The front door was open and gospel music could be heard playing inside. Several relatives were milling about and as Sonny entered the front room he was greeted by sneers and abuse from some of the younger family members. Ignoring them he walked over to Maisie Davidson and offered his condolences. Maisie had travelled over from Trinidad with her family when she was three years old and had lived in the same flat ever since that day. Raised in Hackney, she had suddenly developed a West Indian accent at the age of fifteen. A deeply religious woman, at least when it suited her, Maisie stayed true to her roots in every aspect of her life. Big Boy had been her youngest child and she could never see any wrong in him, as far as she was concerned the police continuously harassed her boy because of the colour of his skin.

"Ya found the murdering bastard that killed me bwoy?"

"No Mrs Davidson but we are working on it, Samuel mixed with some very unsavoury characters and..."

Maisie wore a look of defiance as she raised her hand.

"My son was called Big Bwoy so don't be using his god given name and as for ya working on it, don't make me laugh. It gonna take years and all because our skin aint white."

"I can assure you that isn't the case Mrs Davidson."

"I want ya outta me house and don't bodder me agin unless ya have some news."

Sonny Warren knew there was no point in continuing to reassure the woman and walking from the flat was about to descend the stairs when he noticed Jay Jay Bevan watching all that was going on from the open doorway of his own flat. Walking over Sonny put on his warmest smile and was about to ask the boy some questions when the door slammed shut in his face.

"Fuck off copper; I don't speak to no pigs!"

Sonny grinned and shook his head; there was little

he could do if no one would speak to him. It was always the same and yet they were quick to use the racial card and shout to all that would listen that they were treated as second class citizens. Back in the car, he started the engine and then headed in the direction of Homerton hospital. DD had received emergency surgery and luckily his leg was saved, the same couldn't be said for the reattachment of his right hand. Knowing he'd be disabled for the rest of his life and that his cousin was dead, he felt nothing but anger and had sworn on Big Boys life that somehow he would get revenge. When he saw Sony Warren and Nicky Chilvers, his eyes narrowed and he started to curse.

"Fuck off pigs, I aint got nothing to fucking say to you!"

"Well I've got a few things to say to you Douglas. My word that looks nasty, I bet it hurts don't it?"

"Fuck you copper!"

Sonny grinned when he realised he had really riled the young man.

"Now I know you've all closed ranks and no one will spill their guts but without some help it's unlikely that Big Boys killer will ever be caught."

"Oh he'll be caught alright copper, don't you fucking worry about that."

"I must warn you DD, that if you or any member of your family, try to seek justice for yourselves, I will have your black arses banged up in nick before you can say Bob Marley."

If he'd been able, DD would have left his bed and grabbed this copper by the throat but he wasn't and Sonny had made sure that no one else had heard the remark. Chilvers was staring out of the window and Sonny knew that even if he' heard, he wasn't about to protest. Chief warren was also aware that he was wasting valuable time here and as he left he had one last thing to say.

"If I find out you had anything to do with the murder of Ian Hewitt, well let's just say I will make it a priority to see that you never set foot outside of a prison for the rest of your natural."

With that Sonny walked out of the ward leaving DD staring wide eyed. He had no idea that Ian had been killed but even though the revelation had shocked him, he just shrugged his shoulders and putting in his earphones, switched on his iPod and winced in pain.

It had now been three days since Joey Chambers had paid Tommy Mortimer a visit. Every day Lizzie had asked her brother if there was any news and every day he had shaken his head. It broke his heart to see her so distressed, not to mention the state that his father was in. Mike Chambers idolised his grandson and had now accepted that it was a real possibility that he was going to die. After the falling out with his wife, Joey had eventually returned home but still called in to check on his family every day. Sharon seemed to have turned

over a new leaf and as yet hadn't asked for any
money but Joey knew deep down that it probably
wouldn't last. The kitchen worktop already
contained several magazines on pedigree dogs and
accessories. He wished he hadn't mentioned getting
a dog as his wife was now looking at all the
designer ones that cost a fortune. The previous
night a few cross words had passed between the
couple when Joey had innocently suggested going
down to Battersea and having a look into the
possibility of re-homing some poor neglected
animal. Sharon had told him in no uncertain terms
that she wasn't having some mongrel in her home.
Joey didn't continue to argue with her and had
instead gone to bed early leaving his wife
downstairs. Alone in the front room she could stew
in her own anger for as long as she liked for all he
cared. Within a half hour Sharon Chambers had
calmed down and was now realising that she may
have pushed him too far. Deciding that in the
morning she would be as nice as pie and tell Joey
that she would go to Battersea and have a look, she
then turned in herself. Joey was snoring when she
climbed into bed so sex was out of the question and
Sharon just hoped that her change of heart would be
enough to put him in a good mood the next day.
The following morning Joey was up with the larks
and was surprised to see his wife in the kitchen as
he entered. The smell of bacon and fresh coffee was
mouth watering and he smiled to himself as he

thought that maybe getting into the odd strop with her wouldn't be a bad thing, not if he got a cooked breakfast for his efforts.

"Morning babe, nice bit of bacon do you alright?" Joey nodded as he poured himself a coffee but he didn't speak.

"I was thinking that today me and you could drive over to Battersea dogs home and have a look. You never know they might even have the make of dog I'm looking for."

Joey couldn't stop laughing and Sharon wore a quizzical look on her face.

"What?"

"It aint a fucking handbag Sharon it's a dog and for starters they don't make them they breed them." She was embarrassed now and her face showed it which made Joey instantly feel guilty.

"Anyway I can't first thing as I have to be over at my dad's this morning, so maybe later hey?" Instead of moaning which was what he expected to hear, Joey was taken aback by his wife's next sentence.

"Of course you do I wasn't thinking and anyway there's nothing stopping me going on my own. I'm sure if I see one I like, they will hold it for me and we can go back together later."

Joey grabbed a bacon sandwich from the plate.

"Sweetheart if you see one you like the look of then get it. Now I really need to get off, our Lizzie was expecting me ten minutes ago."

When Joey went up to get dressed, Sharon took a seat and tried to think of a way she could get her hands on a pedigree pooch without her husband knowing. She could sell a few things as he never noticed what was new and what wasn't or she could ask her dad. It had been ages since she'd tapped her parents up and she was sure they'd go for it, with any luck they might even buy her a dog as a present. When Joey entered the kitchen again and took a swig of his coffee Sharon was all smiles and as he kissed her on the lips she willingly kissed him back.

"I'll see you later babe and good dog hunting."

"Give my love to Lizzie and the others."

"I will."

As the front door slammed Sharon Chambers curled back her lip in distaste. She hated his family and it made her sick that she had to be so nice to them. With any luck they would all get struck down with kidney failure and then she could have her Joey all to herself, for a moment the thought made her smile.

As usual the front door to his family home was unlocked and Joey called out as he walked inside.

"Only me, anyone about?"

There was no answer and he thought it was strange as his sister usually replied with 'tradesman's entrance round the back if you don't mind'.

Opening the kitchen door he was surprised to see his father sitting alone at the table.

"Everything alright Dad?"

Mike Chambers looked up into his sons face and his eyes were sad. Instantly Joey knew that something was wrong.

"What is it? What's wrong and where's our Lizzie?"

"Michael took a turn for the worse this morning and Lizzie's just gone off in a mini cab to the hospital. I suppose I should have gone with her but I just couldn't face it son."

Mike began to cry and walking over Joey knelt down and took his father in his arms. It felt so wrong but at the same time so right, Mike's age was really starting to show and it was an added worry to his family. Instead of the tall upright man that they all knew and loved, he had in the last couple of weeks, aged beyond belief and Joey didn't know how much more the old man could take. When he felt that his father's tears had subsided Joey stood up.

"I don't suppose there's any news on our Steve is there?"

"Nothing! Lizzie spent most of yesterday on the blower to the British Embassy."

"No joy then?"

"Nah, they said without Steve's location there was little they could do. Said it'd be like looking for a bleeding needle in a hay stack and as much as it guts me, I know they're right."

Joey took a seat at the table and as he held his head in his hands his father tenderly touched his arm.

"Everyone's doing all they can Son."

"I aint, I feel fucking useless Dad but I don't know what else to do."

"There aint nothing you can do."

Joey looked up and into his father's eyes. He didn't know if he should share his thoughts and even if he did, the chance of his father agreeing to such a mad idea was slim. As ideas went it was so far off the chart that most wouldn't even have given it a second thought but Joey was so desperate that he would try anything.

"There is but it aint right but then nothings right or fair in this world is it Dad? It aint fair what Michaels going through and it aint fair that my baby sister has to sit and watch her only child die."

In frustration Joey slammed his fist onto the kitchen table but his father didn't even flinch.

"So what can you do? What idea have you come up with?"

"It's insane Dad and I'd rather you weren't party to it, besides I need to run it past Lizzie first. I've been to see Michaels father and asked him to be a donor but he didn't want to know."

"You're joking! Why the fucking gutless cunt!"

"Tell me about it. Anyway I think I might pay him another visit and try and appeal to his better nature, fuck me I'll beg if I have to, anything to save that kid bless his little heart."

Mike Chambers leant over and patted his son on the shoulder. He had always been proud of his family

204

but never more so than now. His only girl had always been strong and what she'd been through these last few weeks would test a saint but somehow she had dealt with it. Now his oldest was trying anything he could to save his nephew and the thought had Mike once more in tears.

"I think that's a good idea and whatever the outcome you need to go see Lizzie. Out of all of us you can support her the best Joey, she don't need a blubbering old fool like me hanging around the hospital and making things worse."

Joey Chamber left his father sitting at the table but he didn't drive off straight away, instead he sat in his car and thought long and hard about what he knew he was going to have to do. Like he told his dad, he would give Tommy Mortimer another chance but deep down Joey already knew what the answer would be.

CHAPTER SEVENTEEN

At the same time as Chief Sonny Warren was visiting the Davidson's, Detectives Charlie Brewer and Graham Mason along with W.P.C Hill drove towards the address in Hackney but stopped a short distance away and parked in Lyme Grove. The Chief would not be pleased if they arrived back at the station with a trashed car. Tempers were running high in the area and if they left the car on the square it was a distinct possibility that it would be ablaze by the time they returned. Entering the square they felt as though all eyes were upon them but in reality they had yet to be spotted. People were milling about drinking, music was still playing and now an old oil drum had been dragged into the centre of the square so that a fire could be lit. Charlie didn't like the look of things and could remember back to the troubles of two thousand and eleven. He'd been off duty when the rioting had reached Hackney and the sheer violence and anger had shocked him to the core. Taking refuge in Maddigan's pub on Mare Street the mob had swiftly passed by but not before putting in one of the front windows. The result was Charlie Brewer receiving a cut on his cheek due to flying glass. Even now when he looked in the mirror and saw the scar it brought back terrible memories of that night. Back then it had only taken a day or two for things to escalate to such a degree that the whole country had watched with baited breath and right at this moment the tension was once more electric. Charlie decided that after they had visited the address and gone back to the station, he would pull the chief to one side and let him know exactly how things were. If Sonny chose to do nothing then that was up to him but Charlie wasn't about to sit back and let events take place without at least telling someone. Bobby's on the beat were thin on the ground in this neck of the woods so it was unlikely that the Met knew what was really going on. The two detectives and Karen crossed the square and began to climb the stairs of Pitcairn house. Believing they had entered without being noticed, they were shocked as they walked along the open air landing, to hear someone shout out from below 'fucking filth are here again'. Graham was aware of his partner's fears and when they reached the Hewitt's flat he rapped hard on the door. John opened up almost immediately, it had been a long sleepless night and Sue had only just nodded off on the sofa. Desperate for her not to be woken he was about to give abuse to the caller but as he opened up, instantly recognised the Old Bill.

"Mr Hewitt?"

"That's me."

"I'm Detective Mason and this is Detective Brewer we're from the station at Stoke Newington. Could we come inside Sir and have a word?"

"Sure but try and keep it down only the wife has

just fallen asleep. We had a bad night and since our Ian went missing her nerves are in tatters."

Graham gave Charlie a sideways glance but luckily John didn't see it as he had already turned and walked into the hall. Leading all three officers through to the kitchen he quietly closed the door.

"Do you have any news about our Ian?"

Charlie Brewer, now over his earlier onset of anxiety, took the lead and gently taking hold of Johns arm he steered him towards the table. John already knew what they were about to say, he'd known the minute he'd opened the front door. You didn't get two plain clothes coppers come knocking at your door for anything trivial, especially in this neck of the woods and when the obligatory woman copper accompanied them, it was bound to be bad news. Maybe he had wanted to deny it and that's why he was acting so cheery. If he denied it to himself and the coppers didn't speak then he wouldn't have to accept that it was really happening. Standing up he looked Charlie Brewer directly in the eyes.

"I don't think I want to hear this do I?"

Graham Mason stepped forward. Two years earlier he had completed a bereavement course and instantly knew that the man was going into melt down. Taking a seat at the table he asked John Hewitt to join him.

"Sir I think you know why we are here. The body of a young man matching the description of your son has been found in the vicinity."

John's own upset was absent from his mind as all thoughts were instantly for his wife.

"Oh my god! She'll do her nut!"

We cannot rule out that its Ian, therefore we need you or your wife to accompany us to the hospital to identify the body."

"You mean the morgue don't you?"

"Well yes Sir, now are either of you able to come with us?"

John started to rub his hands through his hair as he thought of Sue and how she would be when he told her.

"I need to go and speak to my wife, fuck me this is going to kill her."

"Take your time Mr Hewitt, we'll wait here."

As John walked towards the door Graham Mason motioned with his eyes for Karen Hill to follow the man. Their home was small but it still didn't stop John from making the walk last as long as he could, anything rather than face his wife and tell her it was a distinct possibility that their son was dead. As quietly as he could he turned the handle to the front room door and walked inside. The noise still woke Sue Hewitt and stretching out her arms she yawned. John was a good man and she'd been so ratty and angry with him and he didn't deserve it. Seeing the ashen look on his face Sue sat bolt upright but when she saw Karen Hill in her uniform, she went straight into panic mode.

"What is it? What's wrong John?"

John began to cry and she was instantly on her feet and wrapping her arms around him.

"Come on sweetheart, tell me what's happened."

John sniffed loudly and wiped his eyes with the cuff of his jumper.

"Oh Sue, the police are here and a body's been found and."

"So? It doesn't mean that it's our Ian. After all that aggro downstairs last night it could be anyone."

"Darling they want us to go and identify the body."

Sue pulled away and walked over to the window with a look on her face that was filled with confusion. Her brain had gone into self preservation mode and she was now in complete denial.

"Why, why would you say that? Honestly John, sometimes you talk a load of shit!"

Taking her hand he led her back over to the settee and guided her down until they were both seated.

"I aint going to tell you to keep calm because I know there's no way you will be able to but you have to get a grip love, you have to face up to reality."

"The two detectives in the kitchen say the body......"

John didn't get to finish his sentence before Sue began to scream and wail. Graham Mason and Charlie Brewer both looked at each other and even after all they had been witness to in their time on the force, nothing could stop them feeling the raw emotion of a mother's heartbreak. Anything John

210

said didn't seem to help and his wife was nothing short of hysterical. Her cries could be heard below in the square and for a few seconds people stopped what they were doing and looked up. It wasn't their pain and like most human beings they quickly lost interest and went back to the dancing and drinking. Karen Hill walker over and gently smiling at John Hewitt, sat down on the other side of the sofa. Sometimes a woman needs to feel the arms of another woman around her, needs to know that someone else might just have an inkling of what they are feeling. Karen offered soothing words to Sue and slowly the tears began to subside, at least for a while. When the crying stopped Charlie Brewer turned to face his partner.

"Sometimes I fucking hate this job."

"You aint alone there my friend. Give them a few minutes more alone and then we'll go in."

John was at a loss but suddenly an inner strength seemed to fill him and taking his wife's hand he spoke gently but firmly.

"Sue you have to stop this. Like you said, we don't even know if it is our Ian but if it is then we will deal with it just like we always do, together!"

His words seemed to register and she flung her arms around her husband's neck. Nestled into his chest she began to cry again but this time they were gentle tears.

"I can't go, you'll have to."

Again John took control and his words momentarily

shocked his wife.

"We will both go! It's nothing to do with me being scared or anything, although in all honesty I'm shitting it."

"So then why do I need to go?"

"Darling if it is him and you don't see him then in your heart you will never accept it. This is going to be the hardest thing we will ever have to do but we will do it and together."

The sobbing began again but this time it was controlled, almost as if she had to do it, had to release the terrible pain that was building up inside her. A few seconds later and the door to the front room opened. Detectives Brewer and Mason walked in but they didn't speak and only nodded solemnly to the couple. Sue gave a weak smile and then surprised them all when she spoke.

"I need to get washed and dressed and then we can get off, the sooner we do this the sooner we will know and it will be over."

John followed his wife through to the bedroom and when the door was closed Graham Mason turned to W.P.C Hill.

"How do you think she took it?"

For a moment Karen couldn't believe the question she'd just been asked and wanted to give a sarcastic reply. The man was either heartless or emotionally dead to even ask such a thing but knowing that a report would be put forward regarding her performance today, she held her tongue and

212

informed detective Mason that it had gone as well as could be expected. In less than five minutes John and Sue were changed and had now rejoined the officers. Exiting the stairwell all eyes were upon them but this time nothing was shouted out. Everyone had heard Sue Hewitt's screams and although they didn't know what had occurred, knew it must have been something bad. Charlie Brewer led the couple to Lyme Grove and when they were all seated in the car, he sped off in the direction of Whitechapel. The traffic was heavy due to the time of day so it took twenty minutes before the car pulled up at the rear entrance to the Royal London Hospital. After walking along a short corridor, Sue Hewitt looked up and saw the words 'Mortuary'. She stopped dead in her tracks as her whole body began to sake uncontrollably. Doubling over she retched once and the cup of tea from earlier splashed from her mouth and onto the linoleum floor. Filled with embarrassment she rummaged in her handbag for a tissue to try and clean it up. Charlie and Karen Hill both took hold of Sue's arms but it was Karen who spoke
"Come on Mrs Hewitt, don't be worrying about that. Someone will be here in a minute to clean it up."
Sue began to cry and as they gently led her away she kept looking back over her shoulder at the mess on the floor. John Hewitt walked slowly behind with Detective Mason but he hadn't said a word for

ages. It cut him to the core to see his wife like this
and he was well aware that there was worse still to
come. As they walked along Karen held onto Sue
with one arm and with the other, gently rubbed
Sues back in a comforting way.

"I'm so sorry Officer; I don't know what came over
me."

"Honestly don't worry about it; it's just the shock
coming out. We'll take a seat over there and the
Detectives will go and see if they're ready for us.
Meekly Sue did as she'd been asked and after John
sat beside her he placed an arm tenderly around her
shoulder. It only took a couple of minutes before
the door opened and Charlie Brewer appeared.

"If you'd both like to come this way."

As Sue stood up her knees buckled but John and
Karen Hill were ready for it and grabbing her with
both arms, sat her back down on the chair.

"Maybe this wasn't the best idea after all. Why
don't you wait here while I go and do it?"

Sue would have given anything to have been able to
agree with him but she knew deep down that if she
didn't look, didn't satisfy herself that her boy was
gone then she wouldn't ever have a day's rest.

"Thanks darling I really appreciate it but we both
know that I have to do this."

Standing up again she took hold of her husband's
arm and together they walked through the swing
doors into the mortuary. The viewing room was
small and on one wall hung a pair of purple velvet

214

curtains that were drawn shut. The detectives waited until the door was closed and then turned to the Hewitt's. Graham was the one to ask the question and the words seemed to get stuck in his throat.

"Are you ready?"

When Sue nodded her head Graham Mason pressed a small switch on the wall and the curtains began to open. Sue Hewitt stared ahead wide eyed and then suddenly began to howl just as she'd done back at the flat. Banging her fists on the glass she screamed out like a wounded animal and when there were no more screams left, her palms opened onto the glass and she slid down the wall in a crumpled heap.

John Hewitt stood sobbing and when he glanced at Charlie Brewer, he looked like a broken man. Johns voice was almost begging as, he asked if they could touch their son and the Detective felt as if his own heart would break.

"Give me a minute and I'll see what I can do."

Charlie didn't know what state Ian's body would be in and he wanted to see for himself before allowing the couple inside. It was one thing to view someone through a glass panel but another when you were within touching distance and the wounds were horrific. Luckily the pathologist had temporarily reconstructed Ian's skull and after heavy bandages were applied, Ian Hewitt apart from a lot of bruising, looked as if he was sleeping.

John and W.P.C Hills gently lifted Sue from the

215

floor and John then embraced her tightly. He didn't speak as there were no words of comfort he could offer; instead they just stood holding each other crying. A few moments later and the detective reappeared.

"If you'd like to follow me Mr and Mrs Hewitt?" The man's words hit John full on and he thought to himself how strange they sounded 'if you'd like to', there was nothing in this whole world he'd like to do less than go and touch his dead son. Following behind the Detective, the couple were led through a side door and into a small room that contained Ian's body. Sue ran over and draping herself over her lifeless son, the sobbing began all over again. John knew that she had to do this, had to release as much of the pain as was possible and as his wife cried he gently stroked the top of Ian's head. Sue kissed Ian's cheeks over and over again and as her tears fell she removed a tissue from her cuff and tenderly wiped her sons face.

"Come on baby, wake up for mummy. Ian mummy's here come on sweetheart wake up." This was far too much for John to bear and walking round to his wife he held her hands and turned her to face him. Sue's look was one of pleading as she roughly tried to pull away but John held her wrists firmly.

"He can't hear you darling you know that. Sweetheart you have to accept what's happened and say your goodbyes."

"But I don't want to."

"And you think I do? Look there's nothing we can do for him babe and you have to get that into your head. Our boy has gone."

"But he looks just like he's asleep!"

Gently he took hold of her arm and led her towards the door. Just as they were about to exit Sue took one last lingering look over her shoulder and the tears came again thick and fast. The detectives drove the couple home and Charlie Brewer walked them back up to the flat. As soon as the door was opened Sue disappeared into the front room leaving John standing in the hall with Charlie.

"Can I ask you a question?"

Charlie Brewer nodded his head but hoped that he was wrong regarding what John Hewitt was going to ask him, he wasn't.

"How did my boy die?"

"The report we received indicates that your son was hit several times on the side of the head with a heavy blunt instrument of some kind."

"I really don't understand all this; I mean who would want to hurt him he was just a kid."

"Believe me when I say we will do our utmost to catch the culprit. There's a whole task force that's been set up down at the station. Would you like me to arrange a victim support office to come and stay for a few days, just until you get your head around all of this."

John shook his head and smiled slightly in an

217

almost grateful manner that made Charlie Brewer feel guilty.

"There aint no need. I'll take care of her now, I should get back inside."

As the men said their goodbyes, Detective Brewer told John that as soon as they had any news they would be in touch. Closing the front door John lent back and for a few seconds stared up at the ceiling. He really didn't want to go into the front room but knew that he had no choice. As the door opened Sue glanced up and her tearstained face looked lost. John couldn't remember ever having seen his wife like this and he wondered just how she was going to cope. Sitting on the settee beside her he once again took her in his arms and they clung to each other as they cried. John fell asleep and when he woke the room was in darkness, looking round for his wife, he panicked when he couldn't see her. With hardly any sleep the previous night he was exhausted but hauling himself from the sofa he made his way to their bedroom but it was empty. Hearing the sound of crying he pushed open the door to Ian's room. Sue was curled up on her son's bed with one of his childhood teddy bears gripped tightly to her chest. John walked over and sat down on the mattress.

"Hi babe."

Sue gave a weak smile but her face looked tortured.

"You managed to get any sleep?"

"Not much, you?"

"Surprisingly yeh."

"What time is it?"

"Just after ten. We've got some whisky in the cupboard, shall I pour us a glass each? You never know it might help you to sleep."

Sue wearily nodded and as her husband left the room she got up and followed him. Standing in the open doorway she watched as he poured the drinks.

"I've been thinking John, we're up to our eyes in debt and we aint even got enough money to bury our only child."

Handing her the drink he gently tilted her chin up so that they were looking directly into each other's eyes.

"I don't want you worrying about that, somehow I will find the money. We'll sell everything we've got and our boy will have the send off he deserves."

"But we owe thousands on the credit cards so really all this new stuff aint ours."

"Do you think I care about any of that? Fuck the credit cards, they can't get blood out of a stone so what's the worst they can do, make us bankrupt? So fucking what, after what's happened to us I don't give a shit what they do. First thing in the morning I'll start selling the stuff off and then we can go down to the funeral directors and get the ball rolling ok?"

As much as she was hurting and as broken as she felt, Sue Hewitt couldn't love her husband any more than she did right at this moment. Further hurt was to follow when the couple would later be informed that for a while at least, Ian's body would have to stay at the mortuary until the police investigation was concluded.

Just as the Hewitt's had finished identifying the body of their son, Chief Sonny Warren and Detective Nicky Chilvers arrived at the Den. Sonny's mobile began to ring and he instantly accepted the call.

"That's the news I expected Chilvers! We have a positive ID on the boy."

Rapping hard on the front door, it was Joyce Lambert who let them in but not before moaning and calling out for them to 'hold their bleeding horses. Joyce was an east ender through and through and as she opened up, instantly knew they were Old Bill. She wasn't rude but neither was she overly friendly. When Sonny informed her that he wanted to see Tommy Mortimer, Joyce led them up the stairs without a word being spoken. Knocking on the office door she hoped that Tommy had been watching the camera and was already aware who his visitors were. She needn't have worried; Tommy was all smiles when the officers entered.

"It's the police to see you Mr Mortimer."

Tommy knew that the woman was a busy body and would have hung around, desperate to know what was going on.

"Thanks Joyce, you can get on with your work now."

Sonny Warren introduced himself and Nick Chilvers and then revealed that Ian Hewitt's body was the one found at the rear of the club.

"Terrible business Officer I must say but I suppose they are the times we're living in."

"When did you last see the boy and what time was it?"

"Yesterday and I believe it was around lunchtime."

"So after Mr Hewitt left these premises you didn't see him again?"

"No I didn't, didn't have any reason to. Ian was a lovely lad and didn't deserve what happened to him."

Tommy's last sentence was spoken from the heart as he really didn't think Ian deserved the wrath of Taffy Jones.

"Do you know of anyone that would want to harm Ian?"

Tommy shook his head.

"Like I said, he was a good lad and I hope the bastard who did it gets his just deserts."

"You said 'the bastard' how could you possibly know that it was just one person?"

"I don't officer, it was just a figure of speech."

Sonny knew that something wasn't right here but exactly what, he couldn't put his finger on.

"For the moment that will be all Mr Mortimer but I can assure you that at some time I will be back."

With that Sonny and Nick left the office and Tommy instantly began to bite down on his thumb nail. He could tell that this wasn't over and there was just something about the way the officer had said he would be back that worried Tommy. Joyce Lambert was polishing the kiosk in the downstairs foyer as the men descended the stairs. About to step outside, Sonny stopped and walked over to her.

"Its Joyce isn't it?"

"Yeh so what?"

"There's no need to be defensive love, I was only asking. Is there anything you can tell us about the Hewitt boy?"

"Not really, I hardly knew him. His Mum and Dad came to see Tommy the other day but apart from that I don't know anything."

Sonny thanked the woman and as he and Nicky stepped outside he turned to face his colleague. Nicky Chilvers was useless when it came down to the practical side of policing but on the theory he usually had a good gut feeling.

"So Chilvers, what do you think?"

"Well to be honest I aint really got a feel for the case yet but he's definitely not telling us the truth. I think if the budget allows we should do a forensic sweep of this place."

"You know what Chilvers; I totally agree with you."

CHAPTER EIGHTEEN

Joey Chambers carried out his father's wishes and had spent all day at the hospital. Michael seemed to be getting worse by the hour but the boy had tried not to let his mother see how sick he was. When Lizzie popped down to the hospital shop to get more magazines and crossword books, Joey took the opportunity to have a chat with his nephew.
"So how you feeling Mikey?"
Michael stared at his uncle and for a few seconds studied the man's face. Out of his three uncles Joey had always been his favourite and he looked upon the man as a father figure. He loved his grandfather but Mike Chambers had always been soft with him and when Michael needed some discipline in his life, Joey had been the one to administer it in a strong but kindly way.
"Like a sack of shit."
"Well that's told me but I suppose it was a stupid question really."
Michael reached over the bed and with as much strength as he was able to muster, grabbed his uncle's wrist.
"Uncle Joey I need to ask you something before me mum comes back."
"Fire away Mikey."
"When I'm gone I want you to watch out for mum."
Joey didn't like the way this conversation was going but at the same time he realised the boy had to have

his say. Since his diagnosis they had all focused on his treatment and had talked of nothing but donors. None of them had bothered to ask Michael how he was feeling inside regarding all that was happening.

"Mikey don't say that, if your mum heard you talk like that it would break her heart."

Suddenly Michaels face became serious and as he tried to pull himself up the bed he spoke in a strained voice.

"Don't you think I don't know that, it's why I'm talking to you and not her. I know I aint got long and I want to put my affairs in order."

Joey could feel his own heart breaking, his nephew was only eighteen and yet he was speaking like a man of far greater maturity. The only trouble was Joey didn't want to hear the words that were coming out of his nephew's mouth.

"You don't know that Mikey, they could find you a donor at any minute. We all have to keep our hopes up and stay positive. There's also your uncle Steve when we finally manage to track him down."

Michael laughed but it was more like he was scoffing at his uncle's words than anything else.

"If you're trying to convince me, you aint doing a very good job. The chances of a donor with my blood group are way less than slim. As for Uncle Steve, if they do manage to find him and it's a bleeding big if, the chances of him being a match are about as likely as you winning the lottery. Look me mum's going to be back in a minute so let's not

224

waste anymore time. Can you bring me in a notepad, pen and some envelopes? I'd like to leave some letters for everyone, you know, to read after I've gone. Please don't try and white wash over this Uncle Joey as times running out and everyday could be my last. Now will you do it for me?"

"You know I will."

Joey could feel a lump forming in his throat and wanted to leave before Michael saw the tears in his eyes.

"I'm going to get off now, so I'll call in and see you tomorrow. If I miss your mum on my way out, tell her I'll see her later."

Joey bent down and kissing his nephew on the cheek, silently prayed that it wouldn't be the last time they spoke. Outside in the cold clinical corridor Joey Chambers let the tears fall, not exactly the head of the family, he had still always made sure that everyone was alright and safe. Now he felt little short of useless as this was one family trouble that he couldn't sort out, or could he. The stupid idea that had begun to form in his mind a few days ago and he had no doubt that it was stupid, suddenly surfaced again. Joey wiped his eyes and headed in the direction of the exit. He was about to walk through the automatic doors when he met his sister on her way back from the shop.

"You off now Joey love?"

"Yeh, places to go people to see you know how it is."

Lizzie studied her brother and clearly knew there

225

was something troubling him.

"You alright Joey?"

It had always been impossible for him to hide anything from his sister and there and then he knew that if he didn't share his thoughts with someone he was likely to go mad.

"Not really."

"What's on your mind?"

"Can we go for a coffee? Michaels fine for a while and there's something I need to talk to you about and it can't wait."

Lizzie Chambers didn't argue or question her brother further, she trusted him implicitly just as she'd always done right from childhood. Linking her arm through his, they headed in the direction of the cafeteria. Joey found them a seat at a quiet corner table where they wouldn't be overheard and after Lizzie was seated he joined the queue at the counter. Five minutes later he placed two hot cappuccinos onto the table and then sat down.

"So what's so urgent that you needed to speak to me now?"

"You know I went to see Mortimer?"

"Yeh and the wanker said he wouldn't help our Michael, so what's new?"

"Well I'm going to see him again, maybe this time I'll have more luck."

"I wouldn't count on it but I suppose it won't do any harm to ask, although there's no reason why that bastard would have changed his mind. Joey I hate that bloke and not because he raped me, if he hadn't then I never would have had my Michael would I? I hate him because he's scum and I can't for the life of me understand any human being that won't help to save someone's life, especially when that someone's your own child."

As Lizzie studied her brother's face she knew there was something more that he needed to get off of his chest.

"What else Joey?"

"What do you mean?"

Lizzie wanted to get back to her son and not play silly buggers with her brother asking twenty questions.

"I know you only too well, so will you just spit out whatever it is that's playing on your mind."

Joey was having second thoughts and was about to protest that he didn't know what she was talking about but one look at her face told him not to bother.

"Ok here goes but you aint going to like it."

"Let me be the judge of that."

"If Mortimer refuses to help then I've come up with a plan but oh Lizzie it's bad. If I have to go through with it then I don't know if I could live with myself afterwards. On the other hand if I do nothing I don't think I could live with that either."

For a moment Lizzie Chambers was silent and Joey knew that she was digesting all that he had said. In reality he hadn't said very much but Lizzie was as

sharp as a razor and without him going into detail she had worked out what he was talking about.
"Joey I love you very much and I hope you know that?"
"Of course I do."
"Good, then whatever you do is fine by me but I would never put pressure on you to do anything you weren't comfortable with. That said, my boy is my world and I'd gladly trade my own life for his. I suppose what I'm trying to say is, whatever's bothering you, you have to look at it from a different angle."
"I aint quite sure I know what you mean?"
"Look, treat it like you're in a boat, our Michael and Tommy Mortimer are in the water and you can only save one of them so which one would you choose?"
"Don't be bleeding daft, there would never be a choice it would always be Michael."
"Then I suppose there's your answer my darling brother. Now I have to get back to the ward. You take care and I'll see you tomorrow."
Lizzie kissed her brother on the cheek and then walked off to see her son. Joey stayed in the cafeteria for ages thinking about what he had to do. He decided that before he put his plan into action, he really would give Tommy Mortimer one last chance to step up to the plate and be a man. As he left the hospital through the main foyer he stopped at one of the leaflet stands and picking up a card slipped it into his pocket. Now feeling slightly

better, Joey Chambers set off for Hackney and the Den. Arriving at just after ten pm, the road was busy with youngsters out enjoying themselves. People were starting to spill out from the pubs as they set about heading off for one of the clubs where they could continue partying until the early hours. No one took any notice of Joey as he parked up his Range Rover and then crossed the street and went into the Den. After all these years Rita Vertigan was still working in the front booth. Her lipstick was still the same shade of scarlet, her hair still a cheap brassy blonde, in fact the only thing that had changed were the added lines that now seemed to cover her entire face. If Lizzie had have been here it would seem to her that time had stood still, luckily she wasn't and Joey wasn't aware that the woman had worked here on the night of his sisters rape. Handing over the ten pounds entrance fee he walked up the stairs. John Newman's 'Love me again' was blearing out and for a second Joey stopped as the tune reminded him of the ones played in his youth. This one was new and a hit but the beat was retro and Joey smiled to himself. Instead of going through the double doors that led into the main room of the club he turned right to where the office was situated. He was nervous as the last time he'd been here it had ended with him staring down the barrel of a gun. Joey hadn't taken any extra precautions this time but he knew that on his next visit, and there definitely would be a next visit, he would be well and truly prepared. He didn't knock on the door and instead turned the handle and walked straight in. As usual Tommy was seated at his desk and as soon as he saw his uninvited guest, reached for the drawer where his gun was kept.

"There's no need for that Mr Mortimer, I aint come here for any trouble."

"Then what the fuck are you doing here?"

Joey didn't bother to close the office door as he knew that the visit would be short and in any case he needed to be able to make a quick escape if the bloke in front of him suddenly decided to do a bit of target practice.

"I'm here on behalf of my sister and your son. I know you made it clear last time that you weren't interested but I thought, well hoped, that you might have changed your mind."

"Not a chance."

"Well it was worth a try I suppose."

"I don't know why you think I owe the fucking kid anything. I mean your sister whoever she was and I really can't fucking remember her, was just a shag. If the stupid bitch wasn't on the pill, well that's her look out."

Joey Chambers was no mug and knew how to look after himself. Over the years he'd never been shy to have a row and right at this moment he wanted to dive over the desk and rip Tommy Mortimer's head off. There was just one problem, the man was only inches away from a gun and Joey knew that as hard as he was, he was no match when it came down to a bullet. Tommy could see that the stranger was thinking and anyone who thought too much could be dangerous and could turn at any second.

"Look pal, I've had enough shit already today so why don't you just sling your fucking hook before my doormen give you a kicking, that or I'll blow your fucking head off you piece of shit!"

Joey raised his palms in a gesture of submission as he backed out of the door. If he'd had any doubts before, they had now well and truly vanished. Joey had no difficulty in accepting that Tommy Mortimer was a cunt and that whatever was coming his way, he deserved. Making his way back down the stairs he was eyed suspiciously by the doormen but nothing was said and as soon as Joey was out onto the street he breathed in a deep lungful of air. What he was planning to do would take guts but he was now positive that it was the right thing to do. Driving back to Notting Hill he meticulously planned out exactly what his actions would be the following day. As he pulled up outside his home he was happy with what he'd come up with. Letting himself inside he called out to his wife but stopped when he heard her talking to someone.

"Come to mummy my little baby, mummy loves you very much. I think I just heard your daddy come home, you just wait until he sees you sweetheart."

Joey walked along the hallway and when he reached the kitchen couldn't believe his eyes. A tiny puppy was perched in a designer wrought iron bed that looked like it had cost a fortune. It was lined with pink velvet pillows that had princess crowns embroidered in the centres and the dog had claimed it as its own. It eyed Joey suspiciously and started yapping and wagging its tail as he walked over. On the work surface sat a Louis Vuitton carry case and matching Versace water and food bowls glimmered on the polished kitchen floor. Joey stared at the animal and knew that there was definitely no way it had come from Battersea dogs home.

"Look at him babe, aint he adorable?"

"How much?"

"Joey he didn't..."

Slamming his fist onto the worktop Joey Chambers was more than angry, he was livid. After all she had said this morning about going to look at a stray and now he had come home to a pedigree pug that must have cost all of a grand.

"Don't fucking start lying Sharon. Now how much has this little lot set me back?"

"If you must know my Dad bought him for me."

"All of it or just the mutt?"

"Don't call him that, his names Coco and to answer your question, my dad bought Coco and my mum bought me the bed."

Joey breathed in deeply trying to contain his anger.

232

He was already struggling with all that he knew he would be facing tomorrow and he really needed to stay calm. The only trouble was, with Michael being so ill Joey hadn't earned much in the last couple of weeks and they were supposed to be tightening their belts. The mortgage cost a fortune each month not to mention all the hire purchase payments for the high end furniture Sharon had insisted on buying. If things didn't change soon Joey knew they were going to face some serious financial difficulties. Walking over to the pet carrier he picked it up by one handle and threw it across the kitchen. Coco began to bark at the mean man and kneeling down Sharon picked him up and cradled him in her arms. She knew she had well and truly overstepped the mark again and just hoped that Joey would calm down but for once her husband wasn't in a calming frame of mind.

"I'm going to ask you one more time and you'd better give me an answer, now how much did this little lot fucking cost?"

"Please stop shouting, the carry case cost eight fifty alright. Coco was thirteen hundred and the bed was a snip at seven hundred but like I told you I only bought the case."

Joey was irate and now continued to shout as he spoke.

"After all your promises and you fucking go and do this. I've had a gutful of you Sharon and if it wasn't for the fact that our Michael was so sick I'd be out of here for good."

Sharon slowly walked towards her husband and tried to embrace him but Joey wasn't having any of it. As she placed her arms around his neck he grabbed her wrists and roughly pulled them away. Sharon winced in pain but the show she put on that he'd hurt her didn't create the guilt she was hoping for. Joey made his way to the door and just as he was about to go into the hall he turned to face his wife.

"And don't bother coming to bed tonight either, you can sleep down here with that little rat you call a dog. When I've sorted everything out tomorrow, that's me and you over with. You've played me for the last fucking time Sharon and I mean it."

Joey slammed the kitchen door and Sharon stood with her mouth gapping open. Over the years she'd always won him round, always managed to get her own way but deep down she knew that this time it was different and she was scared. Pulling Coco closer she tried to work out what he'd meant about sorting things out to tomorrow but she hadn't got a clue. Suddenly the enormity of his last words hit her and she began to cry, only this time they weren't tears of self pity. Sharon Chambers was crying because her marriage was finally over and it was all her own stupid fault.

CHAPTER NINETEEN

Joey hadn't got much sleep and staring out of the window he wondered just how today would pan out. The best laid plans sometimes went wrong and he hoped that it wouldn't be the case for him. Sharon hadn't bothered coming up to bed last night and for that he was grateful, her normal ploy of using sex to get him on side wouldn't have worked and with all that he had on his mind, Joey was doubtful that he would have even been able to rise for the occasion. He could feel an acid taste in his mouth, a usual sign that his nerves were beginning to play up. Hauling himself from the bed he quickly showered and dressing in his oldest clothes, made his way down stairs. Sharon Chambers sat at the breakfast bar nursing her puppy but she didn't speak as he entered. She hoped that he'd had a change of heart but when he completely ignored her, she knew that wasn't the case. In the past she would have begged and pleaded for another chance but she accepted that this time there was no point. Her life would soon have to change and along with that change would be the loss of her cosy lifestyle. In the early hours as she'd lain curled up on the sofa with Coco, Sharon had made a decision, by the end of the week she would pack up her stuff and move back in with her parents. When the house was sold she might have enough left for a small flat in a less desirable part of London but she knew that really

wasn't an option as she couldn't survive on her own. Sharon had always needed someone to take care of her and if Joey was no longer on the scene then her parents would have to accept the responsibility. Her mother would be over the moon to have her only child back in the family home but Sharon didn't think it would be the same for her Dad. He had always complained about the amount of money she asked for and he would now see it as a backward step and a rapid drop in his savings.
"Are you not talking to me?"
Joey just stared at his wife, it was as if he was seeing her for the first time and it had finally registered just what a bloodsucking leach she really was.
"Well I suppose the no reply tells me the answer. Joey, if our marriage is really over, then it's going to take some time to sort things out and we should try and be as amicable as possible. It will make things a whole lot easier to deal with. I'm moving back in with me mum and dad for a while, so I'm going to sort through my stuff first which will take a couple of days."
Sharon waited for a reaction, her husband asking for her to stay, just something to let her know that deep down he still loved her but there was nothing. Joey had just poured himself a coffee and as he took a swig from the mug, nodded his head. Today of all days he wasn't in the mood for talking and pulling on his old jacket he removed a pair of latex gloves from the kitchen drawer. Sharon watched him but

didn't add anything to her last sentence. Holding
Coco tightly she kissed his fur and wished she could
turn the clock back twenty four hours but then
again, their problems had been brewing for a long
time now and you couldn't keep plastering over the
cracks. Maybe things would eventually turn out for
the best and if he missed her enough, he might just
ask her to come home. Joeys mind was too
preoccupied with other things to even give his wife
a second thought and picking up his car keys he
headed into the hall. Stopping at the coat rack he
rummaged in the pocket of his good jacket and
removed the donor card from yesterday. Without a
goodbye, Joey Chambers slammed the front door
closed. Climbing into the range rover he set off for
Hackney but not before he'd called into one of the
numerous second hand shops on Portobello Road.
Choosing one that dealt in all manner of household
objects, he made his way over to the kitchen
utensils. Pretending to browse, he looked through
the large tray of knives and when his hand settled
on one with a fine filleting blade he knew he'd
found what he was looking for. Picking up a toast
rack and some place mats, Joey wanted to appear as
if he was just shopping for items for his home. If
the knife was his only purchase it could raise
suspicions. When the girl at the counter had asked
if he would like them wrapped and when Joey had
told her yes as they were gifts, he handed over forty
pounds. Out on the street, Joey opened the items

and placed the rack and mats into the nearest
rubbish bin. Heading back to the car, he sat for a
few minutes mentally running over his plans and
then starting the engine he pulled out into the traffic
and was soon on his way to Kingsland Road.
Deciding he didn't want the car to be seen too close
to his destination, Joey pulled onto Falkirk Street
and parked at the sports hall. After walking a short
distance he turned left into the back alley that ran
parallel to the rear of the club. He didn't know
what had occurred here but the area was still
cordoned off with police tape, Joey ignored it and
ducked underneath. As he made his way along the
uneven alley he scoured the area looking for any
close circuit television cameras but as far as he
could see there weren't any. Thinking about it, it
was obvious that Tommy Mortimer wouldn't want
anyone to see what went on as he was one of the
biggest dealers in the area. He wasn't expecting the
backdoor to be unlocked again but it was worth a
try. Moving along the outer wall of the club, Joey
reached the back door and removing the latex
gloves from his pocket, pulled them on. Turning
the handle he couldn't believe his luck, someone
was either very forgetful or very lazy and it was a
mistake that would cost the owner dearly. Stepping
inside he walked as quietly as he could through the
rear hall and as he reached the top of the stairs,
could hear a vacuum cleaner being used. Ducking
into the men's toilets he hoped that he hadn't been

seen. Joyce only gave the room a quick onceover and Joey soon heard her lug the machine back down the stairs. Slipping out of the toilets he quietly walked across to the office and pressing his ear to the door listened intently for any noise that would tell if Tommy was in residence. Satisfied that it was too early in the day for the man to show himself, Joey entered the room. The first thing he did was to go over to the desk. Opening the drawer he removed the gun and emptied it of bullets which he placed into his pocket. He needed it to look like a robbery and the roll of banknotes that sat inside would be a good start. Spying the lottery ticket that was still on the desktop, he stuffed it and the cash into his pocket before swiping everything from the desk onto the floor. Looking around the room the next thing to catch his eye was the sofa and he recalled his sister describing the rape to him. Overcome with rage Joey removed the knife and frenziedly slashed at the fabric. For someone trying to remain calm he wasn't doing a very good job and as quickly as he'd started Joey stopped. This wasn't doing anyone any good and it was so out of character but Joey Chambers was hurting and he had momentarily lost it. Breathing in deeply he stood still for a second trying to compose himself. When he heard voices outside he grabbed the empty gun and took up his position behind the door. At the top of the stairs Tommy Mortimer was talking loudly and Joey knew that the cleaner was getting a right ear bashing.

"Now I don't Fucking want to be disturbed Joyce do you hear me? I don't care if it's the Fucking queen herself.'

"Yes Mr Mortimer and I'm sorry about the other day but those poor people looked so upset, my heart really felt for them."

"You're a daft old cow Joyce and if you want to keep your job you won't make the same fucking mistake again. Now do you understand that Joyce?"

Tommy Mortimer had a way of talking down to people and always had to over emphasize what he was saying, his voice was monotonous and he had the habit of using several words when one would have been sufficient. Joyce Lambert only nodded her head but as soon as Tommy turned his back, she sharply shot two fingers in the air and silently mouthed the word 'wanker'. She longed for the day when she could retire, although in reality that wouldn't be any day soon as she hardly had enough to live on as it was. Her state pension only just covered the bare essentials but still she lived in hope of that day, a day when she could tell Tommy Mortimer in no uncertain terms just where he could shove his poxy job. Tommy opened the office door and as soon as he was inside slammed it closed behind him. Joyce didn't hang about after her telling off and was down the stairs like a shot so she didn't hear the words 'what the fuck?' as they left her boss's mouth. The first thing Tommy saw was

240

his favourite conquest sofa that was now in tatters.
Marching over to inspect the damage he didn't
notice Joey Chambers standing beside the now
closed door and he almost jumped out of his skin
when his uninvited visitor began to speak.
"It is a bit of a mess aint it. Sorry about that only I
lost it for a minute, never mind you can always get
another rape couch to replace it."
Tommy had already spun round and his face was so
red with rage that it looked like it would explode at
any minute. Joey couldn't deny that the sight gave
him a small amount of pleasure.
"What the fuck are you doing here? I told you
yesterday what would happen if I saw you again!"
Tommy moved forward towards the desk but
before he had chance to open the drawer, Joey
aimed the gun directly at him.
"You looking for this by any chance?"
When Tommy saw what Joey was holding, the
anger disappeared and was replaced by terror. His
red face that only a few seconds ago had been filled
with rage was now replaced with one of ashen grey.
Fear engulfed him and he could feel his body begin
to tremble and sweat. This bloke, whoever he was,
didn't give up but he had now moved things to a
whole new level.
"What is it you want? Money? I've got plenty of
money and.........."
How the mighty had fallen and as Joey thought
back to yesterday and the conversation that had

passed between the two of them, he started to lose his temper all over again.

"Just shut the fuck up and sit down you slimy cunt!" Tommy did as he was told and as Joey crossed the room, Tommy Mortimer's eyes darted in all directions. He was looking for a way out or at least something to use as a weapon to protect himself but there was nothing. Joey now stood behind the desk and as he pressed the empty barrel of the gun against Tommy's head, he felt like raising it up and smashing it back down again onto the man's skull.

"Look pal help me out here will you? I really don't know what you want from me, unless you're still on about one of my kidneys?"

"It's a bit fucking late to ask me what I want you cunt! You've had plenty of opportunities to help your son but you don't give a toss do you?"

Tommy could feel his throat dry up and he was desperate for a drink of water. Licking his lips he continued to talk in the hope that it might calm the situation.

"If it means that much I'll give the kid a kidney, how's that?"

Joey laughed out loud in a sarcastic way that told Tommy he hadn't got a chance.

"You must think I came off the last fucking banana boat if you think I'm going to fall for that old trick. As soon as I let you go it'll be a case of on your bike cunt."

Tommy was now starting to sweat profusely and as

242

beads formed on his top lip he licked at them with his tongue. The tension was building but he had to keep talking, had to find a way out of this or he knew he was going to die.

"No it won't, I promise it won't now if you just..." Joey had stopped listening and walking around the back of Tommy as he sat in the chair, he placed the man's own gun to the side of Tommy's head. Using his free hand Joey removed the filleting knife. With one swift movement Joey drew the knife across his victim's throat, drawing deep into the flesh so that he ,made sure he hit the jugular vein. Just as Joey stepped back blood spurted from Tommy's neck spraying everything to his right side in blood and for the second time in as many days, the walls were again covered in claret. As Tommy Mortimer's body slumped forward, Joey knew that his task was complete and he watched for a second as blood oozed from Tommy's wound and formed a pool on the desk before slowly dripping down the side and onto the floor. Removing the card from his pocket that he'd picked up on the way out of the hospital yesterday, he twisted Tommy's body so that he was able to place it inside the breast pocket of the man's jacket. After checking that there was no disc in the surveillance recorder, he then walked towards the door and carefully stepped over any blood to make sure that there was no trace on his shoes. Peering outside he glanced in all directions to see if anyone was about but the only thing he could hear was

Joyce vacuuming the downstairs front foyer. Leaving the door wide open Joey made his exit the same way that he'd entered. Standing in the rear yard he suddenly began to shake all over as the enormity of what he'd just done finally hit home. Panting heavily he desperately tried to calm himself and when he thought he'd at last managed it, pulled off the latex gloves and slowly made his way back to Falkirk Street and his waiting car. Climbing inside he placed the gun and knife into a plastic bag and laid them in the car's front foot well. Joey could visibly see his hands shaking as he switched on the engine and just prayed he wouldn't get pulled over by the Old Bill for anything. Turning onto Kingsland Road and then along Shoreditch High Street, he began to relax slightly as he crossed into Whitechapel. Ten minutes later and as he drove along East Smithfield and the Thames came into sight, Joey knew or at least hoped that the nightmare was nearly over. Parking up he grabbed the carrier bag and after using a cloth from the dashboard to wipe all traces from the weapons, he walked over to St Katharine's Pier. Taking a seat on one of the numerous benches Joey sat for a while and watched the boats going up and down the river. It was a bright sunny day and as a gentle breeze began to blow through his hair he started to cry. Ending someone's life no matter what the reason, was about as bad as it got and Joey Chambers didn't know how he was going to live with the fact that he'd done just that. He must have remained on the bench for at least an hour and when he was confident that no one was watching, he reached into the bag and threw first the knife and then the gun into the murky waters, waters that had and would be for many years to come, the keeper of so many horrific secrets.

Finally three hours after he'd first left home he was once again pulling up outside his house. Joey crossed his fingers that Sharon would be out as just the sight of her would be more than he could handle. His luck was in and removing the wad of cash and the bullets that he'd taken from the gun, he hung up his jacket in the hallway. The thing Joey wanted to do more than anything was to shower and try and wash the feeling of guilt from his body. Stepping into the cubicle he let the hot water run down his body as he held his head against the wall. After five minutes he got out but he didn't feel any better. The realisation that he'd taken a man's life filled his every thought and Joey heard the word murderer over and over again in his head. When he couldn't stand it any longer he quickly dried and after changing into fresh clothing, ran from the house. He had to see Lizzie, had to tell her what he'd done and hoped with all his heart that she could make him feel better about himself.

Walking into his old family house, the only place he had ever truly felt at home, he called out but just like on his last visit there was no answer. As usual

Lizzie was at the hospital visiting Michael and as Joey poked his head into the front room he saw his father fast asleep in the arm chair. Deciding to sit and wait for his sister, Joey went into the kitchen and put the kettle on to boil. While he waited he took a seat and crossing his arms on the table top he rested his head on top of them. From out of nowhere the tears began and once they had started Joey didn't seem to be able to stop them. The noise he made must have woken Mike Chambers and he was suddenly at his son's side gently caressing the top of Joeys head. A wise man, Mike didn't ask any questions but he knew that whatever was troubling his son, had to be very bad indeed for Joey to get himself into such a state.

CHAPTER TWENTY

After Joey Chambers had murdered Tommy Mortimer and just before he'd returned home, his wife had set out for her parent's house over in Clapham. At the top of the road she hailed a cab but at first the driver had been reluctant to accept the fare. He eyed the pampered pooch suspiciously and had visions of dog shit all over his back seat. Sharon Chambers assured the man that Coco was a very good dog and if there was a minor accident, then she would happily pay double the fare. It was a distinct possibility that her dog would pee on the seat but she only had forty pounds in her purse and knew most of that would be spent on the fare without any added mishaps. Reluctantly the man agreed and climbing inside Sharon sat back for the journey but kept Coco on her lap just to be on the safe side. The traffic was heavy and as she watched the meter ticking over she began to worry when she had visions of having to ask the man to stop so that she could walk the rest of the way. Luckily that didn't happen and as the cab passed over Battersea Bridge she let out a sigh of relief. The roads wouldn't be as busy now that they had crossed the water and with the cabs meter showing twenty two pounds she was optimistic that there would be enough money to pay her fare. Stopping outside the red brick Victorian terrace on Turret Grove, Sharon let out a sigh of relief. The fare totalled twenty seven pounds fifty and Sharon handed over three ten pound notes but was too proud to ask for any change. In fact the cabbie was a little put out when a further tip wasn't offered. Climbing out of the vehicle with Coco she grabbed her handbag and had only just closed the door when the taxi sped off. Standing alone on the street she now had a sense of what it was going to be like not having any money and she didn't like it. Checking her purse before she left home she was dumb struck when she saw that all her credit and debit cards were gone. Joey wasn't normally spiteful but maybe he had thought she would rack up more debt just to piss him off and had Sharon thought of it first, she might just well have proven him right. The front door to the house was painted in a high black gloss and the brass door furniture shone out in the morning sunlight. Just like herself, Sharon's mother was overly house proud and liked everything to be just so. Straightening her clothes she rang the bell and hoped that it would be her mother who answered. Her luck was in and as she opened up, Linda Jackson smiled from ear to ear.

"Hello my darling, what a lovely surprise. Oh just look at him, aint he adorable."

Linda put out her arms and taking Coco from her daughter, began to shower him in kisses.

"Don't stand there on the doorstep sweetheart, come on in."

Sharon looked over Linda's shoulder and could see

248

her father standing further along in the hallway and his expression wasn't good. At the same time Linda looked into her daughters eyes and could see the onset of tears. Placing Coco onto the floor she took Sharon into her arms.

"Hey hey love, whatever's the matter?"

Suddenly all the emotion of the last twenty four hours brimmed over and Sharon Chambers started to cry and for the first time in as long as she could remember, the tears were real and heartfelt. Linda placed her arm around her daughter and led her inside. Coco was making himself at home and after peeing on the hall rug had now decided to attack the bottom of Derek's trousers. He forcibly tried to shake the dog off but Coco had locked his teeth into the fabric and was holding on for dear life. Linda and Sharon were oblivious as they passed the supposedly head of the household, who was acting as if he was fighting off a wild beast, and went into the kitchen. Derek knew there was trouble on the horizon and bending down he grabbed the dog with both hands and yanked him upwards. Coco yelped out in pain and began to snarl at Derek but Sharon's father wasn't put off. Marching over to the toilet that was situated under the stairs, he opened the door and after throwing Coco inside, went to see what had brought his daughter over.

Derek and Linda Jackson had purchased the house shortly after getting married and over the years had turned the place into a palace. Because it was a

Grove and not a common or garden street, Linda had always thought she was more upmarket and had raised her daughter to think in the same way. Derek loved them both more than anything else in his life and worked tirelessly as a cab driver in the city to provide all that they had needed but his daughter was cut from the same cloth as his wife and she always wanted more. The income he earned from having his own black hackney was way above the wage of most other people in the area but Linda and Sharon spent money as if it was going out of fashion. Now Derek was more than interested, he was actually worried that whatever had gone on and whatever was being discussed behind the closed door, was going to cost him dearly. Entering the lavish kitchen he saw that the women had taken up residence at the table and as his wife noticed him out of the corner of her eye, barked her usual order.

"Derek don't stand there like a bleeding spare part, put the kettle on! Can't you see our girl is upset? I don't know, honestly men are neither use nor ornament, come on jump to it!"

There was no please or thank you but he still obediently did as he was told.

"So sweetheart, what's all this about?"

Sharon grabbed her mother's hand and as she squeezed it she began to cry again. Between sobs she was just able to talk though her words were muffled and at times difficult to understand.

"Joey don't want me anymore, he says our marriage is over. Oh Mum whatever am I going to do?"
"The bastard! Where the fuck does he get off rejecting my girl? Fuck me it aint as if he's from good stock now is it; I mean the Chambers are a dysfunctional lot and a right mess of a family. I tell you what, why don't you....."
Linda didn't get a chance to finish her sentence. The room went silent when Derek slammed the teapot down onto the worktop and it cracked in two. Hot tea spilt everywhere and ran down the crisp white units and onto the floor. Linda was about to give her husband a right ear bashing but when she looked into his face knew he was about to explode. It was a look she hadn't seen that often during their marriage but when she had, knew that he was going to kick off and it wouldn't be a pretty sight.
Marching over to the table he placed his palms onto the surface and leaned in close so that he was only inches from both of their faces.
"You are two nasty bitches and you should both be bleeding ashamed of yourselves."
Linda looked at her husband with daggers but he wasn't put off, for once he was going to have his say and they were going to listen. As his wife went to speak Derek held up his hand and glared at her at the same time.
"The Chambers are one of the nicest families I've ever known and the one thing that stands out above all else, is the fact that they all love each other and

251

would do anything for anybody so don't let me hear you bad mouth any of them again, do you hear me Linda?. As for Joey, he idolises the ground you walk on and if he's called it a day, then all I can say is you must have really pushed him. For fuck's sake Sharon just look at all you have! How many other girls of your age live in a beautiful house in fucking Notting Hill, not to mention all the designer gear you wear? So what's caused it then?"

"Joey says I think money grows on trees and he can't keep up with me, he says he's knackered and I've drained him and he can't take any more. I suppose he has got a lot on his mind what with Michael being so sick."

Linda immediately came to her daughters defence and started mouthing off but it was short lived. "Darling that aint no excuse, I mean the boy is only his nephew for god's sake! I think he's just a tight bastard! I'll tell you what you need to..."

Derek was now even angrier and lifting his right palm, slammed it down onto the table.

"You won't tell her fuck all! For once in your life will you just keep your fucking trap shut woman! You're too fond of dishing out orders and while we're on the subject of spending, she gets it from you. I know exactly how the poor sod feels and I admire his guts! I'll tell you this for nothing; I wish I'd had the balls years ago to do what he's done. Now Sharon, if as you say your marriage is over then yes you can come home but don't think I'm going to be a meal ticket again like poor old Joey's been. If you move back in here, then there's going to be rules. For a start you can get a job as there aint going to be anymore free rides. As for that yappy little sod in the lav, you can sell him. He's already pissed on the hall rug and I aint having my house turned upside down for a four legged rat. Now you two can argue all you like but I won't be changing my mind and if you push me too much further Linda, you'll be forced to get off your arse and find a job as well. I'm going into the front room to read me paper, let me know when you've made up your mind what it's going to be."

Derek Jackson disappeared into the hall and as he passed the toilet door and heard Coco whimpering he loudly shouted out 'shut the fuck up'. Sharon stared at her mother and was very surprised she hadn't said more but Linda knew when she was on a hiding to nothing and Derek was so angry that there was no way he would ever back down.

"So love what's it to be?"

Sharon sighed and her heart sank when she again thought about what her father had said.

"Looks like I aint got a lot of choice in the matter but oh mum, can't you get him to change his mind about Coco?"

Linda Jackson rubbed at her cheek as she thought, it really was out of character for Derek to behave in such a way and she was stumped as to what to do. If they both towed the line then maybe her husband

253

might just soften a bit. They would have to be careful how they approached the subject and for the next couple of days at least, they wouldn't be able to push the matter. Softly she spoke to her daughter but her eyes were serious, a sign for Sharon to really take notice of what she was saying.

"Go and tell your dad that you agree to everything and ask if he will run you home to get your stuff. Leave Coco here and if he says anymore about selling the dog, well we'll just have to cross that bridge when we come to it."

Thirty minutes later Sharon Chambers once more sat in the back of a cab only this time she didn't have to worry about paying the fare. Pulling up outside the beautiful house in Notting Hill Derek switched off the engine and accompanied his daughter inside.

"I've already packed my stuff Dad; it's just a matter of bringing the cases down."

As Derek waited for her he walked from room to room and surveyed all that the couple had achieved. It was a crying shame that it would now all be lost but deep down Derek didn't blame Joey one bit. Derek loved his only child but he was also the first to admit that she was spoilt, greedy and didn't have an ounce of compassion in her. Her lifestyle and the way she treated Joey had finally caught up and was now biting her hard on the backside. Although it pained him to think such a thing, his daughter was now getting her just deserts.

254

When Sharon had lugged three suitcases down the stairs without any help and when her father had placed them all into the cab, she ran upstairs and returned to the hall carrying a black refuse bag.
"What you got there?"
"Well when I was packing I had a good clear out and this is the stuff I won't ever wear again so I'm going to put them in the bin."
"You'll do no such thing young lady! There are people out there desperate for clothes; we'll drop them off at the charity shop on the way. You know it wouldn't hurt you to do a bit of bleeding charity work instead of sitting on your arse all day. I hope it might just make you realise exactly what you have if you see how the other half are forced to live and most through no fault of their own I might add. Some poor bastard's aint had a life of luxury handed to them on a plate by marrying a mug like Joey Chambers."
Sharon rolled her eyes upwards but didn't want to upset the apple cart any further so she didn't argue and as she was about to walk out of the front door, spied Joey's dirty work jacket hanging on the peg. For months she'd been nagging him to get rid of it and now was the ideal opportunity. Grabbing the tired old garment she placed it into the black bag and then walking outside, slammed the front door shut and posted her house keys through the letter box. As the cab pulled away she could feel a lump form in her throat, the house was her dream home

255

and now she had to say goodbye to it and move back in with her parents. Her friend Steph was going to have a field day when she found out about this and Sharon felt nothing but shame.

The volunteers at the Notting Hill branch of Help the Aged were over the moon with the donation and they were just about to thank Sharon but she'd disappeared before they had a chance. It was bad enough actually donating things but if any of her friends had recognised Sharon Chambers coming out of a charity shop, she would have been mortified. Grace Harrod worked at the shop two days a week; she'd lived locally all her life and loathed all the rich people that now inhabited Notting Hill. Her dislike also included the charity shop's manager Celia Montpelier, a woman that didn't need to work and seemed to look down on her employees, at least that's what she called them but all except Celia were volunteers and received no wages. Grace had now been retired for a couple of years and only came to work for the gossip or to see what she could get her hands on for next to nothing. When the boss was on her day off, Grace would get the items for free. None of the other volunteers dared say a word as the stuff disappeared from the rack into her shopping bag. Grace Harrod had a mean and spiteful tongue and in all honesty she frightened the other more genteel women who worked alongside her. Carrying the black bag through to the back room Grace tipped the contents onto the floor and began rummaging through the items.

"Look 'ere Celia, there's some right good clobber. I've a mind to buy some of it myself and put it on eBay; I could make a bleeding fortune."

Celia, who had been in the middle of balancing the accounts, stood up from her desk and made her way over.

"Grace Harrod, you will do no such thing! These items have been donated for the less fortunate members of Notting Hill and not for your own personal gain. Now could you please return to the shop and start tidying up the rails. Standards seem to be slipping lately and it's about time we all took our responsibilities more seriously."

"What about this lot?"

"That's none of your concern but if you must know, I will sort though these items myself."

Grace Harrod did as she was told and grumbled under her breath as she left but her words were muffled and inaudible. For a long time Grace had been harbouring a sneaky feeling that the manageress was selling the stuff herself but she couldn't prove it. In truth Celia Montpelier was doing no such thing and she was only glad to help anyone in need, especially the local homeless community. At the rear of the storeroom was a rack that held items not deemed fit for resale but Celia wouldn't allow anything to be put into the bin. Twice a week mad Maddy Dumont would call in and collect any unwanted items. It had been an arrangement between the two women for the last three years and it worked well. Celia, unlike most other people, knew that Maddy wasn't mad and that she was in fact the kindest human being that Celia had ever had the pleasure of meeting. Maddy was due a visit first thing in the morning and the rack was really getting full, a sight that would definitely bring a smile to the woman's face. Celia grinned to herself as she placed Joey Chamber's work jacket amongst the other items. Walking back over to the pile of clothing on the floor, she picked up one or two items and thoroughly inspected the labels. Chloe, Gucci and Stella McCartney were just a few of the names and Grace had been right, there really were some very expensive items in the bag but what on earth the old jacket was doing amongst them was a mystery.

CHAPTER TWENTY ONE

Within thirty minutes of Tommy being murdered his body was discovered by Joyce Lambert. After finishing the vacuuming downstairs she'd decided to go up to the kitchen and make a couple of hot drinks in the hope of putting her boss in a better frame of mind. Passing the office and seeing the door wide open, she couldn't help but look inside. What greeted her made Joyce's blood run cold and for a moment she stopped in her tracks and could only stare. Composing herself, she made the sign of the cross and said the words 'dear God in heaven'. Cautiously walking inside Joyce made her way over to the recently departed body of Tommy Mortimer. She tilted her head as she inspected him but didn't try and see if there was a pulse, the gaping wound across the man's throat told her there was no point. Whoever had done this knew exactly what the outcome would be and besides, as far as she was concerned, it was well overdue and her boss had finally gotten what he deserved. Drugs were a nasty business and her motto had always been if you lived by the sword then you died by it. The only thing that did bother Joyce Lambert was the possibility that after today she wouldn't have a job but then there were plenty of other clubs willing to pay the minimum wage for a good dogsbody and Joyce had no doubt that was exactly what she was. Leaning over him and being careful not to get any blood on her jumper, she picked up the telephone and dialled 999. After reporting the crime she then went downstairs to unlock the front doors. Fifteen minutes passed before the police and ambulance arrived and the place soon turned into chaos. Joyce was glad that she'd made herself a cuppa while she'd been waiting because now everywhere was being cordoned off and the kitchen was out of bounds.

Over at Stoke Newington police station things were going from bad to worse. Sonny Warren was up to his neck in paperwork and extra detectives had been drafted in from other departments when the news had come through of Tommy Mortimer's demise. It was now deemed by the head man, that both the murder of Ian Hewitt and Tommy Mortimer were linked, it was too much of a coincidence to think otherwise. Sonny was addressing his team in the incident room and where there had previously been two wipe down boards showing any evidence and links that had been collected, there were now four. There was also a board for Big Boy Davidson but Sonny had decided it had to take second stage and all efforts were now being concentrated on the murders of Ian Hewitt and Tommy Mortimer. At considerable cost to the department, a full forensic sweep was being carried out at the Den. Before Tommy's murder Sonny had been about to put in a request to his superiors but that hadn't been needed as it was now a matter of course. The club was large compared to the usual domestic set up and Sonny had told the team to start with Tommy Mortimer's office. Due to the serious nature of the case and the fact that more murders could possibly follow, the lab had been instructed to view the samples as top priority. Screening normally took between two and four months and that was only if the department was lucky but Sonny Warren was praying for a swifter result. Graham Mason and Charlie Brewer were sent over to the Den to gather statements regarding any information the employees may have about Ian Hewitt and their boss Tommy Mortimer. There was nothing anyone could tell them until it was Dicky Stinton's turn. He was asked when he had last seen either of the men and Dicky told the officers that he'd been on bar duty the night before Ian's body was found.

"He was real worried about something, like he had the weight of the world on his shoulders but he wouldn't speak to me about it. Anyway, a call came through to the bar and Ian was summoned to the office. I didn't see him again after that."

Graham and Charlie thanked the man and told him he was free to go. Charlie instantly got on his mobile phone and called Sonny Warren to inform him that Mortimer had lied and that the boy had gone back to the club on the night in question.

Joey Chambers had returned home to find his wife's keys lying on the hall mat. He picked them up and walking through to the kitchen laid them onto the worktop. He'd spent most of the day at his father's and when Lizzie returned from the hospital they had arranged to go back together for the evening visit. He'd had a change of heart regarding confiding in his sister, she had enough on her plate as it was. Now Joey removed a pad, pen and envelopes from the wall unit he used as an office and placed them onto the work surface so that they were ready to take to Michael later. About to climb the stairs for a quick shower and freshen up, he suddenly noticed that his jacket was missing. Entering the front room he frantically searched it from top to bottom before moving on to the dining room and kitchen but the jacket was nowhere to be seen. His mind wasn't in a good place and even though he'd been positive that he'd hung it up earlier, now he wasn't so sure. Running up the stairs Joey Chambers flung open all the wardrobe doors and didn't even notice that Sharon's side was completely bare. Sitting down on the bed he racked his brains trying to think where it could be and he suddenly realised his wife, for some strange reason, must have taken it. Removing his mobile he dialled her number and anxiously waited for a reply. Sharon Chambers was about to sit down to her evening meal when her phone started to ring. Linda Jackson sighed in a disapproving manner but Sharon totally ignored her mother when she saw who was calling. Getting up from the table she quickly made her way into the hall and closed the door so that her parents couldn't hear the conversation.

"Hi Babe."

"Don't fucking high babe me! Where's my jacket?"

Sharon had been so sure that he was phoning to ask her to go home and her heart sank when she realised that he wasn't calling for that reason at all.

"Joey you sound really irate, look it was old and past its best so I took it to the charity shop with some of my stuff. Dad said there are plenty of homeless people who'd be only too glad of our unwanted clothes."

Joey couldn't believe what he was hearing and angrily shook his head as she spoke.

"Well you can just fucking go down there and get it back, do you hear?"

Sharon could feel the onset of tears but she bit down hard on her lip to stop them. The last thing she wanted was to antagonise him in anyway.

"Babe they're closed now but first thing in the morning I'll go down and see if it's still there."

"For your sake it had fucking better be!"

With that Joey hung up and Sharon was left standing in the hall staring at her phone. Joey mentally went over all that had happened earlier and he tried to think of any items that were in the jacket. The cash was hidden upstairs so that wasn't an issue and he'd disposed of the weapons so there was no worry there, the only thing left was the lottery ticket that he'd picked up from Mortimer's desk and he couldn't see how that would incriminate him in anyway. Now feeling better about the situation he quickly showered and had just finished dressing when the house phone began to ring. Sprinting, he made it downstairs in three rings and just before the answer machine kicked in. At first he didn't recognise who the caller was as they were crying and stammering all at the same time.

"Lizzie is that you?"

Lizzie Chambers calmed herself the best she could but her words still came out rapidly.

"Oh Joey I've just had a call from the hospital, we need to get down there as soon as possible as they think a donor has just become available."

"I'll be round in a few minutes to get you."

Joey hung up and grabbing the stationary and his car keys, he ran from the house. He must have broken every speed limit but luck was on his side and he didn't see one member of the police on his way to Islington. Pulling up on Ritchie Street, Joey didn't have to switch the engine off as his father and sister were already outside standing on the kerb. As soon as they were in the car and the doors were closed Joey sped off in the direction of Bart's hospital. The car screeched to a halt and Lizzie ran on ahead but Joey stayed by his father's side, Mike was too old to run but he did his best to quicken his step. When the men entered Michaels room Lizzie was sitting on the side of her son's bed holding his hand.

"Any news?"

"Not yet Joey, we're waiting for Mr Armstrong to come and tell us what's going on."

Joey smiled at his nephew and winked.

"See Mikey, I told you that you shouldn't give up." Michael gave a smile but it was feeble to say the least, oh he was happy that he was going to get a chance to live but since yesterday he'd felt so weak and was slowly loosing the will to fight. It was strange but he really didn't mind, he was so drained and if the only alternative to death was a life spent in a hospital bed, then he really would be happy to die. His thoughts weren't something he would ever let his mother know but deep down he had a hunch that his uncle Joey knew how he was thinking.

As soon as the organ donation card had been found in Tommy Mortimer's pocket, his body had been moved to Bart's. After blood had been taken and it was established that he had a rare group, the transplant team were placed on standby ready to harvest as many organs as they could. Finn Armstrong was over the moon when the call came through that the deceased was a match for Michael Chambers. It was something he didn't think would ever happen but he hadn't passed that on as it was crucial that the patient and family remained positive right up until the end. Now he was on his way to Michael's room to pass on the good news and he had a real spring in his step. As Finn entered he wore a wide grin on his face.

"Well Michael, looks like lady luck is shining on you. We have a donor that is a perfect match; in fact it couldn't have been a better match if you were related to each other."

As the words left the consultants mouth Lizzie shot her brother a look that silently said 'oh my god'. Her mouth was wide open and she couldn't believe what she'd just heard.

"My team are busy harvesting at the moment and as soon as they're finished we'll be taking you down to theatre."

With that Finn Armstrong left the room and Lizzie nodded towards the door which let Joey know in no uncertain terms that she wanted to speak to him outside. When they were alone in the corridor Lizzie turned on him sharply.

"Please tell me you didn't."

"Didn't what?"

"Don't play fucking silly buggers Joey; you know exactly what I'm talking about."

Joey tried to take hold of her arm but Lizzie Chambers wasn't having any of it and roughly shrugged him off.

"Look Sis, the bastard deserved it and now Michaels got a chance. Aint that what you wanted?"

"You know it is but not at the expense of someone else's life. Where the fuck do you get off playing God? No one has that right Joey no matter how much they want to help another person."

"Look you didn't know him."

"Didn't I?"

Joey wished he could take back the words, his sister had suffered terribly at the hands of Tommy Mortimer and it now seemed as if he was dismissing what she'd been through as trivial.

"I know you did but I didn't mean that. Lizzie he was a cunt through and through and like you said, I thought about the boat scenario."

Now Lizzie was really angry, it felt as though Joey was trying to wriggle out of what he'd done and was using her as a scapegoat but she wasn't going to allow that to happen.

"I didn't mean it literally and you know that so stop trying to pass the fucking buck!"

Joey didn't know what else to say, ever since he'd killed Tommy Mortimer he'd been in turmoil and the one person he thought would understand was now condemning him. The only thing to console him was the thought that after Michaels transplant, his sister would be so grateful that she would forgive him and things would go back to normal.

Lizzie Chambers studied her brother's face and could see that he was struggling but at the same time she couldn't believe what he had done and wondered if there was another side to him, a very bad side that she had never known existed. Only able to muster a weak smile she then walked back into the hospital room. Her father was still sitting beside Michael and he was reading out crossword clues to his grandson. Michael was doing his best to answer but Lizzie could see that he didn't really want to.

"I think that's about enough for now Dad, he looks tired so maybe we should let him rest."

Michael grinned at his mother and she could see that it was his way of saying thank you. The next two hours were tense as they all waited for the surgical team to come and nerves were frayed to say the least. Since their earlier conversation, no words had passed between Joey and Lizzie and it didn't go unnoticed by their father. He knew that whatever had been said outside in the corridor couldn't have been very good. Out of all of his children, these two were the closest and Lizzie was a very giving and trusting girl so Joey must have done something bad. Mike wanted to ask them what was wrong but this was neither the time nor the place so he decided to wait until they got home. Thankfully Michael had fallen asleep when the door opened and Finn Armstrong's secretary entered and approached Lizzie.

"I'm sorry to trouble you Miss Chambers but Mr Armstrong is requesting that you go to his office."

Lizzie didn't question the woman further and as she followed her outside, looked over her shoulder at Joey silently asking him to go with her. Two minutes later and the secretary escorted them into Finns office. After she'd offered them tea and they

268

had both declined, she disappeared into the reception area to continue her duties. Lizzie instinctively knew that something was wrong and as they waited she reached out and grabbed her brother's hand.

"I'm scared Joey."

"I know you are but let's just wait and see what he has to say."

As if on cue Finn Armstrong then walked through the door and took a seat behind his desk. This was one of the hardest things he had ever had to do and he wasn't looking forward to it one bit.

"I'm sorry to drag you down here Miss Chambers but I thought it best that we had this conversation away from the ears of Michael and your father." Lizzie's nerves were now in a terrible state and she just wished that whatever he was going to say, he would just get on with it and not drag it out any longer.

"There is no easy way to say this, so I suppose it's best if I just come straight out with it. I'm very sorry but the transplant will not be going ahead." Lizzie clasped her palm to her mouth and as she gulped, tears formed in her eyes. She was so upset that she couldn't talk so it was Joey who continued with the conversation.

"But why? I don't understand, I thought you said it was a perfect match?"

"And it is but we have to follow protocol. Look when any transplant is carried out there are legal

obligations that the hospital has to follow. It seems
that blood tests were carried out as soon as the body
was brought in and somebody jumped the gun
when the donor card was found. It has since been
looked into further by the hospitals legal team and
I'm sorry to say that the donor card hadn't been
signed. Personally if it was up to me it wouldn't
matter but there's no way the hospital would ever
agree to that, it would leave them open to numerous
court actions."

"So all of this has been for nothing then?"

Lizzie shot her brother a look. She knew he wasn't
referring to the weeks of waiting they had endured
and she was now scared he was about to reveal all.

"Like I said Mr Chambers, I'm very very sorry but
it's out of my hands."

Lizzie stood up and wiping her eyes thanked Finn
Armstrong and then walked towards the door.

"Come on Joey, we have to go back and break the
news to Michael."

On their walk through the corridors to Michaels
room Lizzie and Joey didn't speak and Lizzie hoped
that her brother could just hold it together long
enough so that they could tell Michael without any
further upset. Joey opened the door and went
straight over to his nephew's bed and when Mike
looked at his daughter for an answer, she could
only shake her head. Michael was a bright boy and
could sense something was wrong but strangely he
wasn't worried and right at this moment all he

wanted was for his family to go home and for him to be left to sleep.

"Aint good news is it Uncle Joey?"

"Afraid not Mikey."

"It's ok I don't mind, I mean it was a long shot in the first place. We'll all just have to keep hoping and maybe another donor will come up."

Lizzie could feel her eyes fill with tears, she was so proud of her boy and like he said, they all just had to keep hoping even though they knew that Mikey had been handed a death sentence and it was just a matter of time.

"Don't cry mum, I'm fine honestly. Why don't you all go home and then I can have a sleep because I'm right tired now."

Lizzie sniffed loudly and nodded her head as she did so. Kissing her son she told him she would be back that night for visiting. Mike Chambers waited until they were all in the car until he asked the question that had been bothering him for the last hour. Turning in his seat so that he faced both his son and daughter he spoke in a calm but firm voice. "So you two, what's going on and don't bother telling me that it's nothing because I know that aint the truth."

Both Joey and Lizzie were in agreement that what had gone on between them wasn't something their father should know about. If Joey Chambers didn't get caught, then it was a secret that would stay with them and only them until the day they both died.

Lizzie nervously coughed as she spoke.

"Dad it isn't anything for you to worry about, what with all the tension and Joey and Sharon splitting up, we just got a bit ratty with each other but we're alright now aint we Joey?"

Joey Chambers turned to his sister and smiled and at the same time winked. He knew she meant what she was saying and if she had forgiven him then maybe in time he could forgive himself. Mike didn't push the matter, he was just glad that his kids were talking again. Clipping his seatbelt in, he stared forward.

"Come on Joey what are you waiting for. I need a good strong cuppa; my throat is a dry as a nun's fanny."

"Dad!"

They all laughed and as Joey Chambers fired up the Range Rover, the mood for a while at least, was happier.

CHAPTER TWENTY TWO

Finding Ian Hewitt's body was still playing heavily on the mind of Madeline Dumont and as a result she hadn't got much sleep but when her alarm burst into life at six thirty am, Maddy stretched out her arms and then got straight out of bed. Her routine had been exactly the same for the last ten years and she wasn't about to change it now. Even though her age was making her slow down somewhat, there was no way she would ever give up the work she did, well not until they put her in a box and that she hoped was still a long way off. Making her way through to the small kitchen she put the kettle on to boil and while she waited removed six china saucers from the cabinet and placed them onto a tray. After she'd made herself a cup of earl grey tea she poured milk onto the saucers and then peered out of the French doors. The once meticulous garden was now very overgrown but that wasn't what she was looking at. They hadn't arrived yet but everyday she could have set her watch by them. Glancing at the wall clock, Maddy saw that it was six forty four and as she watched the second hand tick by she kept peering out of the doors.
"Bingo!"
Six little faces all sitting in a row were now staring back at her and Maddy giggled as she picked up the tray of milk and walked outside. Patiently they waited until the six saucers were in place and then

they all began to drink at once.

"Now take your time and don't be greedy. Oh you are all good pussy cats aren't you."

Maddy had been caring for the local stray cats for as long as she'd been helping the homeless and when one of them disappeared another would instantly take its place. The inside of Madeleine Dumont's flat was as messy as it was on the outside but she really couldn't care less. Piles of clothing filled every work surface and table until they had been sorted and were then handed out each night when Maddy went on what she liked to call her rounds. Today was her collection day and she would visit as many of the charity shops as she could. There was a time when she could have gone on all day but recently her age had begun to catch up with her and what with the night shifts, it was sometimes just too much. When the local cats had been fed and Maddy had drank her earl grey and eaten the one meagre slice of toast and marmalade she allowed herself each morning, she pulled on her anorak and taking her beaten up old shopping trolley out onto the path, closed the front door and set about her daily tasks. Several of her neighbours were outside collecting their milk and newspapers but they didn't give Madeleine Dumont so much as the time of day. It didn't bother her as Maddy wasn't a very social person, well at least not when it came down to the snooty residents of Notting Hill. Making her way to the High street, her first port of call was to Help the

Aged. Pushing open the shop door Maddy wheeled her trolley inside. Grace Harrod was in the middle of tidying the rails when the bell above the door rang out. Glancing up and seeing Maddy, she sighed heavily and muttered under her breath 'get the air freshener out'. Maddy was far from stupid and although she hadn't heard the woman's words, knew exactly what she was thinking. Smiling sweetly as she'd been taught to do by her parents, Maddy made her way over to Grace.

"Good morning Grace and how are you today?" Grace Harrod looked Maddy up and down and dismissed the woman as she spoke.

"Busy!"

Grace then turned her back on the woman and began to furiously rub at the chrome rails. Maddy wanted to sigh but stopped herself, people were so sad when they didn't even have a few seconds to pass the time of day with someone. She was about to ask if Celia was in but thought better of it, Grace was a nasty woman and her aura spoke volumes. Madeleine Dumont had always had a great interest in spiritual practices and over the years had convinced herself that she could actually see people's outer aura. Walking through to the back storeroom she tapped on the door and always one to show her manners and be polite, she waited to be asked in. Celia Montpelier opened the door and when she saw who it was, smiled from ear to ear. Now this woman's aura was about as nice as you could get and Maddy loved her weekly visits.

"Good morning Madeleine and how are you today?"

"Very well thank you Celia."

"Come through and take the weight off of your feet, would you like a coffee?"

Time was moving on and Maddy was about to decline the woman's offer when she thought better of it. A few extra minutes wouldn't make any difference one way or another and after her thoughts earlier regarding Grace, she accepted graciously. Celia Montpelier had excellent manners and not once did she show her distaste regarding Maddy's body odour. In reality it wasn't really a personal hygiene issue but more the fact that her clothes smelled musty. Maddy didn't care when her own belongings got mixed up with the donations, and it couldn't be helped when her clothes sometimes smelled because of it.

"Have you had much brought in that you don't want?"

Placing two cups of coffee onto the table Celia Montpelier sat down and joined her friend, for that was how she'd come to look upon Maddy.

"Well it's funny that you should ask because actually we have."

Celia pointed to the rack at the rear which made Maddy turn and look and when she saw the row of clothes her eyes opened wide. About to thank the woman she was halted when the door opened and Grace Harrod walked in. Seeing the two having coffee together and the fact that she hadn't been offered a drink really riled Grace and although she didn't say anything the look on her face spoke volumes. Staring at Maddy she spoke in a curt rude manner.

"I've been thinking Celia; if we started to wash the clothes instead of giving them away we could make far more money."

On hearing this Maddy became worried, Help the Aged was one of her best stops and without it there wouldn't be nearly enough to go round but Celia's reply swiftly put a smile back on Maddy's face.

"We make enough money thank you very much Grace and shame on you to want to stop giving to the homeless. Without people like Maddy I don't know what this city would do because it's certainly getting worse. Now if you wouldn't mind returning to the shop, we were in the middle of a private conversation."

Grace stormed off and slammed the door as she went.

"Were we?"

"What?"

"Were we in the middle of a private conversation?"

"I just said that and I know it may appear dismissive but that woman really grates on my nerves at times."

"You and me both Celia, now I really do need to be on my way."

Madeleine Dumont stood up and walking over to

the rack of clothes, began to cram as many as she could into her trolley. When it was full but the rack looked as though it had hardly been touched, she informed Celia that she would call in again later that afternoon. Returning home she began to sort through the clothes and was really pleased with the condition and quality of some of the items. She was sure that sometimes Celia included things that could have been sold in the shop and it warmed Maddy's heart that there were still some kind folk left in the world. At two o'clock she set off once more and after collecting the rest of the donations and returning home again, she was absolutely worn out. Taking a seat in the overstuffed armchair, she closed her eyes and fell into a deep sleep.

A few minutes after Maddy had left the charity shop, Sharon Chambers entered. She hated even being here let alone having to ask for something back. Grace Harrod remembered the woman from yesterday and all the items had been of top quality. If the woman had more to bring in and if she was friendly towards her customer, Grace could possibly lay her hands on a few choice things before Celia had a chance to see them.

"Can I help you?"

Sharon looked at the woman and for a moment contemplated leaving and just telling Joey that they didn't have the jacket but she wanted to save her marriage and if going cap in hand to a charity shop would help her accomplish that, then she would do it gladly.

"Oh yes, I brought some items in yesterday and my husband's old work jacket was amongst them. It's really tatty and heaven knows why he wants it but he does. Is there any way you could have a quick look for me and see if it's still here?"

"Why of course Madam."

Sharon could sense that the woman was being smarmy but she thanked her all the same. Grace disappeared into the back room and after informing Celia Montpelier they began to search for the jacket. In all honesty it was like looking for a needle in a haystack as they were receiving so many donations on a daily basis. Five minutes later and as they both approached Sharon, she could tell by the look on their faces that they didn't have it.

"I'm so sorry but I think it might have already gone. If it hasn't been sold, we have a lady that comes in twice a week to collect our unwanted items for distribution to the homeless and it could have been in with the things she took. She won't be in again for a couple of days, when she does I could ask her if she still has it but it's very doubtful I'm afraid."

Sharon thanked Grace but told her not to bother. She didn't leave her name or address and as she walked out of the shop her spirits were low. She had hoped that returning the jacket to Joey would show her in a good light but now he would just be angry and there wasn't anything she could do about it.

At her flat, Maddy only meant to have a quick nap but it was gone six by the time she woke up. Picking out as many things as she knew would fit into her trolley; Madeleine carefully went through the pockets. It was rare for her to ever find anything but she always checked just the same. A few dried up tissues, a sweet that looked like it had been sucked several times and an old lottery ticket was the sum total of what she found and putting them onto the side table, she packed the trolley to capacity and then set off on her way. The nights had begun to pull in but the darkness didn't bother Maddy, she was doing charitable work and if something should happen to her then she saw it as god's will.

Her first port of call was Victoria railway station and Maddy knew exactly where to look for her clients as she liked to call them. The most favoured place to sleep was near to the ventilation grids where hot air was blown out but when those spaces were taken up, the homeless would congregate under the railway arches to sleep. For most it was safer than the shop doorways where they were either being set upon by drunks or moved on by the police. Spying Jock McGregor she walked over and unzipped her trolley. Jock had been a resident here for as long as Maddy had been doing her charity work and he smiled broadly when he saw her approach. He smelled strongly of alcohol but that was nothing new and retrieving a thick Aran jumper she handed it over.

"Here you go Jock, this should help keep out at least some of the cold."

"Miss Dumont, you are a saint and no mistake."

"Don't be so silly Jock I'm only doing what many others do."

"There aint many who turn out on a fucking freezing night like you do."

"Is there much of a turn out this evening?"

"A few down the arches but a lot have gone over to Charing Cross. Be careful Miss Dumont, that wanker Tully's been let out earlier and he's spoiling for a fight."

"I'll be careful, now you take care of yourself Jock and stay safe."

With that Maddy was once again on her way and after she had dished out several coats and jumpers and when the trolley was half empty, she began the walk over to Charing Cross Station. It wasn't unusual for her to cover ten miles a night there and back and sometimes her poor old legs throbbed by the time she got home but there was no way that she would waste money on a taxi. As far as Maddy was concerned it was an indulgence that just wouldn't sit right with her, not when so many other people were in real need. By the time she arrived, several of her regulars had settled down for the night and removing two blankets from her trolley, she handed them over to the first couple of people she came to. Blankets were always gratefully received but they were also in short supply, people seemed to donate clothes but bedding was another matter altogether. Walking along a little further she spied Tully Clement. Swigging from a bottle he was slightly swaying from side to side but she wasn't scared. Tully Clement was homeless whenever he chose to be or when his current girlfriend had kicked him out. He was a nasty cruel man who took the opportunity to wind up the regulars at the first chance he got. Old Melvin was standing close to Tully and as Maddy went over to him Tully began to shout out.

"Well fuck me if it aint fucking Mother Teresa herself. You soppy old cow, think you're doing good? Why don't you just fuck off and die you stupid bitch!"

Old Melvin who had lived on the streets for longer than he would ever admit to and must have been nearing seventy years of age, stepped forward and his face was full of rage.

"Just shut up Tully, without this woman we would all probably freeze to death. You come down here whenever the fancy takes you but unlike you, some of us have no choice."

As Old Melvin turned and smiled at Maddy, Tully swung the bottle he'd been holding and cracked Melvin on the side of the head knocking him to the floor. Instantly Maddy was on her knees trying to stop the flow of blood but it seemed to be coming from everywhere. Things were about to get out of

282

hand even further but as Tully staggered and loomed over Maddy a police van screeched to a halt. Tully Clement was bundled into the back and a call was put in for an ambulance to attend. It took several minutes for things to calm down and as the van pulled away, Tully Clements was still kicking the metal panels from inside. Luckily Melvin wasn't that badly hurt and after a few stitches, he was now enjoying a nice warm bed on one of the wards and looking forward to a hot breakfast in the morning. Tully wouldn't experience such luxury, a cold cell, single blanket and a cup of stewed tea along with a charge for assault was the sum total of his night under arrest. It was such a regular occurrence that the few hours of community service he would receive for kicking off didn't bother him in the least. When the scene was at last clear and the police had made sure that Madeleine Dumont was alright, she was once more standing alone on the pavement. More than a little shook up, Maddy decided to call it a night and began her journey home. It was after ten when she placed her key in the lock and pouring herself a large brandy she was so glad to be home. The encounter with Tully had upset her more than she'd realised and as she lifted the glass to her lips, she could see her hands visibly shaking. Switching on the gas fire she sat in her chair and huddled over trying to get warm. It had been a good day what with her collections and seeing some of her old friends down at Victoria but

Tully Clement had spoiled it all and that made Maddy feel sad. Switching on the television to watch the news, she suddenly remembered the lottery ticket. It was a long shot but it was worth a try. Holding her back as she walked over to the table she knew that she wouldn't be able to carry on with her work for much longer and a winning ticket would answer all of her prayers. Pressing the remote until the text page appeared; she moved the arrow down until the correct date popped up. Maddy checked the numbers three times before it finally sunk in that it was a winner and worth millions. For a few minutes she thought about how she would spend it, how many clothes she could buy and maybe even several hot food wagons. Beginning to get excited, she instantly stopped herself when she remembered that it didn't really belong to her and there was no way that she could keep it. First thing in the morning she would return it along with the Jacket and see if the shop would be able to trace the rightful owner, if they couldn't then Maddy decided she would take it to the police station. It was the right and honourable thing to do and in any case she was a strong believer of the saying 'be careful what you wish for'. Things were running smoothly and she was able to do her bit for society, for the moment at least. No, Madeleine Dumont knew she had made the right decision, if she was meant to have a lot of money then it would happen when it was her turn and not before.

CHAPTER TWENTY THREE

Just as she'd planned, Madeline Dumont headed for
the Help the Aged shop but was surprised to find a
'closed due to staff shortage' sign posted on the
door. Celia had a hospital appointment she didn't
want to cancel and Grace Harrod had refused to
come in on her day off. Maddy thought for a
moment and then decided to continue with her plan
B and went straight round to Ladbroke Road Police
station. Walking up to the counter she was given a
strange look by the community support officer who
was on duty. Recently and whether it was down to
old age or simply that she was just so busy, Maddy
was starting to resemble the people she was trying
to help. Her hair hadn't been combed and was
sticking out all over the place and her coat had
various marks and food stains down the front.
Harry Winters had taken early retirement from his
job at the post office and even though the lump sum
had been a bonus, with eight years still left until he
could draw his state pension he needed a regular
wage. When the community position came up he
had grabbed it with both hands. The fulltime
bobby's saw the new staff members as a help but
also a hindrance, especially when they thought they
had the same powers as regular policemen. There
had been plenty of cross words at the station since
the introduction of community officers but it always
went straight over Harry Winters head and in all

honesty he was really enjoying his work, all except having to deal with the homeless. They were more often than not drunk, they smelled and were mostly obnoxious. Maddy glanced down at her clothing and when she noticed the state of her coat, instantly knew what he was thinking. As usual she ignored it and smiling sweetly began to speak. When Harry Winters heard her polished accent he was somewhat shocked.

"Good morning, I wonder if you could help me please."

"What seems to be the problem Madam?"

Again Maddy smiled.

"Well it's not really a problem as such officer."

Harry Winters was somewhat arrogant and judgemental as he looked Maddy up and down. He couldn't smell alcohol on the woman's breath but with a reinforced screen between them which only had a small gap at the bottom, he couldn't be sure she wasn't inebriated like so many of her kind.

"Then what is it? I am busy you know, some of us work for a living."

"I recycle unwanted clothes and hand them out to the homeless and even though I might look like one myself, I can assure you I am not. Anyway I've found a lottery ticket in one of the jackets and I haven't got a clue who it belongs to."

"Is it a winner?"

Harry Winter thought that what he'd said was funny and began to laugh out loud but stopped when he saw that Maddy wasn't joining in.

"That's not for me to say and should the rightful owner claim it then only he or she will know. I have taken the liberty of initialling the back just so that I can prove it's the one I handed in; after all there are some very unscrupulous characters about you know."

Harry didn't like the woman's insinuation but wasn't in a position to complain. Removing a lost/found property form from his folder he began to fill it in by taking Maddy's full name and address. When she told him where she lived he didn't know if she was joking and commented that it was a very nice road.

"It was once officer but not anymore. How long does the rightful owner have to claim their property?"

"By law six weeks but in all honesty it's more like seven the way the wheels roll in this place."

Maddy signed the form and after she was given a duplicate copy, she left the station. The next day she headed for the Help the Aged shop to tell Celia all about it. Luckily Grace wasn't working so the atmosphere in the shop was jolly and relaxed. As soon as Celia Montpelier laid eyes on Maddy she ushered her through to the rear. Making them both a coffee they sat down together and Maddy was just about to reveal all when Celia started talking about a young woman who had called in looking for an old jacket.

"Do you think it was one of the Jackets that I gave to you?"

"It could have been Celia but you gave me so many that it's hard to tell. Why did she want it back?"

"I'm not sure but she didn't leave her name or address so there's nothing we can do about it anyway. From what she said it had sentimental value to her husband that's all."

Hearing Celia's last sentence made Maddy feel better and she then went on to explain about the ticket and that the police said if it wasn't claimed in six weeks it would be hers.

"Was it a winner then?"

Maddy nodded her head and smiled.

"Well good for you Maddy, it's about time something nice happened to you."

"It would be great Celia but not for me, for the homeless, I've always wanted to open up my own little shop to help them all. It's nice to dream but I'm not building my hopes up, I'll just have to wait and see what happens. It is bothering me that it could belong to the woman you mentioned though."

"My dear Maddy, that's something we will never know. I mean can you imagine what would happen if we advertised the fact? They would be banging on the door in thousands saying that it was theirs. I'm sure if it had been the woman's jacket that held the ticket she would have made more of it and at least left her name and address. I think you should put all thoughts of it to the back of your mind and get on with doing what you do best, helping people."

Several weeks had now passed since the murders of Ian Hewitt and Tommy Mortimer. Sonny Warrens department were becoming increasingly frustrated as there were no new leads and everything now rested on the DNA results. When the report finally arrived on his desk Sonny was shocked, for once the lab had taken their instructions seriously and pushed the testing through quickly. Cautiously opening up the large manila envelope he was actually nervous regarding what the report was about to tell him. Sonny needn't have worried and within a few minutes he was running into the incident room and shouting for all of his team to gather round.

"Right you lot! Seems we have a breakthrough, well it's a bit more than a breakthrough. The DNA results have just come back and it looks like we have our killer bang to rights. Ian Hewitt's blood was found in Tommy Mortimer's office so we now have a place of death. What we weren't aware of was the fact that bodily fluid which is suspected to be phlegm and was found on Ian Hewitt's body, was also found on the corpse of Big Boy Davidson. We are now certain that the two murders are linked which is a surprise and our murderer has a dirty little habit, a habit that's going to cost him his liberty for a very long time."

"So it's a positive match Chief?"

"Indeed it is Chilvers. He has form and the man in question is none other than Taffy Jones. I've been waiting to get my hands on this particular evil bastard for years. We already had his DNA on file from a while back when he was charged with grievous bodily harm but the case fell through. He's a slippery bastard and I want you all to take extreme caution, he will use anything as a weapon if it means evading capture. When we go in to arrest him I want armed response as a backup. Go about your work but keep in radio contact as the plan is to take him down tonight. There will be a briefing at three pm, so until then keep your mouths shut. Brewer, Mason, I've got a little job for the two of you."

Detectives Charlie Brewer and Graham Mason once again parked up the car on Lyme Grove and were not looking forward to the visit they were about to make. They were not allowed to breathe a word about the breakthrough regarding the murders of Ian Hewitt, Tommy Mortimer or Big Boy Davidson. As far as the Hewitt's were concerned Sonny had sent them over to St Thomas's square as a matter of courtesy. Even though DD had been interview within a few hours of being attacked, he wouldn't say a word and Charlie Brewer knew that it was for one of two reasons. Either he would soon be out for revenge or he was scared shitless of his attacker, either way Charlie could see that this wasn't over by a long way and just hoped that the suspect was arrested before the Davidson's got to him. As they entered the square Detective Brewer was relieved to see that all was quiet and that the gathering of angry people they had come across on their last visit were no more. Apart from two dogs fighting over a heavily soiled baby's nappy, the place was relatively calm. Rubbish was still strewn everywhere but then that was nothing out of the ordinary for this place. Refuse bags had been split open by the local cats and fried chicken bones and the remnants of french fries now lay rotting on the concrete. Graham Mason grimaced at the sight and it didn't go unnoticed by his partner.

"How the fuck do people live like this? I really couldn't stand it Charlie it would drive me nuts."

"It's just a few that spoil it for the majority. Take the people we're about to go and see, nice decent folk but once you live in a place like this there's little chance of moving anywhere else. The only hope they have is if the council regenerate the area but then the rents will go up and the locals can't afford it so they move out of the borough or if they stay, then the council move them to somewhere even more fucking rank."

"Then they should get a job and buy their own homes."

Charlie looked at his partner with disbelief.

"What? Sometimes you're such a knob Graham."

Three or four young boys on cycles eyed the men suspiciously but they didn't say anything.

"Look at those little cunts; there goes the next generation of no hopers."

"Tell me what chance have they got Graham? You can't blame the fucking kids; their lives are mapped out while their mothers are still pushing them around in prams."

"Then the dirty whores should keep their legs shut, that's what I say!"

No more was said as they climbed the stairwell, after all this time Charlie Brewer still didn't get Graham's sick sense of humour and he was well past trying to explain it. Charlie knocked on the door and then stepping sideways, held out his hand as if to say 'you can do the honours'.

John and Sue sat together in silence and when his wife made no attempt to go and see who was calling, John Hewitt slowly made his way into the hall. Twisting the Yale lock open he peered around the edge of the door and even though he recognised the officers, his face wore a blank expression. He didn't invite the men inside but leaving the door open was a silent invitation. When Charlie and Graham entered the front room the couple sat together on the sofa. The curtains were half drawn leaving the room in semi darkness. Charlie switched on the light and as Sue screwed up her eyes at the glare, he knew she must have been sitting like this for hours if not days.

"Hello Mrs Hewitt, we've come to give you an update on the case although in reality there is little more to tell you. It's been decided that Ian's body can now be released for burial so if you want to start making arrangements the paperwork will be finalised within the next couple of days."

Sue Hewitt looked up into the detectives face and her eyes were pleading as she spoke.

"Do you think you will ever catch the bastard who killed our son?"

Charlie sat down on the footstool directly in front of her and took Sue's hands in his.

"I really can't answer that Mrs Hewitt, we've had cases that remain unsolved for years and then suddenly there's a breakthrough. I aint saying that's what's going to happen regarding Ian but it's always best to stay hopeful. It could just have been a case of Ian being in the wrong place at the wrong time. Now I know that doesn't make a difference to you either way but..."

"You're wrong there Officer. My lad was a good boy and if someone didn't deliberately set out to kill him then I suppose that's something. Cold blooded murder, to me at least, is a very different matter. I know that doesn't make sense to you, it doesn't really make sense to me but I have to have something to cling onto, do you understand that?"

Charlie Brewer slowly nodded his head, as crazy as it was, what she was saying did make sense. As soon as they had left the flat, Sue was on her feet.

"What are you doing sweetheart?"

"We not me! We are going down to Caruthers

funeral directors and get the wheels in motion. Our boy is going to have a fantastic send off."

Initially the couple had planned to arrange Ian's funeral long before now but the lack of money and with no idea when their son's body would be released, the Hewitt's had held off. It was now full steam ahead but John didn't have the heart to remind her that they still didn't have a pot to piss in let alone pay for a funeral. All of the credit cards were maxed out and over the last few days the letters had begun to stack up on the side of the worktop. He hadn't had the energy to open them but all the same, John Hewitt knew exactly what they were. He would keep his promise to his wife and somehow find the money but he was dreading what the total would be. John smiled warmly and tried to concentrate on something else, he was just pleased to see his wife back on her feet..

"Well best we get a move on then."

Sue quickly brushed her hair and pulling on her coat, the couple were on their way in minutes. Caruthers Funeral parlour was situated on Mare street and after pushing hard on the glass door, Sue Hewitt was the first to go inside. The place was eerie and appeared to be stuck in some kind of Victorian time warp. The reception was dimly lit with overstuffed antique armchairs set out in one area for consultations. An overhead bell rang out as the couple walked in and they were soon joined by Eli Caruthers but Sue didn't like the man from the offset. He was smartly dressed in a black suit but his protruding teeth made him look scary almost like something out of a horror film. He was hunched over and continually rubbed his palms together as he spoke, still the couple weren't here for socialising and making sure Ian had a good send off was the only thing that mattered.

"Good morning! How can I be of help Mrs?"

"Hewitt, the names Hewitt and we would like to arrange the funeral of our son. He was murdered and the police have just informed us that they are releasing our boy."

"Oh how dreadful for you both."

It made no difference to Eli one way or another, the only thing that mattered was the amount of money the couple were prepared to spend. Past experience had taught him that the more tragic the circumstance, the more elaborate the send off would be and it was good news for Eli as things had been relatively quiet for the last few weeks. After taking down a few details, he then began the hard sell. John wanted to say that everything should be from the basic range but one look from his wife as he began to speak, instantly made him shut up.

"I want nothing but the best for my only son Mr Caruther's, so can I leave it in your hands?"

"It would be a pleasure Mrs Hewitt but there is a rather delicate matter that I need to speak to you about, the remuneration."

"The what?"

"Payment. I'm sorry and I know it's not in the best taste but we are a struggling business after all. Now we are looking somewhere in the figure of between four and five thousand."

Ian gasped but Sue didn't bat an eyelid.

"That's not a problem. Make all the arrangements and then get back to me with a date. Obviously we would like it to be as soon as possible."

With that Sue got up and made her way outside with John following in hot pursuit. He knew he needed to try and make her see sense, so stopping at the first cafe they came to he ordered tea and they took a seat by the window.

"I aint going to argue with you darling and I know your heart is broken but we really need to talk about the cost of all this."

Sue was about to speak but stopped when her husband gently squeezed her hand.

"I know what you're going to say but sweetheart we just aint got that sort of money, come to that we aint got any fucking money! I can sell off a lot of stuff but it won't be nearly enough, the repo letters are starting to build up and this will just make matters worse."

John hoped he had got through to her and when Sue smiled he thought he had but after the teas were placed onto the table and the waitress had disappeared, she looked at him in a way that told him what he'd said made no difference at all.

"I accept all that you've said John but it's our boy

we're talking about here. I'm well aware that we're in debt up to our eyeballs, so a bit more aint going to make any difference. I feel like my life is over and whether that feeling ever goes is irrelevant. I don't care if they throw me in jail as long as Ian isn't given a paupers burial. He deserves a lot better than that John."

How could he argue with her? Their lives were never going to be the same again and if spending a few grand, even if it was a few grand they didn't have, would make his wife feel better, then that's what they would do and to hell with the consequences. For a few seconds it played on his mind that the funeral parlour would be hit with an unpaid bill but at least they could afford to take the loss and in all honest it was something John Hewitt couldn't worry about at the moment. As he nodded and smiled at Sue, she knew that her husband was in total agreement.

CHAPTER TWENTY FOUR

Sonny Warren had been in a meeting with his commander for over an hour and it was finally agreed that the raid on Taffy Jones's shop would take place at five pm that day. A warrant was issued and now everyone was on tender hooks as the hours ticked by. There was an added risk as members of the public would still be on the streets but it was outweighed by the advantages of carrying out the raid in daylight hours. Every detective in the department was called in and all leave was cancelled. Bulletproof vests were handed out and all men were given instructions regarding what to do and what not to do. Copies of the file on Taffy were issued to everyone and it made for colourful but also very violent reading. Sonny, Charlie and Graham were the first to set off and it was agreed that all officers would park on Brewer Street and then rendezvous on Great Pultney Street which ran parallel to Lexington. Whenever an operation was carried out in Soho parking was always an issue. The streets were narrow so cars couldn't just stop anywhere. The council had been informed in advance that something was happening and two traffic wardens had been put into position so that the area was kept clear. Armed response officers were placed at either end of Lexington in case Taffy Jones tried to make a run for it. Sonny Warren knew it was doubtful as Taffy was a fearless man and would most likely fight it out until the end. At exactly two minutes to five, Sonny Warren, Charlie Brewer, Graham Mason and five uniformed officers began the short walk to the shop. Luckily for all concerned the street was relatively quiet and as soon as they approached the building the uniformed officers barged inside. Megan Jones was seated in her usual position behind the counter and as soon as she heard the door and spied the men, she reached under the counter and pressed the alarm button. Taffy had installed the device soon after moving in and a bell would instantly ring out in the flat above, telling him that there were unwanted guests downstairs. The uniformed men charged up the stairs and attempted to break down the steel plated door with a battering ram but it was a futile exercise. Downstairs in the shop Chief Sonny Warren along with Charlie and Graham approached the counter where Megan was now standing.

"What the fuck are you doing in my shop you scum bags? This is nothing short of harassment; you bastards are always after my boy!"

Sonny walked around the counter and glancing down saw the alarm button. He had envisaged something similar but knew there was no way to stop it. Aware that Taffy already knew that the force was on the premises would now make the situation difficult but not impossible.

"I see you've already alerted your son Mrs Jones."

"Yes I have and he'll be waiting for you."

"Unless he's decided to make a run for it?"

"My boy don't run from no one you cunt! You lot are going to take a beating if I know my boy and it serves you right."

Sonny was now angry and the thought that there would be more than one casualty really pissed him off.

"Cuff her Charlie, there's a pole over there so wrap her arms around it. I'm sure you don't want to miss out on the action because you have to babysit this old bitch?"

Charlie Brewer was a bit taken aback by the chief's choice of words but he instantly did as he'd been told. Just then the door opened and three other uniformed officers entered the shop to make sure no one else came in. Sonny and his detectives, accompanied by an armed response officer, then climbed the stairs to the upper landing. The battering ram was still in use but the officer using it looked worn out and there were no signs that it was having any effect on the steel plate.

"Stop! Just stop will you. It's obvious you aint getting anywhere, did you bring the Jamb spreader?"

One of the uniformed officers nodded his head.

"Yes Sir."

"Well don't just stand there man, get the fucking thing out."

Bending down to a large holdall, the device was

300

removed and placed between the hinge and lock of the door. The mechanism was hydraulic and jacked the door jamb apart pulling the door away from the lock. Within seconds the men had gained entry and as Sonny entered he was still shaking his head at the ignorance shown by those in uniform. All of the officers carried taser's and Sonny hoped that would be enough. No one wanted bloodshed no matter how evil the person was known to be. As officers burst in, they saw the door in front slam and they would soon find out that every door in the entire flat was steel plated. The Jamb spreader was needed on two more occasions before anyone gained sight of Taffy Jones. As they entered the kitchen the first policeman inside was instantly screaming as a pan of scalding water hit him in the face. The man's skin began to bubble and peel as he fell to the floor and someone called out 'get a fucking ambulance'. Taffy then ran through into what Ian Hewitt had seen as a classy library and where Taffy kept his arsenal of weapons should he ever need them. Now dressed in a custom made coat that had carbon fibres sew into the lining, the taser guns proved useless and Taffy Jones stood with his arms outstretched. When he'd seen the amount of officers present he knew they obviously had him bang to rights for something but he was determined not to be taken without a fight.

"Right you cunts, bring it on. I aint under no illusion that you're going to take me down but a few of you fuckers will come with me."

Sonny Warren stepped forward.

"Look Taffy there aint no need for any of this, you've already badly hurt one of my officers. Why don't you come quietly and make it easy on yourself?"

"Easy! I don't do fucking easy you cunts!"

Taffy Jones stood well over six feet tall and his daily exercise regime had paid off tenfold. His body now resembled that of his hero, the notorious criminal Charlie Bronson and Taffy Jones struck the infamous fighting pose that he'd seen in the many newspaper cuttings he'd collected.

"Right take him."

Four officers charged at Taffy all at once but it was difficult as there was only a small amount of space. The first officer took the full force of Taffy's boot as it hit him straight between the legs and he screamed out in agony as he was lifted from the floor. From the side the second officer attempted to grab Taffy around the neck but Taffy rolled his shoulders downwards and the officer's arm slipped off. Rolling his shoulders back again, Taffy's huge fist made contact with the man's face instantly spreading his nose and knocking his front teeth out. As the injured policeman went down, the remaining two officers finally bundled Taffy and were able to wrestle him to the floor. A voice was heard calling out for backup and three more men came running in but not before Taffy Jones's gold teeth had bitten deep into the arm of one of the restraining officers. Taffy wasn't trying to shock; this was for real and as his body thrashed about in an attempt to escape, he spat out a lump of the officer's flesh. Seeing their colleagues hurt made the reinforcements try a different tactic. When the lead man kicked out at Taffy's side the others were quick to follow and swiftly stuck the boot in as well. Now at their mercy he could do little but take the punishment as they savagely kicked out at his arms and legs. The officer Taffy had earlier bitten was still on the floor entangled with the man and even though Taffy was being beaten, he snarled back his lips and once more sunk his teeth into the officer's arm. The screaming was horrendous and it evoked a response that would finally silence Taffy. With all the force he could muster, the policeman kicked out at the side of Taffy's head and he was knocked out cold. The bitten constable lay in shock, blood was seeping from the two vicious wounds and beside him were the lumps of flesh that had been ripped from his arm. As Sonny Warren surveyed the scene, he couldn't believe that one man could cause so much carnage in such a small space of time. He now had four policemen injured and two of those looked bad. One uniformed officer was sitting propped up against the wall, his face almost unrecognisable from the beating he had taken. Taffy was face down on the floor with two officers straddling him and a third was in the process of putting him in hand

303

cuffs. Sonny walked over to Taffy and kneeling on the floor leaned in close just as the man was coming round.

"Right you cunt! I am arresting you for the murders of Ian Hewitt and Samuel Davidson. You do not have to say anything, but it may harm your defence if you do not mention when questioned something which you later rely on in court. Anything you say may be given in evidence."

A few minutes later two paramedics entered the room and went straight over to Taffy Jones which infuriated Sonny.

"Not that cunt! See to my officers first."

When the injured policemen had been taken down to the waiting ambulance, Taffy was at last checked over. No one informed the paramedic that he'd been kicked in the head and much to Sonny Warren's pleasure, Taffy was deemed fit for arrest.

"Right, take this fucking piece of shit out of my sight!"

Back at the station and after Sonny had made sure how the uniformed officers were, he composed himself and accompanied by Charlie Brewer, entered the interview room. Taffy Jones was still handcuffed and now that he was seated at the table and being watched over by two other officers, he didn't look anywhere near as intimidating as he had done back at his flat. His solicitor Gordon Bond was seated beside his client and this was one case he didn't want to represent. Working from home as a one man band, Gordon had been Taffy's solicitor for the last five years. It wasn't for any retainer that he was on as half of the time he didn't receive anything and that included fees for court appearances. Taffy Jones was notoriously mean and the only reason Gordon had anything to do with the man was purely and simply down to fear. His one consolation was the fact that if the police had gone to so much trouble, then hopefully they had enough evidence to put Taffy away for a very long time. Of course he would never voice that fact and he still had to show willing in his defence of his client. Sonny and Charlie sat down on the opposite side of the table and after the recorder was switched on and they had introduced themselves for the record, the interview began. Sonny placed a large folder onto the table and for a few seconds he didn't speak as he flicked through the pages of notes and photographs. Removing two colour pictures he pushed them forward so that Taffy could see them. Looking down he admired his handwork and a broad grin spread across his face.

"Recognise these do you Taffy?"

"No comment."

Sonny pointed to the picture of Ian Hewitt.

"This lad was an innocent kid and you murdered him!"

"No comment."

"You can sit there saying no comment until you're blue in the face Taffy but your DNA was on him

305

and on the body of Samuel Davidson, also known as Big Boy. Dirty little habit you've got there Taffy and I might add, a very costly one."

Sonny then placed a picture of Tommy's body in front of the man. Instantly Taffy eyes opened wide and he began to speak, at the same time Gordon Bond advised his client to remain silent but Taffy Jones ignored his brief.

"No fucking way copper, I aint got nothing to do with that."

Sonny Warren terminated the interview and switched off the recorder, getting up from the table it was now his turn to smile.

"Makes no difference either way Taffy, you're going down for a long stretch and if I can clear up another of my cases by pining Mortimer's murder on you, then all the better. As you well know, Mortimer was involved somewhere along the line. It was you who killed Ian Hewitt in Mortimer's office. I think you returned to the Den and killed Tommy so that he wouldn't be able to squeal!"

"That's a fucking lie you cunt!"

"Like I said Taffy, it makes no difference either way."

As Sonny and Charlie Brewer headed towards the door Taffy was out of his seat in a second but he wasn't quick enough and the two uniformed officers who had remained silent throughout the interview were instantly on him. The restraining method used was a little heavier handed that usual,

Taffy had injured their colleagues and the policemen took great pleasure in making him suffer. Strangely Gordon Bond didn't complain, in fact he didn't utter a single word.

CHAPTER TWENTY FIVE

Ian Hewitt's funeral was held ten days later. The coffin was finished in highly polished mahogany and the floral wreath was the best that money could buy. There was nothing to mar the day and the crematorium was full to capacity with people. Teachers and old school friends that Sue and John Hewitt had never known about, filled every seat. As she entered the sight brought a smile to Sue's lips at the thought of how well her boy must have been liked. Detectives Charlie Brewer and Graham Mason followed behind the couple, the two officers had grown to like the Hewitt's but that wasn't the real reason they were attending, there was always the slightest chance that someone would turn up who was able to shed more light on what had happened. Throughout the service, Sue and John Hewitt clung to each other in the front pew of the crematorium and as 'Amazing Grace' began to play and the coffin slowly began to disappear, Sue shrieked out. It took all of John's strength to stop her running over and climbing onto the coffin of her son. There and then he knew that she was lost to him. When Ian had died a part of Sue had died along with him and John realised that he was never going to get that part back. Emerging from the service the couple were greeted by the detectives and when Sue asked Charlie Brewer to go back to the flat for refreshments he didn't feel he could refuse. To refuse would be like another slap in the face to the couple and for Charlie that would make things seem all the worse. Following behind the funeral car, Graham knew they would have to risk parking on the square and just hoped that they had some wheels left on their return. As John helped his wife out of the limousine, the couple were greeted by Eli Caruthers who was once more rubbing his hands together. John knew that the man wanted paying and he was going to have to try and bluff his way out of things just for today.

"Thank you for all that you've done Mr Caruthers. I will be down first thing in the morning to settle up with you. Now if you would excuse us, I really need to get my wife up to the flat. Please feel free to join us for a bite to eat."

This wasn't what Eli Caruthers wanted to hear but he couldn't very well push the matter. Declining Johns offer, he got straight back into his car and drove off as he had to get back to the office. There was a scheduled appointment with Maisie Davidson in less than an hour's time, her son's body was being released later that day and he didn't want to lose out on the business. Eli couldn't worry about the Hewitt's and in any case he was sure that they would settle up eventually, unlike the Davidson's. It would be like trying to get blood out of a stone from them unless he was paid upfront and Eli Caruthers would definitely be asking for a deposit. Charlie realised what had just happened, he also knew that the funeral must have set the couple back a fair few quid and it was probably money they didn't have. For a second he contemplated having a whip round back at the station but then thought better of it. This scenario was seen several times a year and he doubted he'd collect much money; still it was a nice thought. Sue had been up since six that morning and had worked really hard to put on a spread. Charlie and Graham thought they were going to have to eat for England just to make a dent in it and were relieved when Maureen and Derek Burrell from the flat above called in. It was obvious to the detectives that the couple were a real pair of busy bodies and were only here to see what they could find out.

"Terrible business and no mistake, are you family?"

"No I'm afraid not we're police officers."

Maureen and Derek instantly clamed up and didn't utter another word. They were old school and you just didn't talk to the Old Bill even if it was at a funeral. Charlie had seen this so many times over the years and it still made him laugh. He decided to have a bit of fun at the Burrell's expense and force them to speak to him.

"So how come you two weren't at the crematorium then?"

Maureen looked at her husband but Derek only shrugged his shoulders which put her in an awkward position.

"My arthritis is playing up and I couldn't stand for

that long.   I'm a real martyr to my legs aint I
Derek?"
Maureen didn't give her husband a chance to reply
and once again shrugged his shoulders as his wife
answered her own question.
"I truly am and anyway Sue understands why I
wasn't there."
Charlie knew exactly what Sue Hewitt must have
thought of her neighbours no show. It was a
disgrace and now here they were turning up to see
what free grub was on offer.
"I'm sure she does and at least you can enjoy a nice
lunch without having to travel far."
As soon as the words had left his mouth Charlie
Brewer walked out of the front room leaving
Maureen standing with her mouth wide open.
When she noticed Derek was grinning she was
about to give him a mouthful but stopped when Sue
came over.
"Everything alright? Can I get you another cup of
tea?"
Maureen placed her hand tenderly onto Sue's.
"We're all fine thanks. Darling don't you think you
should take the weight off your feet and have a
rest."
Instantly her eyes filled with tears as she looked into
her neighbours face.
"Maureen if I did that, I think I would just give up
and die."
Sue knew that while they had guests and she was

fussing around making sure everything was alright, then she would be fine. When everyone had left and it was just her and John it would be another matter and she was dreading it.

Several weeks earlier Sharon Chambers had telephoned her husband to inform him that the jacket had gone and she'd waited nervously for him to begin ranting and raving. He didn't, nor did he ask her to come home and that alone told her that her marriage was dead in the water and she should stop wishing for something that was never going to happen. Joey was now only interested in one thing and that was looking after his sister and nephew. Since the devastating news that the donor had fallen by the wayside, they were all hoping and praying that another could be found but it wasn't looking good. Joey had put the Notting hill house up for sale and on the day he was clearing out the last of his stuff, he heard an impatient knock at the door. About to put a clean bag into the bin as Sharon had left it full of rotting food, he was struggling to get it out without spilling the contents all over the floor.

"Hang on a minute cant you!"

Joey cautiously carried the bag to the front door but as he opened up all thoughts of making a mess disappeared. Without a second thought he dropped the rubbish onto the floor and as he clung to his brother he began to sob.

"Fuck me bro whatever's got into you? You aint turned into some kind of poofter have you and

what's with the house being up for sale?"
For a moment Joey couldn't speak, couldn't do
anything but hold onto his brother for dear life.
"I know you're pleased to see me Joey but don't you
think this is just a bit over the top?"
Joey Chambers stood back and Steve could see
weeks of pain etched on his brother's face.
"I think we need to go inside so you can tell me
what the fuck is going on, don't you?"
Seated in the front room Joey revealed all that had
happened to Michael and the fact that a match
couldn't be found. He didn't relay what had
happened with Tommy Mortimer, that had to stay
between him and his sister only.
"So why didn't you contact me?"
"We tried, Lizzie even got the British Embassy
involved but they couldn't track you down either."
"Well we need to get to the hospital straight away so
that I can get tested then."
"Stevie it aint as simple as that. Over the last couple
of weeks Mikey has deteriorated. He's refusing to
have any more dialysis and I think it's getting
towards the end now."
"So what's caused it, I mean your kidneys don't just
fucking fail for nothing or do they?"
"Apparently it's a rare inherited disease called
Bartter Syndrome where the kidneys leak excessive
amounts of salt into the urine. Its normally picked
up in infancy but our Michael slipped through the
net, I mean we always just thought he was a sickly

kid."

"So you mean it's been passed down from dad?"

"No, we were all tested weeks ago. It had to have come from Michael's own father."

"Well why aint he doing his bit?"

"It's a long story Steve, suffice to say that there's no way he can help. Now we really need to get to the hospital."

Within minutes Joeys Range Rover was speeding through the street heading for Bart's. When they'd parked up and were about to enter through the main doors Steve Chambers stopped for a second and grabbed his brother's arm.

"Will he look very different?"

"He's lost weight if that's what you mean but he'll always be our Mikey, now come on we need to get up there."

The two men raced up the stairs desperate to pass on the news that Steve was home and could possibly save the day. Tests were immediately carried out and now all they could do was wait to hear the results. The following afternoon Joey and Steve Chambers made their way up to their nephew's room for a visit. Joey had been at the hospital the previous evening and there hadn't been much change but now entering the room, it was a different story. Michael had deteriorated further overnight and Joey was so shocked at what greeted him. Steve hadn't been a match but as the hours had passed, they all still kept on hoping that a donor would be found and Michael might at least have a fighting chance. Lizzie was tenderly stroking her son's hair and their father Mike just stood staring into space. Looking up and seeing her brothers, Lizzie ran into Joeys arms. He tenderly led her out into the corridor to find out what was going on.

"He's bleeding from his stomach and intestines and Mr Armstrong said it's only a matter of time. Oh Joey whatever am I going to do without him?"

"But there's always a chance that a donor will become available?"

"It's too late Joey; my baby's going to die."

Lizzie Chamber began to sob again, deep wracking sobs and the only thing Joey could do was pull her to him and hold her tight. Michael Chambers held out for another three hours but finally his young body just couldn't take anymore and he slipped away with his family all around him.

Madeleine Dumont's life was about to drastically change. Stepping out of the front door to begin her daily rounds, she was a little annoyed when the wall phone in the hall burst into life. Remembering her manners, her voice was polite as she spoke.

"Hello Maddy Dumont speaking."

"Good morning Miss Dumont. This is Community Officer Winters from Ladbroke Station. I have some good news for you, or at least I hope it's good. The lost property you handed in has not been claimed so you are now free to collect it."

"You mean the lottery ticket?"

Harry Winters hadn't read the form properly but now he remembered the woman and smiled to himself.

"Yes that's correct; will you bother to collect it?"

"Well of course I will, I'll be down straight away." With that Maddy hung up and leaving her trusted trolley behind, set out for the police station. Within the hour she had collected the lottery ticket and was now back home and desperate to continue with her work. For safekeeping, she placed the ticket into the front of her favourite book and then hastily grabbed her trolley and set off. Maddy's mind was filled with excitement and coupled with the fact that she was late, she wasn't paying attention when she attempted to cross the main road. Usually she headed straight for the pelican crossing and the safety of the traffic lights but today and totally out of character, she stepped straight into the path of the oncoming traffic. The white van, whose driver was in the middle of a conversation on his mobile, hit Maddy with force. Luckily he wasn't travelling at an excessive speed but it was still fast enough to do considerable damage. Madeleine Dumont suffered a badly broken leg, arm and had fractured her skull.

As Maddy was wheeled from the ambulance she saw the Chambers family exiting the hospital through the main doors. Lizzie was sobbing and being held up by her brothers and even though

Maddy didn't know the people or what was going on, her heart went out to them and she realised how lucky she had been. Due to her age and the fact that she had no family to take care of her, Maddy was kept in hospital for twelve weeks. In that time no one came to visit and she was constantly harassing the staff to go home as she was worried about the cats being fed. Celia from Help the Aged had called at Maddy's flat several times but when she'd got no reply and the neighbours had been little more than useless, she had given up trying to find out what had happened to her friend. Finally on the day of her release Maddy was taken home by one of the volunteer drivers and had hobbled into her house with the aid of a walking stick. Maddy didn't like it but knew that she had little choice but to get used to the aid as the hospital had informed her that her leg would never heal properly and she would be somewhat disabled. A week later she decided to attempt her rounds but they would have to be a lot smaller and although it went against the grain, she would now be using the bus. Dressed in her warmest coat and as she looked around the messy room for her house keys, she suddenly remembered the lottery ticket. Removing it she smiled and decided today was as good as any to telephone Camelot. Before she dialled, Maddy had placed a dining chair in the hallway so that she could sit as she knew that should it be good news, she was likely to faint and she also wasn't able to stand for long on her damaged leg. The number only rang a couple of times before it was answered.

"Oh hello. I would like to claim a lottery win please."

"Certainly Madam. There are just a few things I need to run through with you before I'm able to confirm a winning ticket. Now may I take your name and then could you give me the serial number that's printed at the top left hand side of the ticket. Its eighteen digits long if that's any help."

Maddy placed her glasses onto the tip of her nose and after giving her name, read out the long list of numbers.

"And now as double confirmation, may I have the five numbers and then the two lucky stars?"

Maddy reeled off the winning combination.

"Right if you can bear with me for a few minutes, the line may go silent but please don't hang up."

Maddy smiled to herself and then sat back to wait but it was less than a minute when the woman once more spoke.

"I'm so sorry to have kept you but there seems to be a problem."

"Really my dear and what's that?"

"Well the numbers are all correct but Camelot have a strict one hundred and eighty day claim policy."

"And?"

"Your ticket has gone over by one day. I'm sorry but there really isn't anything I can do about it, we really do have to follow procedure I'm afraid."

Maddy had a slight smile on her face as she gently shook her head.

"Of course you do my dear and don't you worry about it. I can't miss what I've never had; now you enjoy the rest of the day."

As Maddy hung up she sat back in her seat for a second and sighed. It would have been nice to win, she could have done so much good but it obviously wasn't meant to be. Slapping her thigh she got up and taking hold of her trolley and walking stick, once more set off on her rounds. Entering the Help the Aged she was a little disappointed to see Grace on duty but she didn't show it. Usually she tried to strike up a conversation but this time Maddy walked straight to the back of the shop. Grace Harrod didn't like being ignored especially by Maddy and almost ran behind her to see what she was up to. Gently tapping on the storeroom door Maddy waited and when she heard Celia call out 'come in'; she quickly closed the door behind her just as Grace caught up with her. When Celia saw it was Maddy she smiled in a genuine friendly way.

"Thank the Lord! Maddy wherever have you been? I was so worried about you?"

"I had an accident but thankfully I'm on the mend now. I'm not too fond of this though."

Maddy held up the walking stick and waved it in the air.

"Oh dear! Seriously though Maddy, I'm so pleased to see you but you do look a bit down, is it the result of the accident?"

"Not really, you remember that lottery ticket?"

"Oh yes, how did you get on?"

"Not so good, seems I wasn't meant to win the lottery after all."

"Did the tickets rightful owner collect it?"

Standing her trolley against the wall Maddy wearily took a seat.

"No its mine right enough but when I telephoned to claim it, I was told that I was one day too late. Sometimes things happen for a reason Celia and sometimes they are just not meant to happen at all."

Celia Montpelier was out of her chair in a second and her face was like thunder.

"I'm sorry Maddy but that is no excuse. You work tirelessly for the homeless and receive very little thanks. You could have instantly claimed that money for yourself but instead you did the right and honourable thing and look how you've been repaid."

"But rules are rules Celia, there really isn't anymore I can do about it."

"Well you leave it to me! I have a reporter friend who works for the Standard and I'm sure he would be interested in a story like this. You never know it might even go national."

Standing up Maddy embraced her friend and thanked her. She didn't hold out much hope but just someone else showing her kindness, was as far as she was concerned, payment enough.

TWO MONTHS LATER

True to her word Celia Montpelier had really gotten
the bit between her teeth regarding Maddy's lottery
ticket. She had worked tirelessly with her friend
from the Standard and had eventually managed to
get the Sun and the Mirror on board. Photographs
were taken of Maddy at home sorting through all
the donations and even more showing her late at
night with her trusted trolley handing out warm
clothes to the homeless. After two months and
when they realised Celia Montpelier was on some
kind of mission, Camelot somewhat relented. They
still wouldn't allow Maddy to claim the win but as a
gesture of good will, they were prepared to give a
sizable donation to her cause in the form of a charity
grant. The amount was actually so large, that after
all the paperwork had been completed and with
Celia's help, Maddy was able to lease a small shop
on Craven Street near Charing Cross station and
pay the rent in advance for the next five years.
Celia Montpelier helped out as much as she could
as far as advice was concerned and soon donations
were coming in from all over the country. It took a
few weeks for the word to spread but soon Maddy
found that she needed help. Placing an
advertisement in the shop window for a volunteer,
she was soon approached by her first applicant.
The young woman was very smartly dressed and to
Maddy didn't look the type who would normally

give up her time for free. Still Madeleine Dumont
was nothing if not fare and everyone deserved a
chance. Taking the young woman through to the
back of the shop, Maddy made her a tea and sat
down to conduct some kind of interview.
"So my dear, what is your name?"
"Sharon, Sharon Chambers."
"And why would you like to be a volunteer?"
"Honestly?"
"Well I've always found that it's the best policy, so
yes."
"I'm in the middle of a divorce and living back with
my parents. My father thinks I'm spoilt and that I
don't care about anyone else and I'd like to prove
him wrong."
Maddy had hoped to hear that the woman wanted
to help people, that she cared deeply about society's
lost souls but that wasn't the case and scratching at
her head she was in a bit of a quandary as to what
to do. Maddy decided to give Sharon a chance and
not judge her, so the following day the women met
up at the newly named 'Maddy's Place'. The first
customer through the doors that morning was
David Farnham a regular client of Maddy's from
Victoria station. David was well overdue for a wash
and as he approached Sharon she took a step
backwards and held up her hands as if the man was
contagious. Maddy smiled and making her way
towards them, took over and graciously served her
customer. When David Farnham had left the shop

with a bag of fresh clothing, Maddy put the temporarily closed sign on the door and walked over to Sharon.

"I think we need to have a little chat."

"I'm sorry Maddy and I know what you're about to say but the man was so dirty and he smelled terrible."

Maddy gently took hold of Sharon's arm and led her over to a donated settee that was waiting to be collected.

"Sit down my dear, now tell me why you think that man lives the way he does?"

Sharon shrugged her shoulders, she didn't have the first idea but no matter what the reason, in her eyes there was no explanation for looking and living like that.

"I don't know, I suppose he's a drunk or a criminal?"

"My dear girl, nothing could be further from the truth. David Farnham was once a doctor, no he was more than a doctor; he was one of the top consultants at St Thomas's hospital. Well that was until his wife was struck down with cancer and David just went to pieces. After she died he shut himself away and was eventually released from his position. Months later the bank foreclosed on his house and he was homeless. Having no family to turn to, he was destitute and the few friends he thought he had quickly turned their backs on him when he was no longer a man in a prominent position. Sharon when you've lived on the streets with no money or food, nowhere to wash and get a decent night's sleep, then you soon end up like poor David. We really haven't any right to judge someone until we know their story darling. I mean, there are a few who like you say are alcoholics or criminals but on the whole most of my clients are honest decent people that have been dealt a bad hand and are down on their luck."

When Maddy had finished talking she looked at her helper and could see tears in the woman's eyes. "Now let's not say anymore about it and get back to work, there are plenty out there who need our help."

Over the next few weeks the transformation in Sharon Chambers was amazing. She loved coming to work and had even struck up friendships with several homeless women. Long gone were the designer clothes and makeup and Sharon now turned up for work in jeans and sweatshirts ready to get stuck in and get her hands dirty. Linda Jackson wasn't very happy that her daughter was working in a second hand shop but Derek was as proud as punch that Sharon had proved him wrong, his only wish was for Joey to see her now.

Watching the young woman, Madeleine Dumont felt as though she really had won the lottery, not in monetary terms but she had certainly won life's lottery. Things didn't always turn out how you planned or wanted but sometimes if you were lucky, something good really could come from something bad.

Six months after Michael Chambers's funeral, Sue and John Hewitt stood in Bow County Court on Romford Road. They had been summoned to attend a hearing that would declare them both bankrupt but Sue wore a glass like expression for the duration. Ever since Ian's funeral she had become withdrawn and her life seemed to be running in slow motion. John was at his wits end, nothing he said or did could bring her out of the daze like state and she would just sit all day staring into space. The debt collectors had long since cleared the flat and left only the bare necessities of a bed and a couple of chairs. Old Derek from upstairs had given the couple a portable television but in all honesty it was hardly ever used. With one tap of his hammer, the judge declared the couple insolvent and therefore under British law, bankrupt. It meant nothing to the Hewitt's as after Ian's death they had nothing left to lose.

For weeks following Michael's death, Lizzie had been inconsolable but with the help of her loved ones, she was slowly starting to come to terms with things. Joey had moved back into the house on Ritchie Street and when his own house in Notting hill had been sold he was filled with nothing but relief. After reluctantly giving Sharon her share, he was still left with a comfortable amount that would allow him to take things easier work wise. Dave

Chambers had quickly returned to Scotland as he had work commitments but Steve decided to stay close to home, for a while at least. Sharon Chambers remained at her parents' house and continued to work at Maddy's shop. Her father had allowed her to keep Coco but the novelty had soon worn off. It wasn't like the past when she had grown tired of her designer purchases but simply down to the fact that she was now so absorbed with helping the homeless. For once Derek Jackson didn't mind, he'd even taken a liking to Coco and had decided to train the dog himself. The money from Sharon's divorce settlement could have allowed her to frequent the pubs and clubs of Chelsea in the hope of finding a rich husband but nothing was further from her mind. Instead of wasting the money, she gave a large donation to Madeleine Dumont's cause.

A year later Taffy Jones stood trial at the Old Bailey. The Crown Prosecution Service had dropped the charge regarding the murder of Tommy Mortimer as there was insufficient evidence but as far as Sonny Warren was concerned it wouldn't make a lot of difference. Sentencing Taffy to a minimum term of twenty years, the Judge stated that the length had been set due to the amount of violence used and the future threat to the general public. Megan Jones screamed and cursed when the sentence was read out and after repeatedly being asked to be quiet, she was finally led down to the cells for contempt of court.

To date, the murder of Tommy Mortimer remains unsolved.

THE END

21755569R00191

Printed in Great Britain
by Amazon